HALLOWED GROUND

Hallowed Ground

Published by The Conrad Press in the United Kingdom 2019

Tel: +44(0)1227 472 874

www.theconradpress.com

info@theconradpress.com

ISBN 978-1-911546-67-2

Typesetting and Cover Design by:
Charlotte Mouncey, www.bookstyle.co.uk

The Conrad Press logo was designed by Maria Priestley.

Printed and bound in Great Britain
by Clays Ltd, St Ives plc

HALLOWED GROUND

*the mystery of
the African Fairy Circles*

PAUL TWIVY

Inspired by the people, stories and landscapes of Namibia

for Gaby, my life companion,
and my children Sam, Josh, Max, Eve and Clara

Prologue

Ray County, Missouri, The United States of America
13th November 1833

The rain of the preceding days had cleared, giving way to a beautifully clear air that you could drink like water. It had been hours since the three-day-old moon had sunk below the horizon.

Alice woke up from the brightness inside the tent and called out in alarm.

'Father, don't keep stirring the fire. You'll set the tent on fire!'

'I haven't touched the fire,' he replied. 'The embers are dying. You need to come out here. You'll never see the like of this again.'

At the sound of his voice, high-pitched and trembling, stretched between excitement and fear, the whole family woke and left the tent.

Beth Wall exclaimed on behalf of her young family who were struck dumb.

'My God, the whole heavens are on fire. Is it the end of the world, Edward?' she asked as Alice and her brothers clung to her nightshirt from fear, sucking in the warm scent of her body for comfort.

It should have been the darkest hours before dawn, but the whole sky was ablaze with meteors. They were falling like a rain of fire, twenty or thirty of them ablaze every second. The tracks of light remained visible for several seconds. It was if their eyes were a camera set to a very slow shutter speed. The falling stars seemed to radiate from the North-east, but the sheer number of them confused every sense. The brighter ones left a trail of sparks like sky- rockets.

'Fireworks!' the youngest one cried.

Around the family, camped on the banks of the Missouri river, arose several hundred people as if a graveyard had just disgorged its dead. They were Mormon refugees sleeping out in the open. Many fell to their knees and started to pray.

Occasionally, a particularly bright fireball would explode as it neared the Earth, with a sound that echoed half-way round the planet.

'It's as if every star has cut free from its mooring,' Edward cried.

The plantations were lit up for miles around. The white farmers could be seen calling all their slaves together, many of whom fell on their knees praying, arms held aloft, convinced it was Judgement Day. The owners ran around those whom they had enslaved, begging forgiveness and freeing them. Some were telling them, for the first time, who their mothers and fathers were, who they'd been sold to, and where they now lived. This brought brief tears of comfort to their black, upturned faces, followed by the agony that, now, they might never live to be reunited.

Everywhere, people were screaming and praying.

'There can be no atheists on a night like this,' Beth said. 'Some of these stars as big as Venus!'

'I've seen two as big as the moon,' their eldest observed.

'You see those that just skim the horizon?' Beth asked Alice. 'They call those "Earth-grazers".'

Edward raked up the fire and found more logs. The family lay down next to it, holding each other tight. They watched until the rising sun eclipsed the fire-storm. From the southern states to Niagara Falls and the frozen wastes of Canada; from the land-locked plains of the mid-West to boats adrift on the icy Atlantic, people finally fell asleep at the touch of a new dawn on their skin.

Namibia, 1838, five years later

Captain Alexander dropped the flaming torch, sending light scurrying downwards and plunging the cave into darkness.

What he had seen remained imprinted on his retinas. It raced through his neurones like a train threatening to come off the tracks.

Was he hallucinating? Or had he really seen something that would change the way the human- race looked at itself?

He sank slowly to his knees and felt around the cave floor for the torch. Its coarse hessian tip was unmistakeable on his fingertips, as was the reek of kerosene as he raised it close to his face.

He struggled to remember where he'd put the matches. Then he remembered the feel of them at the bottom of his canvas bag.

His fingers trembled as he tried to strike one. The first match sent sparks shooting down his legs in a brief explosion. The cave lit up momentarily.

The second match was steadier, and he lifted the flame to his torch which hissed and spluttered back to life.

There they were: fifteen or more, almost organic in shape, laid out in niches along the cave.

Then his eyes rose upwards again. There were four paintings on the ceiling. He propped the torch up and tried to sketch them in a notebook, but his hands couldn't stop shaking and he was forced to stop.

If only the Herero men hadn't abandoned him, their superstitions blazing in their eyes, their priest unconscious on the floor. Then he would have had witnesses, help and comfort, and not been left feeling like a madman, utterly alone.

Mind you, they had been right to be afraid. The knowledge was too much to bear.

The Royal Geographical Society, which had funded his mission, would blacklist him. The Church and the Army would call him a traitor. He would be an outcast.

He left the tomb and brought back a platoon the next day to hide the entrance from the world. No-one was ready for this. Perhaps in a hundred or so years they might be…

1

Convergence

September 2019

South African Airlines flight SAA 349, from Cape Town to Windhoek, had suddenly dropped thousands of feet in a matter of seconds over Fish River Canyon.

Coffee, juice and even egg from the airline breakfasts had shot as high as the overhead lockers and was now dripping like a gelatinous rain on the passengers. White trays, plates and cups littered the gangways like moon rocks. Oxygen masks had dropped from the ceiling like yellow flowers on plastic tendrils.

Several passengers screamed. Cabin crew were thrown backwards and then tried to rescue some dignity.

Joe would have panicked more if he hadn't been so exhausted. The overnight flight he and his parents had taken from New York to Cape Town had seemed never ending. They had passed through thunderstorms mid-Atlantic and he'd tried to work out if it was better or worse if a plane crashed into the sea rather than the land. Sea is a soft landing he'd reasoned, but then concluded it must be more dangerous to plunge beneath the waves. He'd managed to shut down his imagination before he drowned in it.

Joe Kaplan was fourteen years old and below the median height of his class, by a factor that he knew exactly. He'd put insoles in the heels of his shoes for a few weeks, until the pain in his calves got too much. He was thin and lithe and the best tactician on the football team, so was probably never in danger of being bullied for his height… it just felt like it. His face was beginning to grow a light down of hair which he examined obsessively in the mirror every morning. He longed for the full-on, hipster beards of his Silicon Valley heroes. Much to his mother's annoyance, and partly because of it, he had grown a long fringe of hair. He often kept his face angled slightly down and to one side, so that the fringe flopped over his right eye. He liked seeing the world but the world only half-seeing him.

He knew the pattern of these long journeys only too well. It had become the rhythm of his life: his parents moved constantly because of their jobs. Joe felt like a citizen of everywhere and of nowhere.

He had followed his usual strategy and stocked up a horde of magazines and snacks as sandbags against boredom: Sudoku puzzles, two paperback editions of 'Impossible Math Puzzles' and bags of Haribo. At least he could take his mind for a run. The first in-flight movie had held him in a spell, the second merely tugged at his attention and the third had felt like a glut and he'd fallen asleep.

Cape Town airport had been a blur to him, drowning in an early morning stupor, but he was still aware of the blissful light pouring in from every direction. Africa was beginning to stir in him even then and soared as their plane headed south again over the sea-swollen Cape, and then turned sharply over Table Mountain, heading north towards Namibia.

'Robben Island down there,' his father, Ben, had said, 'where Mandela was imprisoned.'

It seemed to Joe that the sea around the island glistened, as if responding to his father's remark.

His father always wanted to share knowledge and Joe always felt a duty to show keen. Ben Kaplan was about to be fifty: a fact he tried to hide. He disliked airline safety belts as they reminded him that he was developing a paunch. He was an anthropologist at Columbia University in New York, distinguished but not as distinguished as he'd once hoped. Joe envied his father's beard although Ben had, in truth, grown it to offset his baldness. Joe's mother had once told her husband that his forehead reminded her of a Roman Emperor. Ben had carried this remark proudly in his head ever since as a consolation for having lost his hair.

They'd hit turbulence over a landscape that could stupefy even when it was calm. Fish River Canyon had a deeply cutting river which flowed round and back on itself like a ribbon, creating a Manhattan-like island of solid rock in its middle. Its scale became terrifying as they seemingly dropped into it.

A second jolt, worse than the first, hit the plane like a shockwave.

Other passengers threw their panic-stricken gaze out of the windows and prayed for a steady horizon.

This time it hit Joe with full force. His mind sharpened from stupor to alert. His hand grabbed the seat in front, his knuckles turning white.

'I think it's just bad turbulence,' his mum said, trying to reassure herself as much as him. She wanted to hold his hand, but she knew he would reject it.

Barbara Kaplan was only two years younger than her husband, but it looked like ten, as she frequently reminded him. She prided herself on being slim for her age. Although she had to power-dress for her job, her hair was a rebellion: long, dark-brown and straggly. Her face when it wasn't taut with stress, was all kindness. Her features were strong but balanced. She was shorter than most American women, a trait she worried her son had inherited.

Joe had always been tight inside, even as a toddler. He'd sailed through his bar mitzvah, thank God, because he was bright and conscientious. Yet, Barbara worried that his intensity and awkwardness cut him off from other people. She looked down at Namibia hoping that somewhere here he would find the good friends he deserved and needed.

'Don't worry. These planes can resist massive shocks,' his father soothed. 'We haven't dropped nearly as far as it feels.'

A reassuringly professional voice threaded its way through the cabin and into Joe's head.

'Ladies and Gentlemen, this is the Captain. Please don't be alarmed. We hit an air pocket as we crossed into Namibia, but the turbulence should soon clear. Crew, please be seated for now.'

A few minutes later the plane steadied itself, although small ripples of turbulence still licked its belly. The screams had gone, now slightly ashamed of their own absurdity.

Slowly spines unfurled, fingers loosened, minds cleared, panic dispersed, lips lost their frantic prayers.

Joe's recurring thought that he might 'die in Africa before living in Africa' ebbed to the back of his mind and his breathing slowed. At the corner of his vision, through two port-hole windows, appeared a pattern. It was a tessellation in the sand, a blistering of the landscape like a pocked face. It stretched for mile after mile: circles of different sizes in rows and columns that didn't behave. To Joe it looked like Nature playing havoc with maths.

'Fairy circles,' he heard his father mutter.

16

Freddie strained to see through the lingering fog. A chill had suddenly come over him, brought on by the desolate coastline that now lay ahead.

Freddie Wilde had only just turned fourteen, but this was already the third country he was going to call home. Or was it the fourth? He couldn't remember. He was tall; almost as tall as his father, and his mother feared the ship's railings were illegally low as he leaned over them, straining to see. Freddie's blond hair had been blown into even more of an extravagance than normal by the morning breeze. His face was unmistakeably English, chiselled with deep-set, brown eyes that seemed to treat everyone as the only person alive when he gazed at them. His wide mouth had, until recently, always stayed slightly open, as if he couldn't breathe through his nose. Now it was often shut, to hide the train-tracks that imprisoned his teeth.

'Why have we come to live here, Dad?' Clara, his nine-year-old sister asked, adding, 'I thought Africa was hot!'

Clara Wilde's upturned face never lost its look of curiosity. She drank in every detail of the world. Her blonde, curly hair tumbled half- way down her back and was constant work for her mother to control, if also a source of joy. She had 'puppy fat' cheeks that everyone adored but she hated. Clara's eyes were as big as her appetite, but her mouth was tiny. It was always a shock for people to hear such a powerful voice come from such a modest source.

'It is, darling,' her father Ralph reassured, putting his arms round her in an envelope of warmth. 'Most of the country is beautifully hot. Three hundred days of sunshine a year, they say. But this is the Skeleton Coast.'

'Skeletons?' Clara cried in horror.

'Of ships,' Ralph added to reassure her.

Even at this ungodly hour of the morning, Ralph Wilde looked 'dapper' in his early fifties, to use one of his favourite words. Ever since he was a child, he'd been neat, everything trimmed and in place. Had he not been so charming, this neatness might have alienated his 'scruff-ball' schoolfriends. Freddie had inherited his thick hair from his father, although Ralph's had been a sandy brown since his late teens. He had the smooth and confident looks of a diplomat.

'So, what causes the fog?' Freddie asked, lost in an atmosphere of Victorian London he'd not anticipated. The fog seemed to slide its fingers into his hair, causing a shiver to pass through him.

'It's a meeting of opposites- the cold ocean and the hot land,' one of the officers explained from behind where they stood. Their cruise ship was sailing at a speed gravely respectful of the coast's fearsome record of 'ship-wrecking'.

'And the shipwrecks?' Freddie asked.

'Over a thousand of them, would you believe,' the officer replied. 'That ship in front of you is one of the most famous.'

Freddie put the binoculars to his face again.

'I can see it now,' he cried.

'Let me see,' cried Clara, trying to wrest the binoculars from her brother's grasp.

'Get off, Clara. I'll give it to you in a minute,' Freddie snapped.

The ship looked unreal. A forlorn creature, lop-sided and skeletal, drained of life and purpose. Its guts spilled out sand and rust. It had broken in two, like a miniature Titanic on the seabed. It was difficult to judge its scale because of the vastness of the coast that had lured and snapped it like a toy.

When his father had been given his new posting as British High Commissioner to Namibia, it was Freddie's mother who had suggested arriving by ship. Freddie had overheard her saying, 'Freddie and Clara will love it….so much more memorable than just flying into Windhoek.'

She hadn't anticipated quite how chilling it would be. But then nothing phased Anne Wilde for long. She was five foot ten inches tall and had excelled at netball at school, as well as being academic. Becoming Head Girl had been inevitable. Her smile was broad and welcoming, and her shoulder-length hair had a girlish vitality that disguised the fact she was forty-four.

Freddie saw his parents giving each other a knowing but sanguine stare. Why do parents always assume that significant looks are less likely to be noticed than words, when the opposite is true?

Freddie finally passed the binoculars to Clara whom he generally adored, occasionally resented and often over-indulged.

As the chill passed through his heart, he reached instinctively into his pocket.

The warm wood filled his hand with its familiar shape, the flat disk of the head and the round body with its arms outstretched in an embrace, gave him comfort. It was the lucky charm his grandmother had given him. His father's parents had owned a farm in Zimbabwe when it was still called Rhodesia. That is where his father had been born, before they were evicted.

'What is it?' he had asked his grandmother as she gave it to him.

'It's an Akuaba doll.' She had told him the story, which he now recounted in his head.

Akua, an African woman, was desperate to have a baby: a 'ba' as they call it. She tried for many years with no success. In despair, she went to the local priest. He carved her the doll of a baby, laid it on the altar, blessed it, gave it to her and told her to care for it as if it were her real baby. So, she carried the wooden baby in a pouch as she worked the fields. She talked to it, lay it next to her as she slept. Then, miraculously, she gave birth to a real baby, just as the priest had said. The story spread like wildfire and African women have worn Akuaba dolls ever since.

'Why do you want me to have it?' he'd asked his grandmother.

Then she had fixed him with a penetrating gaze. 'Because, Freddie, I wouldn't have given birth to your father without it. Your father was an African child and therefore, in some way, so are you.'

This phrase had thrilled him at the time, and it thrilled him again now, watching the foggy coast of this ancient continent.

Later, just before she died, his grandmother had asked him to give the Akuaba charm to Clara when she was older.

'It is really a charm for women. I'm sure you understand.'

He had nodded solemnly but didn't understand at all. He felt displaced and angry. So, he never fulfilled his vow to hand the charm to Clara and it remained his guilty secret. Which is why it often stayed in his pocket or was worn secretly under his shirt.

'Everything all-right, Freddie?' asked his father, catching the turbulence in his son's far-away look.

Freddie was startled by his father's searching eyes. They look so like his grandmother's. It is as if he was gazing at her face-to-face, again.

'Of course, why wouldn't it be?'

'Oh, because we're travelling again. More change. More loss of friends. More things for all of us to adjust to. It's hard at your age.'

His father's voice was kind.

Freddie nodded both in agreement and gratitude.

'This is Africa, Freddie. This could be something extraordinary.' Returning to the continent where he was born, filled Ralph's veins with electricity.

Freddie latched on to his father's excitement, picked up Clara and swung her round the deck.

Anne contemplated the foggy shoreline ahead. Something in her ached for the neatly-mown lawns and gentle summers of her Sussex upbringing. Part of her wanted Freddie and Clara to grow up with the same simple certainties. On the other hand, looking at them excited and curious as another country came into their lives, gave her another satisfaction.

'Why does Freddie have to go to boarding school?' Clara asked her mother. 'Why can't he stay home with the rest of us?'

'Because the best school for him only has boarders,' Anne replied.

'But it's so close to us in Windy Hook or whatever it's called.'

'Exactly,' said Anne, and with the logic she sometimes found easy to conjure, 'he is going to be close and so we'll see him all the time.'

'Well, weekends and holidays,' Freddie corrected. 'Anyway, Pumpkin, this means you get to choose the best bedroom,' he said to Clara as she ran at him pummelling hard. Freddie held her in a bear-hug, but rather too tightly. She squealed.

'Careful you two,' said his mother.

Anne sidled close to Ralph and slipped her arm through his. 'We're going to be all-right, aren't we?' she asked him.

'Of course, we are!' he responded. 'Should be docking in Walvis Bay anytime soon.'

Freddie turned back to face the shore and his new home, whilst Clara sat on his knee.

'I don't want you wandering off on your own,' her mother, Ilana, had said as Selima and her father, Darius, left the house.

Yet despite this, Selima could not resist the adventure, the sheer adrenaline of exploring alone.

She loved the coast around Swakopmund. It was a landscape she had grown up with. The sand floated on fleeting currents of ocean air, in millions of red and orange pixels. Yet to a human eye, even the eye of someone as perceptive and alive to the great outdoors as Selima, it never changed in any fundamental sense.

Selima van Zyl has always wanted to be a boy. She hated the fact that her breasts were starting to grow, and she kept them as hidden and flattened as possible. Being fourteen was a pain. The changing shape of her body disobeyed her feelings. She always preferred her black hair to be short and straightened its curls, whenever she could be bothered. It hadn't touched her shoulders since she was tiny. Her skin was dark: more like her mother's than her father's. Her smile was broad and infectious especially when she was outdoors. She had, by common consent, inherited her mother's beauty. Yet, unlike her mother, she was allergic to dresses.

Selima thought of the Langstrand dunes as a vast play-ground. It would be the envy of others the world over if only they could see it. There must be millions of little sandpits and playgrounds the world over she reasoned. How hard it must be to turn them into something magical. She imagined them like the playgrounds in Swakopmund: scrappy spaces in parks and schools, gestures to the great outdoors. To Selima, Langstrand was the playground of giants. She could imagine them, vast and gangly, their thick legs striding across the dunes to the sea.

Her father, Darius, ran sand dune tours for tourists around Swakopmund. Well, he seemed to do many things. Her mother, Ilana, always described him as 'an entrepreneur.' Yet, as she got older, this seemed too grand a term for her father.

Darius van Zyl was a comparatively old father for Selima, already in his late forties. However, his outdoor life made him look younger. He had a rugged look inherited from several generations of South African farmers. They had been tough survivors and so was he: a 'solidly-built', stocky man with broad shoulders. His hair was a dark ginger, and he'd grown and kept, a neatly-trimmed beard since his late teens.

She had watched him, over the years, switch between various hopeless schemes. At one time he had tried to export African parrots to Europe. Then he set up an artisan ice-cream business near the Aquarium. All of them failed. He was cheery though, full of hope, and Selima adored his energy. She worried though in the aftermath of his disappointments, when he spent long periods on his own, staring at the sea from his top-floor study. Even she could not touch him in those moments.

Darius's parents had owned a farm on which her father had been raised. He had told her that, after the Namibians gained independence from South Africa, their land had been 'reclaimed' by the Government and returned to the people.

'It was right to claim it back,' he had said. Yet she always sensed that he was bitter about it. His cheerfulness couldn't hide his sense of being dispossessed. She often thought about how different her upbringing might have been if she'd been raised on that farm. She felt she might have loved it. But then, she wouldn't have had her dunes...

Her father took people in his sturdy, faithful and much-abused Land Rover, for adventures over the dunes. This involved dramatic drives along the beaches, as the South Atlantic pounded and threatened to hem them in with its furious, fast-moving tides. His favourite trick was to put the car on cruise control at low speed and jump out, walking beside the car, with his astonished passengers left in the driverless vehicle.

In the school holidays, whenever possible, and the tourists are willing, Selima went along for the ride with her father, and this was one of those days.

She loved it when Darius let rip and pointed the Land Rover head down a steep ridge, bringing cries of delight mixed with fear, as the passengers went on a roller coaster ride down the vast sandy playground and then back up to wide horizons on the crests.

The highlight of their daytrips was always sandboarding. There were those who treated it like a professional sport, with all the cool and kudos of being 'the new snowboarding'. What Selima loved though, was improvising: taking a front-door-sized piece of hardboard, lying on your stomach, lifting up the front end of the board to reduce friction, and launching yourself face downwards from the top of a large dune.

The speed of descent depended on your angle, the balance of your weight and your degree of nerve. Selima, who had been sandboarding since she was six, had no fear and invariably showed up even the bravest of beginners. In particular, she loved beating boys, changing their swagger to respect. She loved the rush of sand-warmed air on her face as she sped, almost out of control, down to the sandy abyss.

At this particular moment, she had 'duned' beyond her father and his German guests. She was on the top of her own slope, alone, enjoying the rebellion, her mother's voice receding rapidly in her head.

She looked out to sea. The earlier fogs had started to burn away under the African sun, and she could see a cruise ship heading down from the Skeleton Coast to Walvis Bay. She could just make out people on the deck staring out at Swakopmund. She wondered about them and their distant, matchstick lives. Why were they coming to her country? Where might they have sailed from?

Just then she heard the Land Rover top the crest.

'Selima? What the hell are you doing?' Darius shouted. 'I've told you about running off before. I don't want you to be on the dunes alone, especially when I am responsible for other people and they have kindly agreed for you to come along.'

'Sorry, Dad!'

'Now come on. Deputy Tour Leader back to base!' He could never be cross with her for long. He adored her too much and she knew it. Ever since he read her stories, aged six, and she used to pincer him with her legs, she'd known exactly how to win him.

She lifted her sand-board, tucked it under her arm and reluctantly strode back to the Land Rover balancing on the dune edge. She gazed seawards again. There was something about that ship now floating into the distance that she couldn't quite fathom.

'So, is the school you're going to teach at, anything like this?' Hannah asked her mother, as they pushed open the heavy doors of the dining hall. Sarah gazed back at her. She detected excitement and mild panic in her daughter in equal measure as they toured her new school.

Hannah Chiang had her own unique style. From her thirteenth birthday onwards - now a year ago - she had insisted on shopping for clothes alone, or with a carefully hand-picked friend, but never with her mother. She was obsessed with vintage shops and her clothes were an eclectic blend of the hippy-ish and the bygone. Sarah, actually loved her daughter's style. She saw it as a direct inheritance of her rebellion against her own mother. Hannah's mono-lid eyes were a beautiful, crescent shape and a dark, haunting brown. Her olive skin glowed with a burnished health. Asian and English met beautifully in her face and in her gracious, slim body. Sarah's pride interrupted her answer.

'Well, it doesn't have the history of The Augustineum,' her mother replied. 'It's a faith school, like this one, but much more modern.'

'That sounds more like me. I hate being formal, you know that. Like you. Why can't I just be at your school?' Hannah pleaded.

Her mother sighed and linked arms with her.

'Can you think of anything more embarrassing than having

your own mother as a teacher at your school?' her mother asked.

'A few things,' Hannah replied. 'Like my father being a teacher in my school,' she said nodding towards Li Chiang who had stopped in the corridor behind them to ask a passing teacher yet another penetrating question about the curriculum.

Li Chiang had a face as round as a moon. His features were neatly perched on its surface, perfectly symmetrical. His cheeks dimpled when he smiled. His long, thin lips had a small gash at each end like parentheses. He wore fashionably thin, high-tech glasses. He was slim, of average height, with an almost exaggeratedly straight-backed posture like a visiting dignitary.

'Li?' Sarah called out down the corridor 'we're waiting for you... again!'

Li would not be hurried by his wife, or anyone in fact, and his back seemed to stiffen in resolve as he added a supplementary question to his first.

'How his new work colleagues are going to cope I don't know,' Sarah added. 'Mind you they'll probably end up adoring him. So many people do.'

'How much uranium does Namibia actually have?' Hannah asked.

'A lot it seems. That's why he's been posted here. It's just lucky I managed to get a teaching post.'

Li Chiang was a mining engineer, raised in Beijing. He had gone to England as a student, before completing his Masters, back in China. He had met Sarah, Hannah's mother, at University. She was learning Mandarin whilst he was learning English. Their cultures met in the middle, in Hannah in fact.

Li joined them in the Dining hall having exhausted some poor, bedraggled Physics teacher.

The faint smell of over-cooked vegetables for the first supper of term was pervasive, triggering a feeling of faint dread in Hannah.

'Ah, one thing you can always rely on: the smell of school food is pretty much the same everywhere,' her father observed.

The school buildings were mainly modern, but with mementoes of its Victorian past studded around the place in statues, mottoes and stained-glass windows that were re-housed in slightly odd, modern settings. It felt like trying too hard. However, the school also opened out on to beautiful courtyards and a large garden filled with succulent plants, shrubs and hardy trees that had learned to withstand the most disrespectful and frequent of climbers. The garden was beautifully kept and the pride and joy of the school.

'Why the Augustineum? It seems such an odd name for an African school,' Hannah queried as they nosed into its corners.

'Well, many of these schools were started by missionaries,' Sarah observed.

'Indeed,' a voice boomed from behind them 'It's named after the very unlikely-sounding Augustine of Hippo.'

They turned around to see a tall, black, gracious man dressed in a grey, lightweight, elegant suit. His beard was white and trimmed to an elegant shape, like topiary. His hair was a motley of white and grey and elegantly combed back. His face was rounder and more affluent looking than many Namibians. He wore bi-focal glasses perched half-way down his nose like a theatrical prop.

'We know him as the Father of the Church,' he said. 'Luther, loved him, and Protestantism is of course our main religion in Namibia. Our main, *inherited* religion I should say.'

'Fascinating,' her father said.

'Apologies, I should have introduced myself. I am Jacob Ubuntu, Headmaster of this literally august institution. You must be, Hannah,' he said, shaking the hand of his pupil before that of her parents to show his carefully-judged priorities. 'I am delighted to welcome you to Windhoek and to our proud and historical school.' He added cordially, 'Do you know Namibia at all?'

'Only what we have read in guide-books,' Sarah replied, 'which, of course, is very superficial.'

'Useful nonetheless and I am always delighted when someone reads anything about Namibia,' Ubuntu said. 'We are fairly obscure in the eyes of the world. I am very pleased that you are joining our international community here. We spoke, a few times, on the phone. You've moved here because of work I believe.'

'Yes, I am here to plunder your soil, Mr Ubuntu, I am afraid,' her father admitted.

'Ah well, many have done that,' Ubuntu responded. 'Well, Hannah, you will be pleased to hear you are not alone in the school. We have a growing number of Chinese students. Indeed, I've wondered whether I should start learning some Mandarin myself.'

'I can help you with that, sir,' Hannah said, keen to impress her new mentor.

'Excellent,' said Ubuntu, 'I look forward to it. Have you seen your dorm yet?'

'That's just where we were heading,' Sarah intervened.

The Headmaster pointed them in the right direction and

then turned to greet other new arrivals with his gracious tones and carefully considered phrases.

'Well, he seems someone with whom I am happy to trust my daughter's education,' Li said as they walked away.

'I agree,' Sarah responded with the authority and knowledge of a fellow teacher. 'Hannah what do you feel?'

'Yes, I think I like him,' Hannah replied, adding, 'I'm scared though. What if I don't make any friends? What if people think I'm a freak? Here we are, this must be mine…'

Hannah thought that her parents must have been relieved not to have to answer her question. She knew that there was no answer that would comfort her. Anyway, here was her new dorm.

The door swung open on a room that could best be described as basic. She had expected that. The beds had metal frames like hospital beds. There were four of them, arranged symmetrically with wardrobes in between for your clothes and to give some sense of privacy. Hannah felt the mattress on the nearest bed. Unforgiving to the touch but not disastrous. She never had problems sleeping anyway. God forbid she would start now.

'As you're the first, you should claim the best bed,' Sarah suggested. 'How about that one by the window?'

'Good thinking Mother,' retorted Hannah in a mock haughty tone, plonking her rucksack down in a territorial statement.

'I have to be right occasionally,' Sarah responded.

'Hmm. Not necessarily.'

Their banter was tinged with sadness at their imminent parting.

'My God it's upside down,' Hannah cried on nearing the window.

Just outside the dorm window was the most extraordinary tree she had ever seen. The tree appeared to have buried its head deep in the earth, like an ostrich, lifting its roots into the air in an act of defiance.

'Reminds me of you, Hannah, doing your hand-stands,' her mother remarked.

Hannah laughed in recognition: 'It looks in a strop...like a sulky child.'

'Too old to be a child,' her father intervened. 'Those trees can live up to three thousand years old. That's a Baobab if I'm not mistaken.'

Just then, a plane appeared, visible through 'the roots', which were, in fact, the branches, of the Baobab. Hannah recognised the flag on the tail fin as the Rainbow Flag: South African Airways. The plane started to circle, flying so slowly it seemed almost impossible that it would stay aloft. It looked strangely elegant in the pale afternoon sunshine.

Hannah fixed her gaze on it. In the back of her mind a thought started to form: 'Something extraordinary is about to happen.'

2
The Augustineum

Hannah woke with a start. Something was screeching, possibly a monkey outside in the garden but she couldn't be sure. It was a primitive sound and it tore into her sleep. She looked at her watch. She'd been asleep on her bed for over an hour. Still no-one had arrived in her dorm.

The upside-down tree outside her window perfectly expressed how she felt. She smiled, remembering her mother's remark.

She suddenly felt the loss of her parents in a rush of adrenaline, a child-in-the-cot feeling of being unutterably alone. She scrunched up the bedsheets and used them to pull her rucksack towards her. She opened the top pocket and took out her mobile, her daemon.

She opened her photos from that morning, the selfies at the airport with her parents, and warmed. She rolled over, pointed her phone at the baobab tree and snapped repeatedly, raising and lowering it like a periscope, playing with the angles.

A tall man, slim and lithe from a lifetime of hard work, was weeding and raking the garden. Basarwa was dressed in khaki, his shirt pocket embroidered with the school logo. A sun hat flopped over his head like an empty jelly mould. His beard was trim and elegant, his face calm and wise. He turned, as if aware of her gaze, and smiled enigmatically at her. She shot back from the window, embarrassed that he'd seen her.

Then she posted her photos on Instagram, selecting a filter that seemed to do justice to its madness. She added a post on WhatsApp as an insurance policy against being ignored…

'Hey guys. This is the crazy upside-down tree outside my window. Yes, I'm finally here in Namibia in my frankly weird, new boarding-school. Missing you all. Which is a not too coded way of saying "Flood me with loving messages."'

She lay back, waiting for the reassuring ping of responses, but before any arrived, the door to her dorm burst open.

A cockatoo-like plume of blond, unkempt hair, floated into view from behind the opening door. It seemed for a moment as if it didn't belong to anyone. It simply added to Hannah's sense that she was in a dream. The hair was followed by the pale-skinned, sculpted face of a boy peering into the dorm.

'Hello!' Freddie said taken aback at finding Hannah sprawled on her bed. 'I don't think I should be in here… a girl's dorm that is.'

There was something about his grinning, English awkwardness that instantly charmed her.

'Possibly not,' Hannah replied, 'Is that why you did it?'

'Probably, knowing me. I heard that the girls' dorms were down here and for some bizarre reason, I was attracted to explore.'

Hannah was charmed by his coyness even though she realised this was precisely his intention.

'I'm Freddie by the way. Freddie Wilde.'

'As in Oscar?'

'Same spelling, yes. Sadly, not descended. And you?'

'Hannah.'

Freddie walked over to her bed and offered his hand.

Brought up strictly, like me, Hannah thought to herself, shaking his hand. Dad would approve!

'Hannah's a palindrome,' Freddie observed.

'Yes, Baba says I go backwards as fast as I go forwards... like my name. Clearly they called me Hannah in order to make the joke.'

'Baba?' Freddie queried, smiling.

'It means father,' she explained. 'In Chinese.'

'So, what's your surname?'

Hannah laughed.

'Chiang.'

'Hannah Chiang. So, are both your parents Chinese?' Freddie asked.

'No, just my dad. My mum's English.'

'I'm straight up English on both sides.' His voice was poised and middle class, unlike his appearance which was raffish and unkempt.

'You don't say!' Hannah observed, needling him and giggling in equal measure.

'Well, there's some wild Irish thrown in there for good measure of course,' he said, trying to inject some colour.

He sat down on the bed opposite her which creaked ominously under his weight.

'Blimey, let's hope the beds hold up,' he laughed, partly from embarrassment.

'Let's hope *we* hold up,' Hannah said. 'Another country, another start.'

'How familiar is that?' he responded.

They exchanged the knowing look of two nomads dragged around the world by the vagaries of their parents' careers.

'So, how did you end up here?' Freddie probed.

'My dad's a mining engineer. He's been posted here. And my mum's a teacher.'

So, they're not in Windhoek?'

'No…'

Hannah ran her finger over a map of Namibia that she had stuck with Blu Tak on to the wardrobe next to her bed.

'No, they're just here… in Swakopmund.'

'I sailed past there this morning, before we docked at Walvis Bay. Odd looking place. A German seaside resort on the African coast! Who would have thought?'

'I know. But then, things in Namibia do seem odd, jumbled up, don't you think? I feel like Alice in Wonderland. I've tumbled down some enormous hole and… So, wait, did you come by ship then?'

'Yes, my mother had this romantic idea we should arrive in Namibia by sea. Unfortunately, this meant being greeted by hundreds of shipwrecks. Not that you could see much of them because everything was smothered in fog.'

'Fog? Something else you wouldn't expect.'

'How many countries have you lived in?' Hannah asked, her curiosity in Freddie deepening by the minute and her loneliness thawing. Nothing could beat the first, delicious moments of a new friendship.

'I think this is my fourth. My dad's in the diplomatic service. He's the new High Commissioner to Namibia.' He then worried that this sounded like bragging.

'OMG, you're going to be living in the Embassy,' she cried.

'Any parties on the cards?'

'If you'd been to any Embassy parties you wouldn't be quite so enthusiastic. Good food though!'

'Do you have any brothers or sisters?' Hannah asked, as she always did.

An affectionate smile stole across Freddie's face.

'I do. I have a totally infuriating but wholly adorable, nine-year-old sister called Clara. You?'

Hannah felt a knot tighten inside her.

'No. Sadly not...' she replied. She wasn't going to say any more at this point.

They both gazed out of the window, at Basarwa pruning the lushness that enveloped him.

'It's so different here...' Hannah observed.

'I know, wonderful, isn't it?'

Hannah felt uplifted by Freddie's enthusiasm. Someone who had started as a disembodied quiff of blond hair was shaping up to be a half-decent companion.

Joe's Brooklyn accent felt very familiar. The tone of it reminded Freddie of his childhood, of American comedies watched in the sunlit sitting-rooms of his childhood homes, curled-up, pyjama-clad, on the sofa. Somehow, canned American laughter was a reassuring constant in his ever-changing world. America felt cosy to Freddie even though he knew it probably wasn't.

He had found Joe, unpacking in his dorm on returning from his chat with Hannah. Joe's trunk seemed huge and was over-run with stickers like an outbreak of measles: stickers from camps and maths competitions, interspersed with flags from every country where he'd lived.

'Take the bed next to mine,' Freddie exhorted.

'Why? Is there something wrong with it?' Joe had been caught out with dud beds once too often.

'Not to my knowledge. Test it if you like. Are you OK? You look a bit pale.'

'Not really. I don't feel great,' Joe replied. 'We had a terrible plane journey from South Africa.'

'What happened?'

'Our plane hit an air pocket. It dropped several thousand feet,' Joe remarked.

The captain, had actually said, "a few hundred feet", but Joe had no desire for the truth at this point.

'Oh my God, that sounds terrifying.'

Joe took in the sparse dorm once more. He thought it smelt damp. Some of the wallpaper was starting to peel and the paint on the sash windows was flaking. On the walls hung a number of very average drawings of the school. A Namibian flag was emblazoned across the back of the door.

'Is it just me or is this place in need of some paint?'

'Can't say I noticed,' Freddie replied, looking at the room anew through Joe's eyes.

Joe continued to unpack.

Joe took out a stack of mathematical puzzle books. Freddie picked one up and flicked through it. He was sure he couldn't even tackle the simplest one.

'Hey, leave that will you?' Joe snapped, snatching it back.

'Sorry, I was just curious.'

'I don't want these damaged. They have to last me until the next trip back to the States.'

Freddie sighed and lay down on his bed to test it, his worst fears confirmed. Great! A sagging mattress and a grumpy 'room-mate'. His dream combination!

After a few minutes of unpacking and grunting, Joe decided to break the silence, regretting his tetchiness.

'After the turbulence - on the plane - we saw something extraordinary.'

'What?'

'I thought I was hallucinating. There were thousands of them below us in the desert.'

'Thousands of what?'

'Circles in the sand. Like giant freckles.'

'Really?'

'They seemed to be in patterns but indecipherable ones.'

There was an awkward silence as Freddie failed to imagine them and didn't know how to respond.

'Do you like math?' Joe eventually asked.

'Not really. Or rather maths doesn't like me. We tend to use the plural over here…'

'Yeah I know. Just another way you, Europeans, get things wrong.' Joe was tired of the condescension everyone this side of the Atlantic seemed justified in doling out to Americans like him. 'Math is the abbreviation of mathematics. It's not mathsematics is it?' he pointed out.

'I suppose not,' Freddie admitted grudgingly. 'I don't really care because I'm not interested in maths. I find it dull.'

'Dull? My God it's in everything… music, architecture. Look outside, look at the plants. How can you not be fascinated by patterns? I can remember watching splashes of rain on my bedroom window for hours; ripples in the bath; the shape of snowflakes. They're endlessly fascinating…'

'What are?' Hannah poked her head round the dormitory door. 'Ah so this is what a boy's dormitory smells like... I mean looks like.'

'Hannah Chiang...' Freddie said, 'this is Joe Kaplan.'

'Nice to meet you, Joe,' Hannah said, holding out her hand. Joe awkwardly re-balanced his weight, shifting to his left foot. 'I don't shake hands. They're full of germs,' he observed.

Hannah was nonplussed.

Hannah and Freddie exchanged knowing glances and decided to leave Joe to stew and sleep.

There was an opening Assembly for all new boarders, with a speech by the Headmaster.

Freddie and Hannah decided to explore the school and its grounds on the way there. Joe was dragged along reluctantly.

The Augustineum clearly had a distinguished history. Their parents had drummed this into all of them, largely in justification for sending them there. Yet, it definitely, had seen better times. Some buildings, such as the library, were Victorian, once ornate and grand, but fallen into disrepair. Others, however, such as the science block, were modern and proudly bore the names of generous sponsors, former pupils they imagined. It was a hotchpotch of architectural styles and eras.

Some walls were painted in turquoise and burnt orange - the colours of a Caribbean bus-stop. The main quadrangle had an ornamental pool that was clearly once beautiful. A small fountain sadly dribbled at its centre.

If the buildings were a gap-toothed smile, the gardens were a bewitching kiss. Palms were fireworks of green. Kokerbooms - quiver trees - weren't trees at all, but giant aloe plants, their branches searching upwards like elegant fingers. They held their green tendrils proudly to the sky. The ground was covered with succulents that needed little water and had their own beauty with fronds and spikes. Birdsong sprinkled the gardens like a rain.

'Do you know why we love birds singing?' Joe asked.

'Isn't it something to do with being safe?' Hannah half-remembered. She often found her mind was full of remnants waiting to be fetched.

Joe loved sharing facts in the way that some people love sharing secrets. He felt safe with facts. 'Apparently, when our ancestors heard birdsong, they knew that no predators were near. So, they felt secure.'

'I just hope they don't wake me at dawn,' Freddie observed.

Hannah noticed Joe was deflated by Freddie's brush-off.

'You know they've discovered something similar about spiders and snakes,' she added.

'Tell me,' Joe asked, turning to Hannah, their eyes threading.

'Listen, I'm petrified by spiders. Mum says my screams can be heard in the next town and that it's just not logical. Well, they've shown pictures of spiders and snakes to young babies and their pupils dilate in fear. But they don't dilate when you show them pictures of bears, for example, that are just as dangerous.'

'So, what's the reason?' Freddie asked, feeling left out of this frenzy of scientific excitement.

'They think that for millions of years, when we all lived in Africa, poisonous spiders and snakes were our most dangerous enemies,' Hannah explained.

'So, our nervous systems were trained here,' Joe concluded.

Freddie suddenly jumped on Joe, growling in his ear like a wild beast.

'Didn't spot this predator, did you?' said Freddie locking him in a stranglehold.

'Get off me,' Joe screamed with a violence that took Freddie aback.

'All-right, all-right. Just chill. It was only a joke.'

'Why do boys always have to fight?' Hannah said. 'Just behave you two.' She had always been slightly jealous of boys fighting. Girls carried more tension inside themselves, anxiety that boys managed to release.

They had by now navigated the increasingly hot grounds of the school, and, guided by the footsteps and noise of countless others, arrived at the Assembly Hall.

Once inside, they took in the details: paintings of old headmasters; verses and proverbs designed to be inspirational; noticeboards cluttered with society notices and rosters; the slightly shoddy grand piano that looked out-of-tune even if it wasn't. Some of the older pupils were studiously cool, boys greeting each other after the holidays with gripped arms and chest-bumps, whilst girls hugged and shrieked. A row of teachers sat on the stage taking in the new pupils, aware that the new pupils were doing precisely the same.

In the middle of the stage sat Jacob Ubuntu in a high-backed chair. Once everyone was seated, he rose slowly and gracefully. Freddie wondered if this was because of his age or to ensure his gravitas. Since he was a slim man, who appeared agile, he plumped for the gravitas. The hall drained of noise as pupils dropped their excited chatter.

'Welcome to all of you who are new to The Augustineum.

Welcome *back* to all the others. I hope you all had a good break. This is our Spring Term. This will seem odd to those of you used to the seasons of the Northern Hemisphere.'

'Topsy-turvy,' whispered Hannah to Joe.

'The water spirals a different way down the plughole,' Joe noted sotto voce.

The Headmaster continued.

'Here in Windhoek, we are lucky to have reasonably moderate temperatures, although it may not feel that way for some of you. It's one of the reasons this school was moved here and indeed why the capital is here. Capitals need to be places where you can think. However, expect some rain. Some of you will find that comfortingly familiar. I am thinking particularly of the English of course.'

A laugh flickered across the hall like a brief flame.

'At the Augustineum, we pride ourselves on being one of the finest schools in the whole of Southern Africa. Past pupils include a number of Namibian Presidents, Prime Ministers and Mayors.'

'Didn't know they bred horses,' quipped Freddie in Hannah's ear.

She looked at him quizzically.

'Mares!' he said by way of explanation, which kept Hannah in stifled giggles.

Joe found himself wishing he had Freddie's easy charm.

'But I don't want to talk about the school today,' Ubuntu continued. 'Many of you know it already and the newly-arrived amongst you will know it soon enough. All I will say at this stage, is that we are interested in the whole you.'

'Ewe! Now he's on to sheep,' Freddie remarked, throwing

fuel on to Hannah's bonfire of giggles. Joe gave them both a 'Have some respect!' scowl.

'I want to talk to you briefly today about the country in which you are now living and learning... my country... Namibia.'

The sacred respect for his country in Ubuntu's voice made Hannah's heart slow and her muted giggles die in her throat. His passion and seriousness found an echo in hers.

'Namibia is one of the emptiest countries in the world, as you can plainly see when you travel through it. Our population is small - about two and a half million - but our land is vast. Yet, Namibia is never empty of ideas, or of surprises. It is dominated by Nature and not by Man. There aren't many places left on Earth where you can still say that. To walk through Namibian landscapes is to experience what our ancestors experienced: vast terrains in which we are small, vulnerable, stilled by the wonder of the world. To go, as some of you have, from Times Square or Tiananmen Square to the Namib or Kalahari Desert, is to travel 20,000 years back in history; to learn to be alone again; to be the hunted as well as the hunter.'

As Jacob Ubuntu surveyed the rows of alert and still faces in front of him, he knew he had possession of their minds. It electrified him but also gave him an overwhelming sense of responsibility. His throat dried and he reached for a glass of water. Now that he had them, he must etch something deep and lasting in their memories.

Hannah swallowed hard. Joe and others coughed as a release of tension. Freddie crossed and uncrossed his legs and stared deep into Ubuntu's eyes.

'This south-west corner of an ancient continent should

inspire you about what human beings can achieve against the odds. You sit in a land which has been invaded, segregated, dominated, re-named and... shamed. Yet it is now a modern state and I, and many others, believe it could thrive. My fervent hope is that this story, of the country I love, will be your inspiration during your time here. I also hope that you will become ambassadors for Namibia when you leave here: a small but strong community of people who have been touched by its magic and who have learned from its resilient people.'

He paused to take another sip of water. The hall seemed to collectively breathe out for the first time in minutes. The words were etched, the memory placed.

'Now to slightly more mundane matters. Teaching begins tomorrow at 8.30,' Ubuntu continued. 'I will be teaching you all African Studies once a week.'

After Assembly, Hannah, Joe and Freddie found themselves in a cosy corner of the Reading Room. It was on the ground floor of the Boarding House, designed as a relaxation space, a common room for those who weren't in the sixth form. It was Victorian, with dark, wood-panelled walls and bookshelves filled with games, magazines and newspapers from around the world that were 2-3 days out of date. There were books as well, rows and rows of them, much to Hannah's delight.

Bizarre though it seemed in such a hot country, the founders of the school had built a large and grandly decorated fireplace: big enough to have an inglenook: an arched space jutting out from, and surrounding, the fireplace. It was like a little room inside the larger room and the three of them were drawn to its cosiness. You could be private and yet observe all those around you at the same time.

'I thought what Ubuntu said was inspiring,' Hannah said.

'My father thinks Namibia is one of the most extraordinary countries in the world. He's studied quite a few, so I tend to believe him,' Joe added.

'What does he do?' asked Hannah.

'Dad? He's an anthropologist,' Joe replied.

'Anthro what?' asked Freddie.

'The study of different cultures,' Hannah said, keen to impress and hoping she was right.

'Yes. He's a Professor. He wants to study the tribes here. One in particular. He's been looking at the papers of some of the missionaries who came here, a hundred and fifty years ago.'

'Sounds amazing,' said Freddie, conjuring up an image of map-reading and ancient trails that he found intoxicating.

'What about your mother?' Hannah asked, always wanting families to be defined by their mother as much as by their father.

'Ah! My mom is here for different reasons,' Joe replied. 'She works for a hotel company… for people who want 'real adventures.' When they heard that my dad was going to be posted here, they saw it as an opportunity for her to scout for new sites.'

'Gosh, your parents are glamorous,' Freddie exclaimed.

'Oh yes, there speaks the son of an Ambassador!' Hannah retorted.

'Hold on. Your father's an Ambassador?' Freddie said keeling backwards with the kind of laugh that signalled he'd been upstaged, like someone in a card game who'd suddenly been presented with his opponent's unbeatable cards.

'Well yes, he's the UK High Commissioner to Namibia,'

Freddie said, half with embarrassment and half with pride.

'So, how come you're not living in splendour at the Commission?'

'And inviting us to posh receptions,' Hannah added. 'I asked the same question.'

'My parents thought it was better for me if I boarded during the week; even though they're just here in Windhoek. Good for my independence...'

Joe and Hannah both tried to work out whether Freddie was hurt or whether he'd been happy to 'take the medicine.' They were also wrestling with the same question.

'You're so lucky to have them nearby,' Hannah said, trying to make Freddie feel better.' My parents are in Swakopmund. I don't know how often I am going to see them.'

'Why Swakopmund?' asked Freddie, happy to be taken away from his own situation.

'Dad's job. He has to be based there. The mines are nearby. Mum found a job at a school there.'

'What does she teach?' Freddie asked.

'Languages. She's also a translator,' Hannah added, feeling pride. 'She says there are clicking languages here.'

'Clicking?' Joe exclaimed.

'Yes, the clicks are like consonants,' she said, feeling the strangeness of it as she said it. 'Mum played me a recording of it. It's extraordinary. You have to hear it, both of you. I'll find it on my phone for you. What about your mother Freddie?'

'She's a doctor!' Freddie replied. 'But not a witch doctor...'

Joe wasn't sure if he was annoyed by Freddie's verbal juggling or jealous. His skill was with numbers not words. He felt at home with their certainty. Sometimes words felt like a lake in which he might drown. But then he also thought how paltry the permutations of twenty-six letters seemed, compared to the infinite sequencing of numbers!

'Witch doctors don't still exist, do they?' said Hannah.

'Of course, they do,' said Joe, relying on half-understood conversations with his father about local tribes.

'My mother is working with AIDS patients,' said Freddie. 'She says the tribal doctors believe it's a curse on Africa, a plague!'

Their conversation flowed for what seemed like hours, halted only by the bedtime bell. They banished anxiety with laughter. They started to confront the exciting if unsettling truth that they were living in Africa. What kind of Africa, they didn't yet know. But they were about to find out…

3

Sossusvlei

A month later

It was the Augustineum field trip to Sossusvlei, the most spectacular range of sand dunes in the world, the russet-red jewels in Namibia's crown.

Their school coach had set off from Windhoek absurdly early, in the dark and relative cold of a February morning, to get to the dunes at a reasonable time and avoid the blistering heat of mid-day as they climbed. The bleary un-reality of it all only added to the excitement, as they drank in the cold air, slung rucksacks into the gaping mouths of the coach's innards, and fell up the coach steps to their seats.

Hannah, Freddie and Joe sat as far forward as they could. That was always their instinct: in classes, assemblies, queues for lunch and now field trips. It hadn't been Joe's, but he had learned to go along with it. They were enthusiasts.... or 'swots' as other pupils liked to call them. Each had the kind of mind that rarely rested: a fault they encouraged in each other to the point of exhaustion.

After only a month of knowing each other, they were inseparable, swimming as a shoal. Like most close friends, they had a shorthand between them; a store of references to hilarious moments that bonded them ever tighter.

They had been trying to pronounce Sossusvlei from the moment that the trip had been announced.

'Sausage vlei!' Hannah giggled.

'Or Saucisson vlei…if you're French!' Freddie added.

'Or S.O.S. susvlei, if you're in trouble!' Joe concluded.

Hannah fell on to Freddie's shoulder laughing hysterically. Three was an awkward number, especially when it came to sitting on a coach. So, Hannah and Freddie had sat themselves in one row, Joe in the row immediately behind, with the promise of a swap on the next leg of the journey.

Joe felt slightly displaced but covered his tracks with a constant exuberance. His long fringe often came in handy, covering one eye and several emotions.

The coach slowed and stopped by the entrance to the Namib-Naukluft National Park.

'Here at last,' said Joe, jumping up and ready to make a sprint to be the first out of the coach.

'Please sit down,' said the coach driver abruptly 'We are only stopping for a minute…just to pick up our guide.'

Joe sank back down again, his quest for fresh air thwarted.

The coach door swung open with a hydraulic hiss and a blast of sandy, midday air. The driver answered an invisible, enquiring voice from outside the coach: 'The Augustineum trip? Yes, this is it!'

A tall, thin and proud Namibian woman with broad shoulders and muscular arms, climbed the steps with the slow-moving grace of a leopard conquering a tree. Ilana van Zyl's head was angled slightly upwards, catching the full force of the light. Her hair was thick, black and shoulder-length as it tumbled down her long elegant neck. From her ears hung two large earrings: red discs like traffic lights. Her smile was of someone in charge and comfortable with it.

Behind her, wearing a bored, sulky look, was a teenage girl, clearly her daughter. The mother was dressed in beautiful native colours, fresh green against the relentless orange and red of the landscape. Her daughter was boyish and dressed in a blood-red T-shirt and jeans. Her hair was cropped short. Her face was strong and timeless, almost regal.

'Go and sit down somewhere, Selima. There, next to that boy.' She pointed to the empty space in the second row next to Joe.

Joe, intrigued by this beautiful, boyish girl, obligingly moved to the seat by the window and brushed the breakfast crumbs off Selima's seat as a welcoming gesture. Selima settled next to him but refused to look him in the eye, twisting her body to face diagonally across the coach away from him.

The tall woman was now blowing on the coach microphone to see if it was working. Her breath grated on the suddenly erupting speaker system like sandpaper. A few who had been dozing opened their eyes.

'Good morning, everyone,' she said.

'Good morning,' the uneven chorus returned.

'My name is Ilana Van Zyl, and I am going to be your guide here at Sossusvlei,' she continued.

'Ah so that's how you pronounce it,' said Freddie out loud, almost involuntarily, and to the amusement of his fellow travellers.

Ilana laughed with them, which warmed everyone to her. At first, she had seemed too daunting, too proud by half. Now they had some measure of her.

'Yes, it's not one of the easiest names. Someone once said it sounds like a snake sneezing.'

This caught Joe unawares, touched his funny bone, and triggered an unstoppable cascade of laughter.

Selima looked at him, half-attracted, half-alarmed.

'What it means in English is "Dead-End Marsh." So, you might prefer the Afrikaans,' she said smiling.

Selima knew these words as if they were the script of her childhood. She found herself fascinated by Joe. Her sneaky, sideways glances gathered as much information about him as possible: his black American trainers and his rectangular smart watch with which he was clearly obsessed. This was another culture made flesh.

'We are now inside the Namib-Naukluft National Park and we are going to drive to the famous sand dunes, some of the highest in the world.'

Joe plucked up courage and turned to Selima.

'Hi, I'm Joe. Joe Kaplan,' he grunted.

'Selima.' She didn't feel the need to add her surname. Her first name would be distinctive enough and anyway she felt suddenly self-conscious about the link to her mother.

'This is Hannah and Freddie,' Joe added, as they both spun round, proffering a 'high five' through the space between the headrests.

'That's your mum I assume…our guide?' Hannah asked, immediately wanting to validate her theory.

'Do we look alike?' Selima asked 'Or is it just because we came on the coach together?'

'Actually, you have a similar voice,' Freddie offered. 'I think that's how you often recognise families.'

'Well yes, she is my mum,' Selima replied, sounding curter than she had intended. So, she followed it up with a warm enquiry.

'So, you are all at the Augustineum right? That must be so cool. You board, yes?'

'No, we're never bored,' Freddie jumped in, 'that's the whole point.'

'That's why we board,' Joe added.

'Ignore them,' said Hannah 'They give up…eventually.'

Selima laughed, liking Hannah instantly for the way she could handle boys, and decided to plough on with her interrogation.

'Isn't it strange to be apart from your parents though?' she asked.

'It is. But it feels free,' said Freddie, who twisted round to face Selima full-on, slightly to Hannah's annoyance.

Selima, gazing at her mother, who she knew would be checking on her, felt the thrill of this idea pass through her.

'It's also odd and lonely at times,' said Hannah, determined to be more honest than the boys. Then she worried that perhaps only she felt like that.

'I agree,' said Joe. 'It can be lonely. It's like you're drifting sometimes. On a space-walk.'

'Never heard you say that before,' Freddie interjected.

'Perhaps you weren't listening,' Joe replied curtly.

'I wasn't criticising. I just wish I'd known,' Freddie said, remembering a few nights he'd lain awake feeling wretched and abandoned. His parents and Clara were only a few miles away, but it felt sometimes like the dark side of the moon.

Selima was touched by their honesty. She also looked at

her mother with new appreciation.

'Where do you live?' Joe asked.

'Swakopmund,' she replied.

'OMG. That's where my folks are living,' exclaimed Hannah. 'My mum is teaching at a school there. She helps students… with problems.'

'Which school? Which problems?' Selima asked.

'Swakopmund High… learning problems?'

'That's my school. What's her name?' Selima asked.

'Sarah. Well, I suppose she'd be Miss Chiang to you.'

Selima shivered and went quiet. So, she was 'a child with problems' and this was her special needs teacher's daughter. She felt pinned and classified, like a butterfly. It was true of course and she knew it. Yet somehow it was shocking to hear it said, and by someone she'd only just met.

'No, I haven't come across her,' Selima said, hoping she wouldn't blush and that the subject would change.

The road had narrowed to a corridor flanked by dunes, two hundred metres high, on either side. It was as if a Red Sea of sand had parted for them.

'Wow! Look at the size of that!' Joe exclaimed.

Ilana flicked the 'On' switch of her coach microphone.

'On our left is the famous Dune Forty-Five' she announced.

Thirty heads turned as one, as if watching a tennis match.

'I bet it's named after the forty-five-degree angle of the slopes,' Joe suggested.

'Dune Forty-Five refers to the fact that it is forty-five kilometres from the entrance to the park,' Ilana explained.

'That's just so dull,' Joe commented in a loud stage whisper.

Selima giggled in inverse proportion to her mother's frown.

Hannah's arm shot up.

'Are we going to climb it, Miss?'

'No. We are holding out for something even better. We are going to climb the father of all dunes, literally. I am talking about "Big Daddy".'

They stood, open-mouthed, at the base, staring up at its full 325 metres. 'Big Daddy' seemed to taunt them with its size.

'Remember Lawrence of Arabia?' Freddie asked, and then declared, 'I'm not daunted by this.'

He swept a white kufiyah around his head, adjusted the agal, and shook out the headscarf, so that it flowed over his shoulders. His father had bought it for him on a diplomatic trip to the United Arab Emirates.

'Remember Selima of Namibia,' Selima declared, twisting her prized baseball cap around her head so that the peak fell at the back and protected her neck from the overhead sun. She wouldn't have been so sensible had her mother not been there.

The five-million-year-old sand changed colour from orange peel to burnt sienna under their feet as they climbed. The dune's ridge had looked as thin and sharp as paper from below, but was just about fat and wide enough to keep their feet stable when they got to it. What they hadn't allowed for was the sand grabbing your ankles at each step.

It took an hour of tough walking to reach the top, Selima cursing the long piece of cardboard she'd tucked under her arms, on which to ride the descent. By then, their hamstrings were on fire. The ridge, with its hundreds of 'evenly-spaced', indentations, from feet trampling on each side, now looked for all the world like a dinosaur's spine. This strange anatomy continued as hundreds of dunes curved and weaved as far as the eye could see. Some of them looked like bodies turned on their side. The low-hanging sun cast its magic like a lantern, sharp ridges dividing light from shadow.

Freddie, Hannah, Selima and Joe hugged each other with the thrill of arriving at the summit. The view was unforgettable.

'Now you can understand why they call it the "dune sea",' Selima proudly declared, bursting with a love of her country. Surely, however far and wide her new-found friends had travelled, they could never have encountered anything to match this. They might be citizens of the world, but now it was their turn to be humble in her world.

Down below them, at the base of Big Daddy, were the 1,000-year-old, mummified trees of Dead Vlei. Stripped of the veins and arteries of leaves and twigs, the dead camelthorn trees looked like iron: architectural forms twisted into black question-marks against the iridescent blue of the sky. The desolation of the vlei made them shiver, even in the heat of mid-day. These were trees that had died in the eleventh century as William the Conqueror had claimed an exhausted England. Yet they were still standing. Salt killed and salt preserved. Salt didn't forgive. Lot from the Bible stole into Freddie's mind.

The salt pan shimmered with a heat haze as they gazed down at it, giving the illusion of a very shallow lake. Yet there was no water, only hot air shimmering.

'It's like a graveyard for trees!' Hannah exclaimed.

'This is how the whole world will look if global warming can't be stopped,' Freddie added.

They contemplated the fate of their planet in silence.

'Why are you carrying that large piece of cardboard?' Joe asked Selima.

'I am using it to ride the dune.'

'So, it has some hidden aerodynamic properties?' Joe giggled.

'Aerodynamic?' Freddie exclaimed. 'It's about as aerodynamic as a front door!'

'Depends how it's used and who uses it,' said Selima.

They watched a group of their fellow students suddenly release themselves down the steep slopes of the dune as if fired from a gun. Some leaped down, shifting weight from one leg to the other, as if hopping on hot coals. Others jumped with both feet at the same time, enjoying the depth to which their feet sank and the reverberations back up their spines as they landed. Some ran straight down, others went diagonal. Their shadows raced, licking the sand.

'It's a tradition at Dead Vlei,' Selima said, 'to run down as fast as you can, without falling.'

'There's no vlei you're going to be beat me,' Freddie announced, already planning his route with his eyes.

A diagonal is going to be quickest, Joe thought to himself, careful not to divulge it.

'Oh my God,' Hannah screamed.

Her foot had slipped off the ridge and was sucked down by what felt like an opening mouth of sand, its lips and tongue rolling up her leg.

Freddie and Joe didn't notice. There were already locked in an alpha male exchange of bragging rights. They ran along the ridge trying to find the perfect start-point.

Selima thankfully came to Hannah's aid.

'Here, grab my hand!' Selima said. 'Sand can be treacherous, like water. It envelops you sometimes.'

Hannah felt secure again in the grip of Selima's outstretched arm. Selima felt strong and Hannah blushed with pleasure. She looked into Selima's eyes to see if she'd noticed. She was sure she had. They both smiled.

The boys broke the magic with their shouts.

'Hey. Bloody win-at-all costs cheat!'

Joe had pushed Freddie backwards on to his bum to give himself a head start and was running full pelt down the slope at a diagonal, having calculated that the pull of gravity would be more controllable at an angle.

Freddie bounced back up and decided the only way to beat Joe was to run as fast as he could straight downwards.

Freddie knew that you should, when running downhill, just relax your body and let gravity pull you down. Yet, there was nothing rational about running down the largest sand dune on the planet. He felt the exhilaration of warm air rushing against his face. There was a thrill in his legs gaining their own momentum, rejecting his brain's message to slow down. One moment he was fully aloft. The next came the pounding of feet sinking in sand. Then up again like an angel. Down like an earthling. He was just about staying upright and drawing closer to Joe every second, but the pace was too fast. He slipped, fell with full force on to his side and then span like tumbleweed to the bottom. Fortunately, he encountered no stones or tree roots and finally rolled to a halt with a dull thud pounding in the back of his head, but eyes lit by the sky and laughter.

Hannah meanwhile had plumped for jumping with both feet simultaneously, in a series of double thuds, like a kangaroo.

She counted the sand dunes ahead of her as she jumped. Each time she landed she called out a number.

'Twenty-five, twenty-six, twenty-seven…'

Fascinated, she looked ahead at how the horizon lowered and the dunes opposite rose with every jump. The sand felt like a warm trampoline as she rose up, free and happy. Until, that is, she almost landed on Freddie's head, which, upside down, took on the look of a grisly Greek mask.

'Yikes!' she screamed, missing his head by a fraction by falling sideways and away from his outstretched form.

After a moment, they rolled towards each other and laughed with the thrill of surviving the run.

Selima chose that moment to glide past them in a gracious arc, body flat, stomach down, on her improvised front-door of a sandboard. Her muscular arms lifted the front of the board above the sand to avoid friction.

'Well done you two,' she beamed.

Joe, meanwhile, having ended his diagonal run a distance from them, ran to join the happy horde.

Gradually their breathing became less staccato, slowed as one.

They were the last of their group to reach Dead Vlei. They could see the others walking towards the coach in the distance. They gazed around at the medieval trees.

'What can you see?' Selima asked.

'Dead trees and sand?' Joe retorted.

'No, look more carefully,' Selima urged. 'What can you see in the shapes of the trees? I can see an impala, rising- up, on two legs. See, over there!' She pointed.

'I can see a ballerina, leaning forward,' Hannah said, taking up the theme.

'And I see a man walking in a high wind,' Freddie added.

'A serpent trying to bite the clouds,' Selima announced.

'I can see all the letters of a new alphabet, one per tree,' Joe added, 'like a giant pop-up book.'

They searched for each other's forms as they called them out. It was like scanning clouds for shapes, but standing upright.

'Do you think this vlei is what a dead planet looks like?' Hannah questioned.

'Actually, something remarkable happens here,' Selima said, 'about once every ten years. My mum often talks about it to tour groups. I remember seeing it when I was about five.'

The others turned to her, expectantly.

'There's torrential rain. It comes down so hard and lasts so long it feels as if the end of the world has come… like Noah's flood. Then the river behind us – the Tsauchab – floods and bursts its banks. It sweeps out towards the ocean over there.'

She could see the river in her mind's eye, surging like a madman through the desert.

'This vlei fills with water and stays full,' she continued, 'sometimes for up to a year, long after the flood has gone.'

'It's hard to imagine this place alive,' Freddie said, casting his eye over the vast saltpan, cracked like crazy paving as far as the eye could see.

'What's it like?' Joe asked, captivated by Selima's shining eyes.

'It's like nothing you can imagine. The dunes are reflected in the water… as if they had doubles. There are swarms of dragonflies, hovering, held in a trance. There are waterlilies on the lake, and devil-thorn flowers all around edge. Even the birds come.'

They all looked at the desiccated dryness in front of them and tried to imagine the scene in Selima's head.

'Selima, I'm so glad we've met you,' Hannah said, slipping her arm through Selima's. Namibia was coming alive for her.

'Me too,' Selima smiled 'I feel as if I have known you all forever. You just…didn't appear until now. But you've always been there.'

'Let's set up a group… on WhatsApp,' Joe suggested. 'Come on, I'm taking the cover photo for it right now. Selfie time!'

'How are you going to get all of us in, with the sand dunes as well?' Hannah asked.

'Leave it to me,' said Joe.

'Please don't tell me you've got a selfie stick! My mum says they're the tourist curse.'

'What do you take me for?' Joe responded indignantly.

He opened his rucksack, with its multitude of pockets and sewn-in 'I love Math' and 'Silicon Valley' badges. He retrieved a small, neat, zipped-up bag and opened it. It contained every kind of computer lead, charging cable, and adapter imaginable, plus a series of neatly arranged specialist screwdrivers. He unzipped an inside pocket and pulled out a Stanley knife and some silver gaffer tape.

'This is Joe's version of a first aid kit. It's for computers, not people,' Freddie observed.

'Sure, who cares about people? They only have a finite time left,' Joe observed. 'Can I borrow your sandboard?' he asked Selima.

Selima handed it over, an act of trust she had rarely bestowed.

'You don't mind if I just add an extra feature?' he asked.

Joe proceeded to cut the cardboard, fold and tape it, at one end of the sandboard, to make a kind of holder. He then strapped his mobile phone inside it. He picked up the sandboard with the mobile phone carefully taped to its far end. The six-foot distance between him and the phone allowed for the perfect, wide-angle photo.

'This should give us the right field of vision. Right everyone come and stand at this end.'

'There's only one problem,' Hannah observed. 'How are you going to be able to reach as far as the phone to take the picture?'

'Ah. I have a cunning alternative to extendable arms. It's called a timer and it's already set. OK everyone, smile!'

As Joe and Freddie held the sandboard up, they all struck up the crazed poses that social media required. After a few shots, the sandboard started to droop at one end under the weight of Joe's mobile.

'Uh-oh. That last one's a sky shot,' Joe exclaimed, as the board wilted under the weight of his mobile, tilting it backwards.

Photos complete, Joe gave the sandboard back to Selima and returned his mobile to his pocket. He felt accomplished.

As they walked on through the blackened camelthorns, touching the bark for luck, they tried to agree a name for their WhatsApp Group.

'The Augustineums?' Freddie suggested.

'No, that leaves Selima out,' Joe said chivalrously. 'Anyway, it sounds too pompous.'

'Four Go Mad in Namibia?' Freddie offered.

'Likely to happen!' Selima laughed.

'Four Sides of One Rectangle!' Joe suggested.

'No, Joe!'

'I've got it,' Freddie said. 'Just look around us...'

'What?' Selima asked.

'The Four Teenagers of the Apocalypse!' Freddie declared.

Eight feet stopped as one. The name was settled.

That evening, the air was like water: clear, clean, free of sand at last. The temperature was kind, no bite from either heat or cold. They tumbled out of their tents, limbs aching but minds alert.

Selima had persuaded her mother to let her sleep in the same tent as Hannah and not, as was customary, with her. Any hurt Ilana felt was banished by the warmth she felt on seeing Selima find some soulmates. She always worried about her only child spending too much time on her own; or tagging along with Darius.

She had shouted at the four straggling, giggling teenagers - the last to board the coach that afternoon - but it had been a happy shout, its anger just a pretence to please the driver.

'Do you think the rest of us are happy to just sit here in the boiling heat waiting for you four to turn up?'

She felt love for these three strangers who had taken her daughter instantly and instinctively into their world.

The four of them spent early evening at the camp, half-exhausted and half-drunk on friendship; exchanging stories and fragmented notes on their lives; taking it in turns to play music from Spotify and share frustrations about their parents.

Now, a path snaked into the distance in front of them, lit by flares on both sides. At the end of this 'runway', in the near distance, was an enclosure lit from within by fire.

'That's the Boma,' Selima said.

'Boma?'

'They sometimes call it a Kraal as well. It's an enclosure to keep the animals safe. They often use it for special meals.'

'Ironic,' Joe observed.

Selima looked at him blankly. 'Why?'

'Building an enclosure to keep animals safe and then cooking them inside it,' he explained.

'Don't you tell stories in a Boma?' Freddie asked.

'Sure do!' Selima called back, dancing up the path in anticipation.

As they drew closer, the Boma glowed ever stronger against a dark, moon-bereft sky. What was going on inside was hard to see. A wall of wooden stakes, interwoven skilfully, was built around the Boma's perimeter, hiding its innards from view. They could hear well enough though…

There were drums with a beat as steady as a Masaai warrior's heart. There was clapping, its rhythms moving and shifting like sands in a storm. Overlaid on both were cries and whoops that seemed to call for the missing moon.

They rounded the perimeter and entered the Boma via a spiral that opened out like a shell.

In front of them as they entered, were ten Herero men and women singing and swaying like a gospel choir.

'Welcome to you all.
Welcome to you all.
Welcome to you all,
To the Boma.'

It was a warm river of welcome. The sound reverberated

off the inner walls, on which were hung a series of tribal masks for decoration.

In the centre of the Boma was a firepit, its scaffolding of criss-crossed logs ablaze, inside a circle of heavy stones. Spiralling outwards from the fire were lights of other kinds: paper lanterns on the sandy floor; oil lamps on dining tables set in a semi-circle, and finally electric lights which shone upwards into the canopies of the surrounding trees. It was as if the firepit had lit its own solar system and now stood at the centre.

The meal was delicious. There were 'kapana': strips of red meat sizzling on the grill and then dipped in a chilli, tomato and onion sauce. There were 'fat cakes': deep-fried balls of dough served straight from the pan.

'Carnivore's paradise,' exclaimed Joe as he tore into the juicy meat to Selima's amusement.

'What is that?' said Hannah poking at Joe's plate.

'Kudu steak,' said Selima. 'One of our specialities.'

'What? Kudu as in those delicate little creatures that leap around with horns?' Hannah replied incredulously.

'Antelope yes. This is the best game meat you'll ever taste,' said Selima, plunging her fork in and enjoying Hannah's squeamishness.

'Not for Hannah it won't be,' Freddie interjected. 'She's vegetarian.'

Selima spluttered.

'You're what? Vegetarian? But we only get vegetables five months of the year, and, even then, they're tough as old boots!'

'Welcome to Namibia,' Joe said sarcastically.

'Have some fat cakes,' said Freddie, somewhat more helpfully.

'Thanks,' said Hannah, touched by his chivalry.

'How about an ostrich egg?' Selima asked, beckoning to one of the cooks. She knew them all by now.

'If I must,' Hannah cried.

'Makes a big omelette,' Freddie proffered in encouragement.

Fortunately for Hannah they had 'Koeksisters' for dessert: small doughnuts dripping with honey and served with marula ice cream. The other three gave her extra portions.

After dinner came the dancing. First the women danced, then the men. They danced with a short plank strapped to one foot. As their feet stamped the ground, the sound echoed hypnotically around the Boma.

'They use their feet as drums,' Freddie exclaimed to Hannah. 'I love it!'

As the dance continued, the rhythm rose up the length of their bodies. Their legs were covered in shakers, like miniature tambourines. Their torsos shuddered and their arms shivered with rattles. Soon their whole bodies were possessed, pounding on the Earth as if demanding answers from below.

Their faces remained calm and poised though, as if they didn't belong to their bodies.

'It's a kind of trance,' Selima whispered to the others.

When the dancing had finished and the applause had died away, they were all called around the firepit for stories. This was the moment Selima always loved.

Faces glowed, eyes became coals, mouths fell open.

The first storyteller began.

'There was a legendary bushman called Mantis. He was named after the praying creature of the same name. His wife was Dassie, a rock badger and his adopted daughter was a porcupine.

Mantis, like all bushmen, lived without fire, and endured the darkness of long nights and eating meat raw. Until one day he saw the Ostrich take fire from under its wing and dip its food into the flames. The ungainly bird carefully tucked the fire back under its wing after eating, to hide it from the other animals.

The Mantis knew that Ostrich would not give him any fire and so he tricked it into eating from a plum tree, urging it to eat the sweetest fruits from the very top. As the ostrich stretched up on tiptoe, it spread its wings to balance and Mantis stole the fire from underneath.'

'And that,' concluded the storyteller, 'is how we come to have fire to cook our meat.'

Applause rippled through the forward-leaning crowd.

'Now, please tell us if you would like to hear stories on any particular subject,' the storyteller invited. 'We have stories about nearly everything. And when we don't, we invent them.'

There was a short silence which Hannah decided to break.

'Can you tell us a story about the Fairy Circles?'

Selima smiled to herself in anticipation of the reaction.

The Herero fell quiet. The quietness was infectious. It spread like a contagion to the students, and from the students to the teachers, and from the teachers to the animals, until the only sound was the crackling of the logs in the fire-pit.

All faces turned to the oldest of the tribesmen present. His face was as craggy as Fish Rock Canyon and his movements were deliberate like a reptile. He replied slowly and with caution.

'Well, there is more than one story about the Fairy Circles.'

No one was sure whether this was a polite refusal or an invitation for others to tell their stories first.

'Great. Let's have more than one. We have time, don't we?' Joe said, looking at Jacob Ubuntu for approval. Ubuntu's face was facing decisively downwards, however not wishing to engage. Joe feared that he had spoken disrespectfully.

'I mean the night is ours,' he added.

'The night is never ours...' the Elder replied, 'it is always shared with the ancestors.'

'They don't understand such talk,' Ubuntu intervened, worried about the rising discomfort of his simply curious students. 'Why don't you tell them about the Golden Leopard?'

'Very well.'

The Elder drew his seated self, up to its full half-height, and looked for suitable reverence from the young people's up-turned faces. He continued, once he had found it.

'Leopards are sacred to us. They represent the "oba": the power of kings. In fact, they are kings themselves, in their own territories. Kings of the forest, where they haul their prey up into the trees and hang them like trophies. Kings of the desert where they prowl under moonlight.'

He paused as an animal pelt was passed up the line of storytellers and wrapped around his shoulders. The pelt partly covered two bands around his neck. The upper band was made of rings of veld-grass woven through with makalani palm. The lower band was a metal necklace, from which hung, flattened arrowheads. The jewellery glowed with the light of the fire.

Ubuntu leant into the excited audience of his pupils and in a loud whisper said, 'The Chiefs wear the pard's pelt. Especially, when they speak of him.'

'Pard?' Joe whispered in Selima's ear.

'Short for leopard,' she whispered back.

The Elder resumed.

'Leopards are notoriously hard to find. They hunt from dusk until dawn. They retreat just as humans rise with the sun. They are masters of camouflage when they are still, fast as the wind when they run. They live alone, except when they are breeding. They are all rare, but none is rarer than the Golden Leopard.'

He paused to drink from a wooden cup. They watched his Adam's Apple twitch, then rest. Throat cleared, he continued…

'One day a Golden Leopard stalked a Kudu so stealthily that he could pounce on it from just five feet away. He snapped its throat like a twig.'

Hannah winced. A log jolted and fell off the fire, dislodging others. Half the audience jumped.

'Then he dragged his kill, its neck clamped in his jaws, back to his favourite acacia tree. But prowling at the base of the tree, waiting for him to return, was a large lion. Anger inflamed the leopard's eyes and seized his brain. The arrogance of this lordly lion who presumed he could just snatch the leopard's hard-earned prey! As he approached the tree, the leopard let the kudu fall to the ground, but with no intention of surrendering it. His stomach was as empty as a cave.

Lions will nearly always defeat a leopard. They will even, when they have a mind to, pull a leopard's prey out of its tree, from under its very tail. Such arrogance! But the Golden Leopard was cunning. He retreated several paces from the kudu, pretending to grant access. The lion stepped forward and sank his teeth into the prey. But, as he did so, the golden leopard ran forward and jumped on to the lion's back and sank his teeth deep into the muscled nape of the lion's neck.

The lion roared in pain. A roar that shook the ground where they stood and alerted the pride nearby. Undaunted and agile, the leopard grabbed one hoof of the kudu and pulled its leg across the throat of the lion. The lion struggled to breathe. The lion, however, was too strong for the leopard to strangle him. So, after forcing its way free, the lion limped away panting, vowing in its mind to return with the rest of the pride and kill the leopard.

After a while, when the shock had subsided and hunger had risen again to the fore, the leopard dragged the kudu up the acacia and strung it up. After he had feasted and rested, a chill fell across his heart as the moon rose.

The leopard knew that the lion would soon come to wreak revenge, to re-establish his power. A plan formed in his mind. He bounded down the tree and, belly full of meat, eyes defiant, he set out into the Namib desert alone. At first, he prowled, wary of lions. Then he ran. He ran so hard that the unforgiving sand hurt his paws and the wind turned his eyes to a stream of tears. And as he ran, he shook. He rotated his belly, arched his back and shook and shook and shook, until he could feel it in every sinew and tendon of his body.

As he shook, the splashy spots of his coat flew through the moonlit air like sparks from a fire. The leopard ran for a hundred miles, shaking, until all his spots were gone. Where each spot landed, a fairy circle grew. Finally, exhausted, he stopped and looked back at his tracks. There, pulsing under the moonlight, were a thousand glowing circles. It was as if raindrops had splashed from a giant's face, lacerating the sand.

The leopard found shelter by some rocks and slept. He slept for two whole days and nights without waking. When he finally rose, he smelt out a rockpool and drank. Then, looking at his reflection, he saw what he had hoped for. His body was free of all its spots and his fur was pure gold. He looked for all the world like a lioness, and that indeed was how he made himself safe from any more lions.

And, to this very day, the Golden Leopard with no spots, roams the Fairy Circles by night.'

For what seemed like the first time in minutes, Hannah breathed out. The Boma was held in a trance. Even the fire had grown silent under the spell.

Later, when they were lying in their tent, Joe turned to Freddie.

'You know what? The more they tell stories about the fairy circles, the more I want to get to the truth.'

4
African Studies

Jacob Ubuntu taught them African Studies on a Wednesday. It was a passion and a mission for him. His international pupils had rapidly changing lives. They jumped like a bolt of electricity from one country to the next, every two years. He wanted to soak them in his own deep and unfolding culture.

Today's lesson was about the paintings and engravings at Twyfelfontein.

The lesson was held in one of the more modern classrooms, well-equipped for presentations. Ubuntu's eyes were wide and glistening, and they carried within them the bright colours of his reflected PowerPoint slides. Drawings of rhinoceroses, giraffes, ostriches and elephants patrolled across his forehead like silent, ghostly herds.

'We used to think these engravings were made by our ancestors to teach their children how to hunt. Now we think these drawings had a deeper meaning.'

Another slide came up. It was of a lion but no ordinary lion. It had human feet and toes and an unusually long tail which suddenly and impossibly defied gravity by shooting up at right angles and ended in something like a paw. It was child-like in the way it was drawn, but somehow adult in its meaning.

'This is the famous Lion Man,' Ubuntu continued. 'This figure shows the transformation of humans into animals.'

An arm shot up with a question.

'Yes?' said Ubuntu, faintly annoyed that the spell of his excited narrative had been broken.

'Excuse me sir, but how is that possible? Humans can't transform into animals,' a voice asked from the back of the class.

'How long have you observed people?' Ubuntu asked.

'I can't honestly say, sir,' the voice in the darkened audience answered in a shy tremble. 'Perhaps, I haven't.'

'May I suggest that you start observing your fellow humans more carefully. And that you read a book called "Lord of the Flies." Then you will discover how easily humans can become animals,' Ubuntu replied. The room noticeably chilled.

Hannah's arm went up.

'What is at the end of the lion's tail sir?'

Freddie couldn't resist answering out loud 'Is it an improbable ending sir?'

The class laughed in appreciation.

'Thank you for your witty interjection, Mr Wilde,' Ubuntu commented with a withering sarcasm.

'Sorry to interrupt Headmaster,' Freddie replied.

'Interruptions are always welcome when they add something,' Jacob Ubuntu remarked, leaving it unsaid as to whether Freddie's remark could be classified as such. 'I think that Miss Chiang meant T-A-I-L, not T-A-L-E.'

He had already clocked Hannah as a star pupil, an observation confirmed, yet again, by her question. He also knew that if Hannah's parents were pleased with her schooling, word-of-mouth would work its sweet magic amongst the ever-more-important Chinese community.

'The answer to that excellent question is what is called a "Pugmark": in other words, an animal footprint.'

'Why was a footprint important enough to paint sir?' Freddie asked.

'Good question. Does anyone have the answer?'

'That's how they managed to kill and eat. They had to track animal footprints to survive.' Joe's answer was complete and impressive. He wasn't about to reveal that he knew this because of many Sunday afternoons learning about it from his father. Animal tracking was one of Ben Kaplan's keenest interests.

Ubuntu acknowledged the impressive nature of Joe's response and then continued.

'But there aren't just animals engraved on these rocks. There are also strange, geometrical patterns scattered everywhere.'

Another slide came up to illustrate the point. Joe's attention ratcheted several notches higher. His brain always engaged with geometric shapes, silently but rapidly, sifting their repeatable patterns.

'No one really knows what these patterns are,' said Ubuntu, 'but it is thought they may be maps to water sources.'

'Sir, could they be linked in any way to the Fairy Circles?' Joe interjected, forgetting in his excitement to put his hand up.

Ubuntu walked very slowly and solemnly towards Joe, in front of the screen onto which his slides had been projected. As he did so, his face was smeared and distorted by images of the strange geometric shapes from Twyfelfontein. It was as if he had contracted some rare skin disease. Only his stern look prevented another wave of laughter at his sudden 'rash'.

Ubuntu stood tall over the seated Joe.

'Why are you so interested in the Fairy Circles?' the Headmaster asked gravely.

'I am interested in the patterns sir… whether they are mathematical,' Joe continued in order to fill the silence, to make it less awkward. 'I saw them as we flew into from South Africa.'

'What did you see that so fascinated you?' Ubuntu enquired.

'I saw thousands of circles, sir. It was like … I don't know, like acne on a giant face…' Joe described.

Half of those present laughed and the other half felt uncomfortable in recognition of their own skin.

'I thought I started to see patterns in them as we flew over,' Joe explained and then in a pleading tone added 'What are they, sir? I heard the story at the Boma, but what do we really know?'

Ubuntu slowly returned to the front of the class, in order to respond with suitable authority. He pulled himself up to his full height.

'Fairy Circles are one of the greatest, unsolved mysteries of Nature. The circles are circular, bare patches, but with a ring of tall grasses around their edge.'

Ubuntu tapped excitedly at the keys of the classroom computer from which he was projecting. He exited his PowerPoint presentation, brought up Google and searched firstly for a map of Southern Africa, which he rapidly found and then enlarged.

'The circles, tens of thousands of them, appear in a band, or corridor if you like, that stretches fifteen hundred miles.'

He used his steel, extendable pointer as a kind of wand to indicate on the projected map.

'All the way from southern Angola up here, through

Namibia and down here to the Orange River in the North-western Cape of South Africa. This band is about a hundred miles inland. Most of it is very barren. We are not far from them here, actually.'

He then searched the term 'Fairy Circles' under Google Images and brought up some of the most dramatic. There were sharp intakes of breath at the sheer scale of the circles. They had been photographed from hot air balloons and small planes, their silhouettes falling sharp and angular across the intricate patterns.

'What causes the Fairy Circles, sir?' another voice piped up from the back.

This question seemed to momentarily paralyse the Headmaster. He visibly slumped and, as he turned to face the questioner, his eyes betrayed anxiety, possibly even fear.

'The truth is we don't entirely know what causes them,' Ubuntu admitted.

Freddie's hand went up next.

'What do people living near the circles think caused them, sir? We heard the story of the Golden Leopard but what else do Namibians think?'

Ubuntu cleared his throat before answering. He also sat for the first time, on a high stool stationed at the front of the class. He was happy to stand when talking about Science. Instinctively, he always sat when talking about Religion or Culture.

'Well, a tribe called the Himba believe their original ancestor, Mukuru, created the circles. Some believe that they are formed from the giant teardrops of the gods...or their footprints.'

75

Ubuntu's shadow was cast, vast and dark, upon the back-wall of the class by the light of the projector, as if he too was one of the gods walking upon the Earth, raised up high by his stool.

'Other tribes believe that the fire from the nostrils of underground dragons, or their poisonous breath, caused them. Many of them think the circles have magical properties.'

'What do you think, sir?' Hannah asked.

After a long pause, Ubuntu simply replied 'I don't know what to believe. And in that doubt, I am far from alone. They remain a mystery.'

He decided with that wistful phrase to end his lesson.

'Thank you, boys and girls. Next week, we will discuss the early tribes.'

As they filed out, the hubbub of pupils was almost deafening.

It was the last lesson of the day and Joe, Hannah and Freddie escaped into the fading heat and relative peace of the garden.

Hannah, spun round to face them both, walking backwards as she spoke to them. 'There's something extraordinary about the Fairy Circles, something other-worldly. I...'

Hannah's declamation was stopped mid-flow by a sudden collision. She tripped and fell backwards over a large pair of feet in mud-spattered boots.

'I am sorry, Miss,' the feet said.

It was Basarwa, the gardener. He extended both his hands to grasp hers and helped her up. She was mildly grazed but more embarrassed than hurt. Her mother's repeated advice not to walk backwards whilst engrossed in conversation came back to haunt her.

'No, it was my fault. I shouldn't have been walking backwards,' Hannah reassured him, sorry for his anxiety and pained expression.

'Are you OK?' Basarwa asked. 'No bruises or cuts? I have First Aid in my shed if you need it.'

She noticed that his thin, muscular arms were trembling.

'No, honestly, I'm fine,' she reassured as Joe chivalrously checked her legs for any sign of cuts or bruising.

Freddie handed Basarwa back his floppy hat which had fallen to the ground after the collision.

'Excuse me asking, Miss, but did I hear you talking about the Fairy Circles just now?' Basarwa asked.

'Yes, you did. Why?' Hannah asked.

'If you don't mind me saying, you need to be careful. Very careful. Those circles are sacred. Sacred to the San…my people.'

Hannah felt very flummoxed, very Western and very naive, as she gazed into his knowing eyes.

Basarwa continued, gripping her arms more tightly than she would have liked.

'You see…every circle is the grave of a bushman: a bushman killed by the white invaders. They have come, for hundreds of years, preaching their ways, killing us for being different. But we have lasted longer than anyone on Earth, until guns anyway. God has cried a giant tear for each one of us to mark where we fell. If you tamper with those circles, you tamper with the dead.'

That night, Basarwa's face haunted all of them. In the morning they woke exhausted but relieved to hear the birds.

5

Half Term Discoveries

Joe read out the inscription at the base of the statue that overlooked Windhoek, as his father circled it taking photographs. 'Their blood waters our freedom.'

'Powerful isn't it?' Ben suggested, in between snaps.

It was a half-term tradition: Joe was spending a few days at work with his father. They had got up ridiculously early, much to Joe's annoyance. He always looked forward to sleeping in at half-term: wallowing, half-asleep, in a warm bath of his dreams. This morning, his dream had been of Selima and vivid to the point that he felt she was in the room with him when he woke.

Sadly, the figure at the window that had greeted him had not been her, but his father tearing the curtains apart in an unspoken accusation of laziness.

'Come on. We're going to the Museum together. I want to get there early.'

There was little need for this last sentence because Ben Kaplan always wanted to get everywhere early. He was never up and about later than 6 a.m. regardless of when he'd gone to sleep.

Joe had lost count of the times when, in the holidays, he'd accompanied his father to the obscure vaults of a 'Museum of Native This' or 'Anthropological Institute of That'.

This morning, they had duly arrived at the Alte Feste, a

19th century German fort overlooking Windhoek. It was now largely abandoned with a sad museum inside. On the outside though, it glistened a pristine, toy-town white in the early sun. They were standing in front of a statue which Joe could tell, both from the emotion of its figures and its prominent position overlooking the capital, was significant.

A male and female Namibian stood side by side, on top of what appeared to be the half-dome of a skull, but was, in fact, the roof of a traditional hut. The outer arms of both the man and woman were raised to the sky in a triumphant gesture. Dangling from their wrists were the sawn-off shackles of the slavery from which they had just been freed.

'Whose blood?' Joe asked, referring to the inscription.

Ben stopped taking photographs and sat down on the grass next to Joe, staring him squarely in the eyes.

'Between 1904 and 1907, the Germans wiped out most of the Herero tribe and half of the Nama.'

'Why? What happened?'

'Four thousand Germans attacked six thousand Herero men. The Herero were defending forty thousand of their women and children.'

Ben picked up a stick and drew a crude map in the dirt to indicate what had happened.

'The Germans forced them eastwards into the desert. Then they refused them access to water. Ten thousand Herero died of starvation and thirst. Can you believe it? Then the Germans issued the order to exterminate the rest. Those that weren't shot, were put into death camps or used as slaves on the railways. They did the same thing to the Nama.'

Joe cast his gaze to the ground, shocked.

'So, Jews weren't the first people to be put in concentration camps?' he asked after a while.

'No, we weren't,' Ben replied, cupping his hands around Joe's face, lifting it up to his own. He kissed the top of Joe's head in gratitude for his very existence. 'And, tragically, we won't be the last either.'

'How many died?'

'They reckon sixty-five thousand Herero and ten thousand Nama.'

Joe got up and walked round the back of the statue, its true significance now clear. The sky was blue but now it felt dark. He'd had this feeling before, visiting the Holocaust Museum in Israel. From behind, the statue was even more powerful. The liberated Namibians, spines unfurled by freedom, seemed to be hammering on the gates of heaven, demanding to enter.

They both fell silent.

'Come on,' Ben called, deciding to lift the gloom. 'My crates will be waiting for me.'

A few minutes later, Joe was inhaling the musty smells of a storeroom, in the, nearby, Owela Museum. Its walls were bare and cracking, its shelves heaving with labelled antiquities and boxes. They sat at a workbench. His father had ordered a couple of crates to be brought up from the archives. Somehow, his request, made through the University, had got bogged down in paperwork and Joe could see the tense excitement in his father's hands and shoulders, having waited so long.

Ben hovered above the first crate, pausing momentarily, hands held aloft as if in prayer, before diving in with relish.

Joe had often observed his father at moments like this:

picking apart the entrails of different cultures, absorbed to the point of almost disappearing. How could he not admire him as well as love him? But, how often had he also felt put to one side by Ben's all-consuming passion for the past?

That's how it had happened, three years ago, when they were living in California.

It had been the last day of Summer Camp. The heat of the intense summer day was starting to fade as parents arrived en masse to pick up their children.

Lining up to greet the parents as they arrived at the camp car park, was a parade of cheerleaders in two ragged but enthusiastic lines. They sang their way through all the songs: songs that had become the soundtrack of their summer.

Joe gazed at every arriving car, hoping to pick out the familiar roof lines of their family station wagon. Behind each insect-spattered windscreen, Joe could see mothers, over-excited, anxiously trying to pick out their son or daughter's face in the waiting crowd. Fathers stepped out of the cars and arched their backs like cats, trying to stretch out the effects of long, stressful drives and searched for the elusive keys of roof-boxes.

There were hugs and tears aplenty. There were proud, excited, introductions of people's newly-acquired best friends to their parents, with pleased smiles and the criss-crossing of many hands. Dotted amongst these fever-pitched encounters were the inevitable arguments, as returning teenagers confessed to having lost or broken various possessions in the course of camp.

'Your parents here yet?' one of Joe's friends asked, struggling with an overstuffed rucksack.

'No, not yet. They're always late. I'm used to it.' Joe remembered catching a tone of bitterness in his own voice.

'Stay in touch on the Facebook Group yeah?'

'Of course. Cheers bud!'

As the parking lot emptied to a thin straggle of cars and the camp songs faded into the near-silence of the surrounding woods, Joe had started to feel worried. On her last call, his mother had told him that she was away on a conference and so his dad would pick him up.

He tried to call Ben's mobile. It went to voicemail. He texted. No reply. He tried again with the same response.

As his last friend left, his isolation felt embarrassing. Being conspicuously alone made him angry. Camp staff had come up to him to check if everything was all-right and to invite him into their cabin and he'd palmed them off with the same patter. He stayed defiantly sitting on his suitcase. He tried to look nonchalant, but the anger and panic was building inside.

He calmed himself, as he often did when confronted with a difficult situation, by calculating the probabilities of what might have happened. He had read that road accidents in California ran at an average of five a day. He calculated they would be lower in the summer because of better road conditions. He then looked up the population of California on his phone, divided it by two to arrive at a rough car population – two cars per average household of four – and then tried to work out the percentages and mathematical probabilities that his dad had been in an accident.

Four hours later, after finally succumbing to a painfully long and self-conscious wait in the caretaker's lodge, watching a baseball game, his father had finally shown up. Ben had forgotten he was supposed to pick Joe up. He had also been so absorbed in the finds from a recent dig, that he forgot his phone was on silent and failed to notice Barbara and Joe's frantic texts.

Joe could still remember trying to hide the hot tears of rage as Ben drove him away from the camp in silence. None of the profuse apologies from his father could disperse his anger and shame.

Joe struggled back to the present. His father had already picked a variety of objects from the first crate and placed them carefully in sections on the table, like a surgeon laying out instruments for an operation. One of them was a Victorian writing box with initials carved with italicised lettering on the top.

'Who is J.W.A?' he asked.

'General James William Alexander. Well, he was actually a Captain at the time he came to Namibia.'

Joe found himself curious about the range of objects on the table. There were painted rocks; stretched animal skins; spears with broken shafts; primitive cooking utensils now rust-red; a Bible; some old maps and sepia photographs.

'What do you know about him?' Joe asked.

'He was Scottish. Father was a financier who went bankrupt. He went into the Army, first for the East India Company, then the British Army. Travelled the world.'

'What period are we talking about?'

'Well he came to Africa in the 1830's'

'Why was he here in Namibia? The British didn't fight wars here, did they?'

'He fought in one of the Cape Frontier Wars in South Africa, then travelled north and fell in love with it. It wasn't Namibia then of course. He was sponsored by the Royal Geographical Society to explore what they called Damaraland.'

'Which is where?'

'Near here. He became fascinated by the local tribes.'

Joe picked up one of the explorer's notebooks and started leafing through it.

'Uhm. Gloves please,' his father said.

Joe had accompanied his father enough times to know where to find another pair of thin, transparent gloves in his father's bag. He squeaked a pair on. They were tight. He already had bigger hands than his father.

He returned to the notebook. He turned the pages slowly. There were, neatly labelled sketches, in faded ink, of the Herero cooking, hunting, lighting fires and dancing.

'What happened to him?' Joe asked, finding himself intrigued by the man who'd made these meticulous notes and sketches.

'That's the thing. No-one really knows. He wrote several journals, but we only have copies of the first. It was clear that he was enchanted by the Herero. He was also trying to unravel a mystery when he died.'

'What sort of mystery?'

'All we have is a letter he wrote home to his wife. He spoke about visiting somewhere the Herero believed to be a sacred resting place. He asked them to accompany him. When they came close to the spot, the shaman - their priest - fell into a trance. The elders took it as a bad omen, a sign from the ancestors. They refused to go any further. So, he went on alone.'

'What happened?' Joe had sat down on a stool wanting to bury himself further in the story.

'He describes entering an underground tomb. Something

panicked him and he left, vowing to come back.'

'So…?'

'That was the last letter he ever wrote. We don't know if he ever returned. His body has never been found.'

Joe fingered the notebook as his father was speaking. His mind was running.

'Mum, you must control your temper when you meet them. You know what you're like when you get on your high horse!'

Selima was feeling sick from the car journey. It was suffocatingly hot in her mother's small car because Ilana refused, on ecological grounds, to ever switch on the air conditioning. 'Save the planet but kill your offspring,' Selima had once said to her sarcastically, but it had zero impact.

Ilana was in a determined mood as they drove north into Damaraland.

'You don't understand, Selima. This country has only recently found its dignity. We're a democracy but we're also fragile… like so many small countries.'

'Small? I wouldn't exactly call Namibia small,' Selima exclaimed, gesturing to the vast landscapes wrapped around their car windows.

'You know what I mean, small in population. What's worse, we're rich in minerals and that means the whole world and his wife are queueing up to rape our land. Look at all the mines that are springing up.'

'Well mines are one thing. But this is a hotel. A hotel that hasn't even been built yet. I feel just as passionately as you do, about protecting our country. This is where I grew up, where I belong. I'm just saying, don't go overboard…'

'This isn't like you, Selima. Since when were you afraid of speaking out?'

'Look, Mum, Mrs Kaplan - the woman in charge of planning the hotel - is my friend's mother, OK?'

'Which friend?' Ilana asked turning her head away from the road.

'Joe.'

Selima thrilled at saying his name but tried not to betray too much excitement in her voice. Her mother had emotional radar like no-one else on Earth. She was forensic when she detected something.

'Is that your American friend? The one you sat next to on the coach?'

'You don't need to say it in that accusing way. Have you got something against Americans?

'Of course I haven't. Except when they ride roughshod over other people's culture.'

'It seems that most countries have done that in Africa. In fact, America less than most.'

'Look, I know you think I go off the deep end... but Namibia is not exactly short of land and they're planning to build this hotel right next to a sacred burial site. That's what I am trying to stop. Hold on. This must be it...'

They turned off the main road and down a dirt track, the tyres chewing the stones and scattering them as if in anger.

'Slow down, Mum, I'm feeling sick as it is.'

Ilana realised she was venting her anger on the car's accelerator and eased the angle of her foot. Some makeshift huts and tents came into view and a small mechanical digger. They were clearly already excavating ground to test it for the hotel's foundations.

Ilana got out of the car agitated, not waiting for Selima.

Barbara Kaplan was seated at, what the architect had laughingly called, a draughtsman's desk, but was actually more like a wall-paper pasting table. Sprawled in front of her were print-outs of Excel spreadsheets - her constantly shifting budgets - with jottings pencilled in the margins like angry graffiti. Next to those lay floor plans and elevations for the hotel, held down at the corners by pebbles and, in one case, an ostrich egg. The use of the egg only further exacerbated Ilana's growing sense of outrage when she spotted it.

Selima felt faintly sick at meeting Joe's mother for the first time in these circumstances. She knew from the way that Ilana had stormed out of the car that this was going to be painful.

She would hang back, disown her if need be.

She saw her mother extend her hand, which at least suggested a polite start.

'Mrs Kaplan?'

Barbara looked up from her plans.

'Yes. Guilty as charged.'

'Pleased to meet you. I'm Ilana Van Zyl.'

They shook hands.

Ilana gestured behind her.

'This is my daughter, Selima. She knows your son, Joe. They met on the field trip to Sossusvlei.'

Barbara looked piercingly at Selima. Any friend of her son was of immediate interest to her.

'Nice to meet you, Selima. Joe's talked about you often.' She wasn't sure he had, but it sounded like the right thing to say.

Selima tried not to blush or to feel too pleased.

'So, you're at the Augustineum as well?'

'No,' Selima replied. 'My mother was the tour guide on a school trip. That's why Joe and I met... and Hannah and Freddie.'

'I see,' Barbara said, trying to work out why a tourist guide and her daughter had arrived at their reconnaissance site. 'Well, welcome to our rather makeshift site. There are some rather uncomfortable stools tucked under here.'

Barbara pulled two of them out from underneath the table.

'There you are. Please, do sit. Can I get you some tea?'

Selima was about to say yes, parched from her mother's suffocating car, but her mother cut across her as the words were forming in her throat.

'That's very kind but no.'

'Then please at least have some water'

'Thanks!'

Selima poured water from the jug for her and her mother and gulped, not just from genuine thirst, but also to fill the horrible pregnancy of the ensuing silence.

'Mrs Kaplan...' Ilana began, as they sat around the table.

'Please. Call me Barbara.'

'Very well. Barbara, I believe you are planning to build a hotel here. Is that correct?'

'Yes. Well, my employers are planning to build a hotel here to be precise. We build what are usually called boutique hotels.'

Ilana wasn't getting any more comfortable. Selima decided that staring into the bottom of her water glass was preferable to watching her mother squaring up to this new adversary.

'You see, Barbara, although being a tourist guide is my job, my passion is conservation, the environment, sustainability, whatever you wish to call it.'

At the mention of these words, Barbara's heart sank. It was, a roll-call, of now sacred terms, with which she was all too familiar: from the protesters who always appeared whenever they had built their hotels around the world. She respected their views, indeed agreed with most of them, but it spelt headaches, more pressure.

Selima thought she saw Barbara's shoulders tense. She also noticed a heavy sigh which Barbara then sought to smother with reassuring words.

'We pride ourselves on our sustainability. It's paramount in all that we do.'

Barbara didn't even convince herself. She was aware that she was protesting too much, papering over the cracks of her boss's patchy environmental track record.

'We only use wood from FSC forests,' Barbara continued. 'No hardwoods. We use materials such as bamboo. Our brick is often re-constituted…'

Ilana put her hand up in a traffic warden gesture indicating that Barbara should stop her litany.

'I am not worried about your use of materials or your building methods. Indeed, I am reassured by what you have already said. My concern is something different. Are you aware of the nature of this site?'

Barbara hesitated. Did Ilana mean the soil or rock type? Or the views? The remoteness?

'I am not sure what you are referring to. Do explain.'

'I am referring to the fact that this is on the edge of an ancient burial site. A site sacred to the local tribespeople. Even the limited disturbance you have caused up until now has caused them great distress,' Ilana explained.

'No one has said anything,' Barbara protested.

'They're hoping you will go away. They find it difficult to confront foreigners.'

Barbara pulled herself up to her full height as if she were an accused prisoner in the dock about to deliver her own defence.

'There is nothing marked here to signify anything sacred… nothing on the landscape itself, nor on the maps that the local council has provided.'

Ilana pulled herself up to an even fuller height in response.

'That's because in Namibia, the maps that matter are in people's heads, in their collective memory. No planning clerk will give you that information. Although I keep lobbying that they should.'

Selima raised her eyes from her water glass, looked at her mum, her ardent posture, her passion, and felt a rush of pride. The justice of her mother's cause prickled the back of Selima's neck.

Barbara stood up and surveyed the terrain in front of them. There was nothing to indicate a burial ground. However, she cast her mind back to some work she had done in rural Australia several years earlier, when Joe was young.

They had been surveying another possible hotel site. The Aborigines had pointed a few hundred metres away to 'their larder, their food store'. She looked and saw only flat sand. After shrugging her shoulders and protesting, they took her over to the spot they'd indicated. After digging down a few feet with their cupped hands and some improvised spades, they pulled out 'provisions' kept cool in the damp sand, well below the burning surface. This was their 'fridge'. It had made her realise that not everything important below the ground was signalled above the ground.

'So how were we supposed to know this?' Barbara asked, trying not to sound too defensive. She was respectful by nature, but this was irritating her in the boiling heat. This was first-class inconvenience, and she could already envisage the rows with her boss, as it all unfolded and a new site had to be found.

'That's why I came here,' Ilana answered. 'I came here because I suspected that you didn't know and to stop your mistake from getting worse, from spreading like a stain.'

'We've started negotiations on the land,' Barbara said in an irritated tone.

'There are plenty of sites not far from here that would suit. In fact, they might well suit you better. They have better views, better transport links. We can help you locate them.'

'Look, Ilana, I appreciate everything you are saying but…'

At that moment a gruff voice cut her off.

'Mrs Kaplan, there's something you need to see…'

A head appeared from beneath where they were sitting. But even before the face appeared, the unmistakeable twang of the voice had made Selima and Ilana sit bolt upright.

'Darius?' Ilana exclaimed.

'Dad?!' Selima echoed.

Darius looked sheepish and shoved the spade in his hand trenchantly into the soil as a vent for his embarrassment. He was sweating.

'What are you doing here?' Ilana pressed.

'I told you I was helping out, driving, for an American company.'

'Yes, but I didn't know that you were also digging test excavations for a hotel. Or that it was here.'

Barbara, who had felt on the back foot before, now felt on two back feet. This family seemed to have surrounded her in their various ways and, to make matters worse, were now in conflict with each other.

'Darius, I had no idea,' Barbara said, 'that your daughter and my son knew each other.'

'Neither did I,' he replied defensively, 'until this moment.'

Selima's gaze darted between her two parents. She could see that her mother was struggling with this 'deceit' by her father. Equally, she could see that he was flummoxed and probably innocent of any crime. She always felt for his vulnerability.

'But, Darius, you are helping to explore foundations for a hotel that can never be built here,' Ilana protested, looking at him with a burning piety that Selima could see made her father defensive and angry.

'Well it certainly can't be built here now,' he said.

'What do you mean?' Barbara asked, trying to keep up.

'Come and have a look,' he replied, signalling for them all to follow him.

'Selima, I'm not sure you should come.'

'Don't be ridiculous, Dad!'

They all followed him down a straggly trail. A pit lay ahead, where they had been excavating. It was the size of a small swimming-pool and about as deep. In the corner of the pit, a worker stood as still as stone. At his feet lay what looked like a long and ragged bag of clothes.

As Selima got closer, she realised it was a military uniform of some kind. Inside the uniform was a skeleton, the shrunken remnants of the full-bodied man that had once filled it. The ribs protruded from under the jacket. Boots encased its skeletal feet, splaying them outwards with their weight and giving the corpse a sinister, clown-like appearance.

'I'm pretty sure it's a British Army uniform,' Darius said, circling the body. 'Victorian. You can tell from the VR on the buttons.'

'Not the burial site I was imagining,' said Ilana.

'Burial site?' Darius asked.

'There's supposed to be a tribal burial site here,' Ilana explained.

'Well, that may be beneath of course. We haven't dug that deep yet,' Darius pointed out.

Barbara found herself held in a grim fascination with this corpse. She knelt as close to it as she could bear.

'What's that wrapped around the… neck?' she asked, pointing. She hesitated to use the term as the neck was long gone.

'That's what I've been pondering,' Darius chimed.

'It's a Herero garland,' Ilana said with some certainty, kneeling close to the corpse. She knew tribal ways well and had studied them as part of her degree. 'It's a garland of honour. You can tell from the gemstones.'

Selima gazed at the gemstones dulled by the soil, strung together in a long, still-unbroken necklace. The contrast between their strong colours, muddied though they were, and the black of the decaying uniform, could not have been greater.

'This soldier was honoured by the local people when they buried him. That was rare,' Ilana commented.

Selima was silent. She was fixated by one thing. The jaws of the skull were wide apart, gaping. Perhaps all skulls buried for this long were like this, she didn't know. But it was as if this soldier, whoever he was, had died from a sudden shock, his jaw locked in horror, at the moment of his death.

'I must call Ben… my husband… Joe's father,' Barbara said, trying to gather her wits. 'He's an anthropologist. He'll be able to unravel what's happened here.'

'We have our own anthropologists in Namibia,' Ilana said defensively. 'Darius, what are you doing? Leave it…him… alone,' Ilana called out.

Selima watched fascinated as her father gently slid his hand into the inside of the skeleton's jacket and felt inside the pockets for clues to his identity. She didn't share her mother's squeamishness. If Darius hadn't investigated, she probably would have done the same.

He pulled out a Victorian pocket watch and rubbed it clean with his sleeve. It was in remarkably good condition. He turned it over, finding an inscription on the back.

'What does it say, Dad?'

'It's got some initials and a date. J.W.A. 1829.'

Freddie's father had worked in grander Embassies but none more interesting than this one in Windhoek. Spending a day with his father at work was always awkward, wherever they'd been in the world. He had often been palmed off with photocopying or filing of some particularly pointless kind. He was rarely allowed into meetings. They were 'confidential' and 'Government business' which he understood but resented. So, he eavesdropped when he could but was usually disappointed or confused by the fragments he picked up.

Once, he had accompanied his father to 10, Downing

Street. It was late afternoon on a Sunday and so the place seemed eerily quiet. His mother was away for the weekend with Clara, and so Ralph had no choice when the emergency summons came, but to take Freddie with him.

Downing Street was like a Tardis. From the outside it seemed a very modest, terraced, Georgian house, but once you were inside the famous front door, it all opened out. The door had swung open without them knocking which struck Freddie as quite magical. No wonder people liked these powerful jobs if doors opened automatically as you approached.

The Prime Minister had returned early from Chequers and Ralph was needed.

'Wait here,' his father said, 'and don't move. You've brought something to read, I hope. They're very strict on security here as you can imagine. I won't be long.'

If only Freddie had got £5 for every time he'd heard that one. He sat in a dark, unremarkable waiting-room and tried to read his book. He went into the toilet, excited by the idea that Prime Ministers had sat on its old-fashioned wooden seat. Then he wandered down a corridor leading to number 11.

Staircases seemed to appear in odd places like an Escher drawing. Computers and photocopiers lay silent, apart from one person in a far corner tapping furiously at the keyboard. He looked up momentarily as Freddie appeared, looked vaguely quizzical and then returned to the notes he was typing.

Returning to the entrance hall of Number 10, with its black and white, chess-board flooring, Freddie half expected the White Rabbit to run across it and disappear through a hidden door, pursued by a breathless Alice. He noticed that the man on security behind the front door was now nowhere to be seen.

It was too tempting not to creep down the central corridor further into the house. After all, how cross could they be with a stray ten-year old boy? He was already formulating lame excuses in his head. His heart raced as he crept down the corridor.

He stood in front of double-doors that seemed significant (he later learned it was the Cabinet Room) and heard voices from inside, including his father's. He quickly turned right fearing the double-doors might suddenly open and reveal him. He came to a very grand staircase with ornate banisters. On the walls stretching above him were portraits and photos of every Prime Minister. It looked too imposing to walk upstairs, so instead he proceeded down.

At the foot of the stairs he found a magnificent globe. It rested on a stand on the marble floor and must have been four or five feet tall. On the perimeter of the globe itself was a key to every flag of every nation in the world.

He leaned forward and spun the globe on its axis. Fortunately, it made practically no sound just the quiet shuffling of longitudes and latitudes. He thought about how many countries he had already visited, indeed lived in. He was struck by how manageable it all was when you could spin and control the entire world and race across continents, with your fingertips. It was so different to the actual, overwhelming impact of arriving in another country: the feeling on your skin, the unexpected smells, new horizons, gabbled languages. He had feared each new beginning and yet loved it as well.

He was so absorbed by his games with the globe, that he failed to hear the approaching footsteps.

'And how did you find your way here young man?'

He spun round. It was a policeman wearing a white shirt

and dark blue, bullet-proof vest. Attached to his vest was a walkie-talkie which periodically crackled into life with a burst of static.

'Sorry, sir, I am here with my father and I seemed to have got lost coming back from the toilet.'

'Who is your father?' the policeman replied, enjoying his authority.

'Ralph Wilde, sir. He's a High Commissioner.'

Freddie felt he sounded like a spoiled brat as he said these words. He was sure the policemen would feel the same. He felt just as ashamed of his privilege as he did at being caught.

'Is he indeed? Well I suppose that makes you a High Commissioner's son then,' the policemen goaded.

'I'm sorry, sir. I didn't mean any harm.'

'Come on then, let's take you back to where you're supposed to be'. His voice seemed to have softened at Freddie's tone of remorse but also of respect. Not like the snotty politician's kids he normally had to herd.

'My mum says I am always poking my nose where I shouldn't. Curiosity killed the cat.'

'Ah yes, but not the Downing Street cat. Have you heard about Larry the number 10 cat?' The policeman was enjoying this interlude in his boring Sunday afternoon.

'No, but I imagine he's allowed to roam anywhere?' Freddie said.

'He is… because of his role as mouser, you see,' the policeman explained.

Freddie was then treated to a tour of the grandest rooms in the house, many of which faced on to the garden at the back. Freddie's head was whirling by the time he was reunited with his pale and stressed father waiting by the front door.

'There you are, Freddie. Where on earth have you been? I told you not to move.'

The policeman intervened.

'And he didn't sir. I took pity on him, sitting in that dark waiting room for hours, so I gave him a tour. Sorry if that's caused you any alarm, sir.'

'Not at all. It's extremely kind of you. I'm very obliged officer.'

Freddie had never seen his father back down quite so quickly. He had made two mental notes at the time. One was 'Always be respectful to policemen.' The other: 'If you don't go wandering, you're bound to miss out on the best things in life.'

That's why today, whilst his father was embroiled in endless meetings, Freddie had ventured into every nook and cranny of the High Commission. He'd talked to the gardener about the vegetable patch and why the grass had started to scorch. He had helped the cook prepare a jug of iced smoothies in the basement kitchen. He had toured the digital photographs of Namibian tribes that his father had insisted should replace the old-fashioned paintings that preceded them. He had even tried to read a framed copy of the Namibian constitution.

Now the afternoon was rolling towards its conclusion and Freddie was fading. He was trapped in the boiling hot office next door to his father's. He could hear animated voices and realised that his father had mistakenly left the door to his office open. He could see through a gap between the door and its frame, into the room.

Ralph Wilde and a few of his team were gathered around a small table in the centre of which sat a triangular conference phone with speakers embedded in each of its three tentacles. A rather grating and very English voice was blasting out from the speakers.

'Look, Ralph, I cannot stress enough the importance of our trade with Africa post Brexit. We are talking about "Global Britain" here. It's the first time that we've ever had a department dedicated to international trade. That tells you how seriously we're taking it.'

He heard his father replying in a tone Freddie knew only too well from family rows: rising tension just about held in check, like floodwater building up behind a dam.

'I appreciate that, Minister, and we have strong, bilateral trade agreements between Namibia and the UK that will survive Brexit. I'm just not sure how much more you can expect from a country as small as this.'

'Well, more uranium for a start. We're in a race with the Chinese and others as you know. It's vital for nuclear energy, which is the only way we're going to meet our carbon emission targets. Then there's the gas from Kudu…'

'The copper at Tsumeb…' Ralph added

'Greater access to diamonds wouldn't go amiss either.'

'I've grasped all of that, Minister. But with the greatest respect, Namibia's trade with the EU dwarfs their trade with us. When we leave Europe, it's going to make things much more complex.'

There was a pause. Freddie felt worried that his father had overstepped the mark and was about to be slapped down by the Minister. If so, the repercussions on the family would last for days.

The Minister's voice, when it returned, was slightly chilling.

'We have a solution to that in Namibia. Who leads Europe?'

'Germany… well and France.'

'Exactly. The Germans and Namibians have been negotiating for three years now, but it seems that Germany is pulling back from admitting its genocide in their former colony. They fear the legal repercussions apparently. They don't want to admit to a state crime.'

'I have spoken to a number of the Namibian negotiators and they won't give up,' Ralph replied. 'They want a formal admission, a "deep apology" as they call it… and reparations. And I don't blame them.'

'Well, Ralph, anything you can do…'

'What do you mean, Minister?'

'Anything you can do to make matters worse for Germany can only help the British cause and benefit British trade.'

Freddie could see his father take a deep breath and grip the sides of his chair before replying.

'I will not use matters of this importance to win us trade favours, with the greatest respect, Minister. It would be unforgivable.'

There was another ominous silence. Freddie could see his father's team shift uncomfortably in their seats.

The voice on the speakerphone was quiet and menacing.

'I suggest, High Commissioner, you reconsider your position.'

Freddie had rarely felt such pride in his father. He could not understand the detail of what had been said but he knew the spirit of it. He would have rushed through the open door and hugged his father, were it not for the fact that it would have revealed his eavesdropping.

'How can you bear to read in this heat?' Li asked.

Hannah looked up at her father as he mopped the sweat from his brow. She'd always noticed how sensitive his skin was. It was an exact barometer of his feelings. When he drank alcohol – usually to 'de-pressurise' as he put it – he came out in a rash. This was embarrassing, when they had friends round for dinner. Her own skin was unresponsive most of the time: a healthy shade of brown. Except she bruised easily: a Chinese vulnerability her mother had told her.

'How can I bear *not* to read, you mean?' Hannah replied. 'It's the only way I can stop thinking about the heat.'

They were in her father's makeshift office – hut to be more accurate – on a site being tested for uranium deposits. The hut had a portable air conditioning unit, but it was next to useless as it wheezed away like an asthmatic.

'Bloody thing,' Li said as he bashed it for the umpteenth time, hoping it would somehow trigger a higher fan speed.

'Hitting it won't help,' Hannah said, as if dealing with a child.

'I tell you what, don't become a mining engineer when you grow up. Do something more civilised. Something you can have some control over.'

Hannah gazed at him. She'd never heard him be quite so damning of his job.

'It must be exciting sometimes though, Baba. You never know what you're going to find. At least you're not stuck in an office all day.'

'No, I'm stuck inside this blasted Portakabin watching my wall-charts go further and further into the red. We're way behind schedule. Perhaps it was a mistake to agree to a posting here.'

'How can you say that? It's magical here.'

Hannah surprised even herself with the strength of her feelings.

There was a loud banging on the door of the hut.

'Come in,' shouted Li.

A helmeted man in heavy duty overalls and a high-vis jacket popped his head round the door.

'We've hit something, boss.'

'Please tell me it's something positive,' Li retorted.

'I think you need to come and see. It's ... disturbing.'

'Oh great!'

Of all the words that Li didn't want to hear at this precise moment in time, these were possibly the worst, as Hannah could tell from the manner in which he tugged on his protective boots and whipped his helmet off the rack, almost tearing the peg off with it.

'I'm coming with you,' she said, jumping up.

'Hannah, it might be dangerous.'

'I don't care. I want to be with you, and I want to escape from this heat. At least it will be cool down there in the mine shaft.'

She'd heard his torrent of complaints every night at dinner and was beginning to worry about him. He was so stressed that her mother had insisted on taking regular blood pressure checks with their machine at home.

His company was badly behind schedule with the test digs. His wall calendar 'looked like a car crash'. His re-calculations were daily, as were the flood of emails from HQ in Shanghai demanding updates on 'progress'. There was no way Hannah was going to let him face another problem alone.

The outdoor heat hit them both like a furnace as the door

of his hut swung open. The light bleached their eyes.

A short walk later, they were at the makeshift lift used to descend to the test shaft. The doors were slammed shut with full force. God help anyone whose hand accidentally got in the way. Hannah had learned the brutal, mechanical world of mining from many previous days spent with her father. It repelled and fascinated her in equal measure. The zig-zag metal patterns of the lift door reminded her of her grandmother's apartment in the French quarter in Shanghai. She wished they were there now, smelling a New Year banquet ever more vividly as the lift ascended. Instead, they were descending into darkness and cold.

By the time they arrived at the bottom with a metallic clang, Li had mentally filed through every possible disaster: flooding, broken shafts, impenetrable rock. Every possibility except the one he now confronted.

In front of them, under the harsh lights that illuminated the dig, lay a half-exposed, bonfire-sized, hillock of bones and skulls. They were used to finding artefacts and skeletons as they dug ever deeper, peeling back the layers of Time. Finds were usually interesting for a few hours, days even, as they sat in the ring-side seat of History. But then, weeks of frustrating delay followed, as archaeologists and museums, scraped, classified, photographed and boxed the artefacts. This though was different. Its scale was overwhelming.

Hannah stopped in her tracks.

'This isn't all of it, boss. There are more skeletons. Hundreds. Maybe even thousands,' one of Li's team said. 'Some of the local men were shaking. I've sent them up to the surface to get some air.'

'How can there be so many?' Hannah gasped.

'Who knows? A battle? A plague of some sort? A drought?' Li conjectured.

'Excuse me sir,' a miner said softly 'Some of the jewellery we've found amongst the bodies are from the Herero tribe. I recognise them. My mother is Herero.'

'Oh my God,' Hannah said in a sudden realisation that froze her blood. 'The Genocide.'

Clara was fed up with crayons and her drawing. She looked round her mother's hospital office, hoping to be inspired. She didn't find much. There were large posters showing where the muscles and organs of the body were, which would have been interesting if she hadn't seen them countless times before. There were smaller posters encouraging people to stay healthy and have regular check-ups. A white-board was covered with scribblings about 'duty rosters' and 'beds available by ward.' Her mum was sitting at a computer, tapping in notes.

'What is that smell, Mummy?' Clara asked.

She couldn't work out what it was. It was something she'd sometimes smelt on her mother's clothing when she came back from the hospital. Or occasionally in the back of the car when her doctor's bag had been half-open at Clara's feet.

'I don't know, darling,' Anne Wilde replied without looking up. 'I probably smell it every day so it's hard for me to know. It could be the disinfectant they put on the floors. Or the smell of the laundry, the fresh gowns and sheets.'

'No, I like the smell of laundry.'

'Well, I'm not sure then. It could be the alcohol swabs we use before injections.'

'Would I have smelt that when you gave us our vaccinations?'

'Yes, darling!' she said smiling at Clara and hoping to calm her. 'Yes, that's it.'

Clara always had to get things settled. She couldn't be at peace until she'd solved something. She knew that her mum recognised this obsession and found it irritating, but Clara couldn't stop herself.

Clara didn't really like hospitals and this hospital was no different. She was aware that most of what was going in a hospital was hidden from a child and it made her feel uneasy.

'When are we leaving?'

'When I've finished my shift,' Anne said as she sorted through some patient notes.

'What's Freddie doing with Daddy?'

'He's at the High Commission.'

'Is it called High because it's on a hill?'

'No, darling. Although that would be logical wouldn't it? The trouble is that not much in Government is logical. That's why they end up with silly names for things.'

'Isn't it boring being in an office?' Clara asked. She remembered how Daddy had told her he'd spent most of his day in 'meetings'. But, when he tried to tell her what meetings were, she couldn't see the point of them.

'You've had a much more exciting time coming here to the hospital with me.'

There was a pause during which Anne hoped for some appreciation.

'It hasn't been that exciting,' Clara observed.

'Well, you enjoyed meeting the patients. And, I must say, you cheered them up. So, you've done a good deed.'

'What is AIDS, Mummy?' Clara had been longing to ask

her, ever since she heard the nurses talking about it. 'Is it some-thing to do with hearing aids? Like Grandma's?'

'No, darling. AIDS is a horrible disease...' Anne struggled to find the words to explain the dark shadow that had fallen across so many lives. How was it possible to convey something so devastating to a child? She got up from her desk and walked over to where Clara was sitting on an unused examination table, swinging her legs. She sat down next to her.

'Yes, but what is it?'

'Well, AIDS stands for "Acquired Immuno-Deficiency Syndrome".'

'What on earth does that mean?'

'It's caused by a virus called HIV. It weakens your body's means of defending itself.'

'How do you catch it?'

'Well you usually catch it by having sex with someone who's already got the virus. Or a blood transfusion. But what is especially tragic is that mothers can also pass it on to their babies, either in the womb, or after they're born: through breastfeeding them.'

'You mean that breastfeeding your baby can kill it?'

Clara was horrified and her incredulity made her mother's throat close when she wanted to speak. The cruelty of this truth seemed unbearable coming from her youngest child who was still so vulnerable. She put her arm round Clara and pulled her close.

'Only in those circumstances darling. Normally, breast-feeding is the perfect thing to do for your baby. Which is one reason why this disease seems so cruel.'

Clara loved feeling the warmth of her mother next to her and the squeeze of her hand.

They sat in silence for a few moments.

'Is that why you wanted to be a doctor?'

'Yes.'

'I couldn't be a doctor. I'm not a good enough person,' Clara concluded.

'Well, first- of- all, you are good…. most of the time. But secondly, you don't have to be a saint to be a doctor, you just need to be practical and to listen carefully. If you listen carefully, the patient will always give you the diagnosis… usually without knowing it.'

'How many people are dying of AIDS?'

Anne paused, wondering if Clara needed to know the truth, and deciding that she did.

'Millions.'

A staff nurse burst into the room, looking agitated.

'We've got another case. I thought you'd want to see.'

Anne got up and swiftly followed the nurse. Unbeknown to her mother, so did Clara… through two sets of swing doors and on to a ward.

A woman was lying almost motionless in bed.

'We've given her a sedative,' the nurse said as Anne approached the bed, took the patient's wrist and timed her pulse.

'Blood pressure?' she asked the nurse.

'A hundred and forty-five over a hundred.'

She read the patient's name from a clipboard at the end of the bed.

'Mrs Onwate? How are you feeling?'

The patient turned her head with the slow, patient movement of a tortoise crossing a hot lawn.

'I'm feeling better now, thank you, doctor.'

Anne found her humility and patience heart-breaking.

'Do you mind if I examine you?'

Mrs Onwate shook her head.

Clara watched intently, as her mother gently turned down the sheet and lifted the patient's gown. It reminded her of how gentle her mother always was, whenever Clara herself felt ill.

On the woman's stomach were several scorch marks. It looked as if she had been burned by boiling water.

'Have you burned yourself at all? While cooking?'

'No, doctor, they just appeared in the last few months.'

Anne looked significantly at the nurse and vice versa.

Same as the others, the nurse thought to herself.

'But she must have been burned,' Clara blurted out.

Her mother spun round, aware of Clara's presence for the first time.

'Clara, I told you not to follow me on to the ward. You shouldn't be seeing things like this at your age.'

'Why? At what age should I be seeing it?'

Clara's question seemed to floor her mother.

Later that evening, when they were back at home, Clara had drawn a picture of hundreds of people running into a fire. When her mother saw it, she shrieked.

'That's hideous, Clara.'

She tore the picture into several pieces and threw it into the bin. Clara burst into tears. Later, Anne felt shocked at her own reaction, went into Clara's bedroom and lay down next to her, holding her hand, until they both went to sleep.

Selima felt ambiguous as she walked up the gravel path to the

Chiang house in Swakopmund.

It was a relief to get away from home. Her mother and father had been bickering for most of half-term. Her mother couldn't get over the deceit that Darius had been working for an American hotel company without telling her, especially given the location of the dig.

On the other hand, she also felt awkward going to see her special needs teacher. Teachers should never be seen outside of school grounds. Their private lives should remain invisible. It was bad enough bumping into one of them in a supermarket. Going to their home added a whole other dimension of embarrassment.

She rang the bell.

'Hello, Selima. Do come in,' Sarah Chiang said.

'Thank you, miss.'

'We'll just go through here, into the sitting-room.'

The house seemed quieter and darker than her own. There was a sense of emptiness that Selima couldn't quite fathom. Everything was arranged beautifully: books stood like soldiers in alphabetical order; Chinese silk paintings were hung in perfect symmetry; Shanghai Tan fans were spread open and delicately nailed to the walls; photographs of former homes from around the world stood neatly spaced on shelves. How different to the colourful mess of her own home!

They entered the living-room and sat opposite each other. Sarah shut the door and sat in a chair with a notebook open in front of her. Selima sat alone, bolt upright, on a three-person sofa, feeling small.

'How are things?' Sarah asked, determined to try and relax her stiff pupil.

'Fine,' Selima said.

'Are you feeling any more confident with your school-work?'

'I think so. I still have to read lots of things through several times.'

'Do the letters still float around?'

'Yes. But your suggestions have definitely helped.'

'Have you tried wearing the coloured glasses I lent you?'

'No, Miss. Will it really help?'

'It helps some people.'

Sarah paused, gauging Selima's mood and pondering how to find a way into her trust.

'Don't get me wrong when I ask this, Selima, but do you get irritated with yourself?'

Selima felt grateful for the understanding these words betrayed.

She nodded vigorously, catching sight of a Chinese lucky cat with a nodding head and up-raised paw in the mirror. It seemed almost to be mocking her.

'How much attention did the school pay to your dyslexia, before I arrived?' Sarah asked.

'I had one special teacher before you. But she didn't really explain it to me. Not in the way you have.'

Sarah felt gratified she'd had some impact.

'Look, Selima, dyslexia is much more common than many people realise. It was often missed in the past. As many as one in ten people suffer from one form or another. It can make people feel stupid or slow. But some of the cleverest people who have ever lived, were dyslexic.'

'Such as…?'

'Well, Einstein for one. He was fired from his first few teaching jobs for appearing to be stupid. Then he invented the theory of relativity. It just goes to show. Dyslexics often have special talents. They are great musicians or engineers or architects. They can see or hear things most people can't. They need to experience things though, be hands-on, not just be taught through words.'

This all chimed with Selima. Long ago she had forsaken books for the great outdoors. Books were too hard and so sand dunes and trees had become her words, landscapes her stories. She also loved tinkering with things. One day her mother went ballistic when she'd discovered Selima trying to take the washing machine apart. Her father had just laughed, in fact seemed to be rather proud of her.

'Can I be cured, Miss?' Selima asked.

'You mustn't think of it as an illness, Selima. Think of it as having a special set of eyes and ears that see and hear things differently.'

'What if I just want normal eyes, Miss?'

Sarah's heart broke inside for this vulnerable girl, who, like all other dyslexic young people, simply wanted to blend in. She paused.

'When do you feel at your strongest, Selima?'

Selima didn't have to hesitate.

'When I'm out in the dunes, or swimming in the sea… or driving in my father's jeep. Or helping him fix an engine.'

'Then try to take that feeling of strength with you in the classroom. Be patient and strong. Think of a sentence as like an engine you sometimes have to strip down to make it work.'

Just then, the door to the sitting-room burst open and a book dropped to the floor, splashing its pages.

'Hannah, how many times have I told you not to come into the sitting-room when I have a pupil here?'

Hannah stared open-mouthed.

'Selima! Oh my God,' Hannah exclaimed.

'Hi Hannah!'

Sarah was taken aback.

'How come you two know each other?'

'We met on the school trip to Sossusvlei' Selima explained. She had known that this encounter would happen at some point, ever since Hannah made the comment on the coach about her mother being a special needs teacher.

'But hold on,' Hannah said, 'when I asked if you knew my mum, the special needs teacher, you said no.'

'I didn't want you to think…'

Sarah understood immediately and intervened.

'No-one wants to be defined by so-called 'special needs', Hannah. It's a ridiculous term, demeaning. It should be banned. Selima has dyslexia like many other students.'

'I'm sorry, Hannah, I shouldn't have lied,' Selima said.

'Don't be silly. I would have done exactly the same,' Hannah said, sitting down on the sofa next to her.

Seeing the two girls light up in each other's presence, Sarah decided to abandon the extra lesson and bow out.

'I'm going to make some supper and leave you two girls to chat. You can stay if you like Selima.'

As soon as she'd left the room, Hannah and Selima burst into giggles and Hannah fell on to the sofa and swung her legs over Selima's.

'This is so weird,' Hannah exclaimed.

'Not as weird as it is for me,' said Selima. 'Your house is

amazing. It's so tidy.'

'That's my dad. He's obsessive.'

'Yes, but you've got things from all over the world in here.'

'True, but, I often wish we'd just stayed in one place for longer. This must be my …' she counted through them in her mind, '… fifth home.'

'Perhaps you'll settle here.'

'I doubt it.'

Selima felt a rush of sadness at her friend's honesty.

'You've got so many books,' Selima said gesturing to the bookcase that almost occupied an entire wall.

'Books are my friends,' Hannah replied. 'When I was younger, other children had friends, I had books.'

'Didn't you have any friends?' Selima asked, surprised but comforted by Hannah's honesty. As an only child, Selima had often felt lonely.

'Yes, I had a few friends. They also had books as friends.'

Since she was five, Hannah had counted stories as companions: walked the paths of their words, fallen headlong into their illustrations, been hugged by their covers.

People were stories too of course. Indeed, older people, like her grandparents, were whole libraries of stories. But people weren't as open, as revealing, as expressive or as succinct as books.

'I love languages,' Hannah confessed. 'My parents brought me up to speak Mandarin and English. Chinese letters seemed like paintings to me. I loved watching my father scratch away with a calligraphy pen. I used to ask him "Are Chinese characters actually pictures Baba?"'

'What did he say?' Selima, thinking of her own father who

would always rather be making something rather than writing or reading.

'He used to pick me up, put me on his lap, point to the letters, and say "Well little one, this is the character for mountain - Shan - and you can see that it looks like a mountain." And it does. Look I'll show you.'

Hannah got up excitedly from the sofa and went to a writing desk. She pulled out a sheet of creamy-white paper from a drawer and a calligraphy pen from a pot. She grabbed a book from the vast bookshelf to use as a rest and returned to the sofa.

She drew the three upward strokes, the largest in the middle, and a cross stroke to show Selima. Selima immediately felt she would rather have learned a language like Chinese where the letters were like pictures.

'But then, we can add another character underneath…'

Hannah drew an elegant blend of lines underneath as Selima gazed on entranced.

'Now these two characters together have a totally different meaning.'

'What do they mean?' Selima asked.

'They mean … Mountain Mist. And what happens in a mountain mist?'

Hannah put down the pen, paper and book, covered Selima's eyes with her hands and blew cold air on the back of her neck, making her shiver.

'You get lost and lonely in the mountain mist!' Hannah shrieked in her ear.

They both fell about laughing.

'That's what my dad used to do to me. He's so good at calligraphy. He learned it as a child. I suppose, being an engineer, he's good at practical things.'

This was the explanation her mother had given her many years ago. It seemed to Hannah to be plausible and so she accepted it, repeating it for the rest of her life.

'I always wondered why I was an only child,' Hannah confessed. 'Did you?'

'Yes,' Selima said. 'All my friends had siblings. I told them I was jealous. Then they used to laugh and tell me hideous stories about fights and being forced to share.'

'Mine too. But I was still jealous. One night I heard my mother sobbing through the bedroom wall and Baba trying to soothe her. The next morning, I saw streaks of dried blood on the bathroom floor and fresh blood in the toilet.'

'She'd obviously had a bad period,' Selima said.

'No, she had a miscarriage. I didn't understand at the time, but I didn't want to ask. I remember she stayed in bed for two days, touching her tummy all the time in a slow, circular motion.'

'How sad,' Selima empathised.

'Then one day, when I was nine, they told me I was going to have a baby brother or sister.'

'Oh my God, you must have been so excited,' Selima said.

'I was. I kept thinking of the adventures we'd have together. I wanted to make him or her a present, something special. Then one morning, it came to me. I would make the baby a book. Not an ordinary baby book with pointless questions about time of birth, or weight, or with spaces to glue in locks of hair. A real book.'

'You wrote a whole book?' Selima asked in amazement.

'Well, it was quite short, but every day I added drawings

or little stories to it. When I'd finished it, I went out to our garden in Shanghai and picked some leaves from our mulberry tree to press in the middle of it.'

'What happened?'

'It seems like a day from another universe now. When my mum went into labour, time seemed to slow down, almost stop. I remember sitting down at our piano to try and pass the time. I decided the black notes were for boys, the white for girls. I went up and down the keyboard. In the end, I was thumping them out of frustration. Then Baba appeared. He looked as pale as a ghost.'

'What did he say?'

'He said "Hannah... your mother is all-right. But I'm afraid the baby was stillborn."'

'What does stillborn mean?' Selima asked, knowing already from the chill in Hannah's voice.

Hannah uttered the single syllable.

'Dead.'

They sat in silence staring at the wall. Selima now understood the emptiness she had felt in the house.

'Two weeks later, I remembered the baby book and where I had hidden it. I took off the blue bow and pink tissue paper and opened it. In the middle of the book, where I had crushed the mulberry leaves, there was a brown, dead silkworm. I buried the book in the garden, under a tree. I didn't touch another book for a year.'

Sarah, who had walked back to the sitting-room to tell the girls that supper was ready, heard Hannah's story through the open door. She stood silently in the hall and wept.

6

The Skeleton Coast

Ben Kaplan sat at the breakfast table sifting through Darius's photographs, sometimes turning them to examine the body's position from a different angle. Occasionally he reached for a magnifying cube and placed it over a detail of the picture. The whole family had gathered in the kitchen the morning after the find.

Joe patiently watched over his father's shoulder.

The remains of the family breakfast were scattered over the scrubbed, wooden table like the remains of an archaeological dig. Barbara brought over a cafetiere of fresh coffee.

'How far down did they find the body?' Ben asked.

'I'm not sure. Six feet perhaps,' Barbara replied.

'The details of the uniform have largely gone, but there's probably enough to identify it. I'll need to check in regimental records, try and find a match,' Ben said.

Joe picked up the Victorian pocket-watch and turned it on to its front.

'It's got to be him, Dad,' he said staring at the faded initials carved on the back.

'Who?' Barbara asked, feeling excluded, as she often did when Joe and his father got into a huddle over something.

Ben sounded as if he was writing the headlines for an obituary.

'James William Alexander. Scottish Captain of the British Army. Fought in one of South Africa's Frontier Wars and then came to Namibia to study the Herero and Nama.'

'Joe, how do you know about this?' his mother asked, trying to break into the charmed circle of knowledge.

'When I went with Dad to the archives at half-term, his was one of the boxes we emptied. Dad told me his story. It could be another person with the same initials...'

'It could be. Never rule out coincidence. And never get prematurely excited about anything. Those are two things I have learned over the years,' Ben reflected.

Joe was pleased to have his caution validated.

'What about the date on the watch though? 1829. I thought you said he was exploring here in the 1830's,' Joe challenged.

'He was. 1829 would be the date when he was given the watch... or perhaps when he purchased it and had it inscribed,' Ben pointed out.

'Of course!' said Joe. 'I was thinking it was the date he had died.'

'Most people do. It's a very interesting phenomenon,' Ben said. 'The tendency is to think of anything with a date stamped on it that's found in a grave as the date of burial. It's the way our minds initially grasp it. But there's a whole preceding history in a grave. It has its own chronology, running backwards from death to birth.'

'So, if this is the person you're thinking of...?' Barbara asked, wedging her way into the conversation.

'If it is him, we know that he was revered by the local tribes,' Ben replied.

'So that would explain the garland around his neck?' Barbara added.

'Exactly. We also know that he was exploring a secret burial ground when he died.'

'So, this site is that burial ground?' Barbara suggested, finding herself now as wrapped up in this Victorian secret as her husband and son.

'Ah but no, it isn't,' Ben said emphatically.

'What do you mean, Dad?' Joe asked.

'You remember what I told you, Joe. He was searching for a sacred burial site that the Herero would not go anywhere near. They refused to accompany him. So, since we know from the garland that he has been buried and decorated by the Herero…'

'We know that this can't be the site he was pursuing: the one they were too afraid to go near,' Joe said, pleased to be able to follow the logic of his father's detective work.

'Precisely. Barbara, how much of an area have they excavated round the body?'

'I couldn't say exactly, but not much. As soon as they had uncovered the body, they downed spades and found us.'

'Good. Do we know if they have left the site untouched since then?'

'We put tarpaulins over the body and left the site with "No Entry" signs dotted around. There's always someone patrolling the site. So hopefully not.'

'Excellent. Let's just hope the Ministry hasn't sent in their own archaeologists.'

'It's quite possible they have,' Barbara started to explain. 'Ilana…'

'My friend Selima's Mom,' Joe intervened, explaining a

crucial detail his mother had failed to mention.

'Yes exactly, thank you, Joe,' Barbara continued. 'When I mentioned getting you to come and examine the site, Ilana said that Namibia had its own anthropologists.'

'In which case, I need to phone the Ministry and stop them jumping in with both feet. We also need to get a permit from them to examine the site. That could be tricky. I've got to know a few people, win their trust, but they're not senior enough to have clout.'

'Wait!' Joe had a brainwave. 'My friend Freddie's father is the British High Commissioner. Couldn't we ask him to help us? He must be well-connected into the Government.'

'Well it's worth a try,' Ben replied.

'If we get a permit, we can go at the weekend,' Barbara suggested.

'Can we go with Hannah, Selima and Freddie?' Joe pleaded.

'It's too many people,' Ben objected. 'You need as few people disturbing a site as possible.'

'Hold on, Dad. Selima's father, Darius, was the one who found the body in the first place. Her mother is an expert on tribal customs. They could be incredibly helpful to you. What's more, Hannah's mother is a linguist. She studies dialects. She might be able to help with any translations. They live in Swakopmund and so does Selima's family. I'm sure we could stay with them if I asked.'

'And what about Freddie and his family?' Barbara asked.

'They live in Windhoek. I can't leave Freddie out, and if his father's going to help us…'

'Ok, we'll see. Can you get Freddie's father's number for me? I'd like to speak to him as soon as possible.'

'Of course.' Joe started to message Freddie on the WhatsApp Group.

'In the meantime, why don't I speak to Ilana and ask them for a good bed and breakfast in Swakopmund,' Barbara added.

The door to Ralph Wilde's office was opened with a definite vigour.

'Ben Kaplan and his son to see you, High Commissioner.' Ralph's secretary was always efficient and polite, qualities on which he had already learnt to rely.

'Thank you, Tulela. Please show them in.'

Joe was curious to meet Freddie's father. He had already formed a mental image of Ralph: very English, eccentric, probably with a cut-glass accent and slightly stern. He had also imagined him wearing a suit regardless of the weather. So, he was somewhat taken aback to find him wearing a crisp white shirt and no tie. His trousers though had been so well-pressed that you could have cut paper on their creases, and his shoes were polished enough to pass muster on a parade ground.

'Pleased to meet you, Mr Kaplan, and, you must be Joe…' His voice was soft, assured and light. They shook hands.

'Joe, Freddie's next door looking very bored. I'm afraid I've run out of even vaguely interesting jobs to give him. Why don't you relieve him of his chores? You can go in through that door.'

Joe opened the internal door into the next room, deliberately leaving it slightly open.

Freddie was sitting at a computer screen, painfully entering data of some kind. On hearing the door open, he turned around, grateful for any kind of distraction.

'Joe! Thank God. Entertainment at last.'

121

Freddie walked over to him, clasped hands and slapped shoulders.

'Glad you think so. I thought perhaps you'd had enough of me by the end of last week.'

Freddie reeled back and looked at him quizzically.

'Why on earth would you think that?'

'My strange obsessions,' Joe said. 'I thought perhaps they were boring you.'

'I don't find them strange or boring,' Freddie reassured. 'In fact, you've shown me whole new ways of looking at things.'

'I have?'

'Of course. Now, please find something interesting in this data my father's given me to crunch.'

Freddie got up, sat Joe down in his chair in front of the computer, then dragged a second chair to be next to him. They had already forgotten the awkwardness of their fathers meeting for the first time in the room next door.

'So, you're an anthropologist Freddie tells me...' Ralph beckoned to Ben to take a seat opposite him at his meeting-table by the window.

'Correct, yes. The cliché tells us not to dig too deep into the past. Well, I can't dig deep enough.' Ben was tired of how often he had said this by way of an introduction, but it remained, nonetheless, true.

Ralph poured them both a glass of iced water from a jug, freshened with lime, and passed one across.

'I am imagining, Namibia is a treasure-trove for someone like you.'

'You're not wrong. I'm a child in a sweet shop here.'

Ralph laughed. 'So, how can I help?' he asked.

'My wife, Barbara, has been excavating on a potential hotel site in Damaraland. They unearthed the remains of a Victorian soldier, whilst doing a test dig on the foundations.'

'How inconvenient!' Ralph commented. He added a coda on seeing Ben's discomfort with his remark, 'Inconvenient for them, but highly revealing for you I suppose…'

'And that is my point. I think he may be a very distinguished explorer. Someone on the trail of something remarkable that he started to write up in his journals. I need a Government licence to examine the body and dig further around the site.'

'Well, I'm only a couple of months into this job, so I am not entirely familiar with all the branches of the Namibian Government. My guess would be that the Department of Arts and Culture or Land Reform will be the places to apply.'

Ralph walked back to his desk, sifted through some plastic folders and removed a document.

'I have the organisational charts here…'

'There's a further complication,' Ben intervened. 'It relates to one of Freddie and Joe's friends…'

Joe was enjoying playing around with the trade data Freddie's father had given him to analyse, converting it into charts it to make it more comprehensible. But he was not so engrossed as to miss his name being spoken in the next-door room.

'Did you hear that? I think they're talking about Selima,' he said to Freddie.

'If we move a bit closer to the door, we can hear everything,' Freddie suggested.

'There's a Namibian girl that both of our boys have befriended,' Ben continued. 'Her name is Selima. Her mother is Ilana Van Zyl, a tourist guide who led their school outing to Sossusvlei. She's on the war-path about environmental damage and preserving Namibian culture.'

'Sounds admirable,' Ralph commented.

'I like your dad already,' Joe whispered to Freddie. Freddie smiled and put his finger to his lips.

'It is admirable, but she wants local anthropologists to be given the right to examine the find, not me.'

'You think that I can stop them in some way. Is that it?'

'It's not so much a question of stopping them, as helping me get an urgent licence to work alongside them. I want to go back to the dig this weekend.'

'Yes! Go for it,' Joe whispered from behind the door, fist-pumping.

'Please don't take this question the wrong way, but on what grounds do you qualify?' Ralph asked Ben.

'I am a recognised expert on the Herero,' Ben answered. 'If I'm involved in the dig, I can also draw on the expertise of my academic peers back in America and the UK, in decoding what we find. I'm attached to the University of Columbia in New York.'

'I see your predicament,' Ralph replied, 'but it's possible that by interfering I might make them even more determined to keep foreigners out. It's their country, their soil, their find.'

'But it's not their corpse,' Ben pointed out. 'It's the remains, of a British, well Scottish to be precise, soldier. As the British High Commissioner, I imagine you have the rights to ask for the body to be returned to Scotland. There are almost certainly living descendants who would want the return of the body.'

'And before it is returned, I, as High Commissioner, naturally want to ensure that none of his possessions…' Ralph chimed in, cottoning on to Ben's line of argument.

'…are taken or despoiled,' Ben finished Ralph's sentence for him. 'Precisely. You understand the situation perfectly, as I hoped you would.'

'Your dad has got to win a medal for inventing diplomatic arguments,' Freddie whispered, returning the earlier compliment paid to his own father by Joe.

'I will see what I can do,' Ralph said.

Ben shot his hand across the table and shook Ralph's, trading a look of mutual resolve.

'One other thing. I'd like you and your family to come with me at the weekend…if you feel you can,' Ben continued.

'Come with you? Is this for me to provide you with diplomatic air cover? Because…'

Freddie burst in through the part-open door, behind which they had been listening. This took Joe somewhat by surprise, who stumbled in after him, his prop having been removed. The fathers tried to look stern at their eavesdropping but were already both smiling inwardly at their sons' shared conspiracy and their friendship.

'Dad, please say yes. Joe and I really want to go. Mum and Clara can come too. Come on, you said we need to get out of Windhoek more. What better opportunity is there than this?' Freddie was never less than comprehensive when trying to persuade.

'Well, it certainly beats another weekend at the club being thrashed by your mother at tennis. We need to check she isn't on duty at the hospital first. Where would we stay?'

'Hannah and Selima's parents both live in Swakopmund which is near to the site. I'm sure we can stay with them.'

'A weekend by the seaside. What could be better?' Joe chipped in.

Things moved on apace as they had to. Ralph used his Deputy's connections into the Ministry of Arts and Culture to obtain a licence for Ben to examine the site. What's more, it was agreed that he would have a clear week in which to examine the site without local archaeologists, providing that a member of the National Anthropology Museum could be present to supervise.

Anne Wilde was on weekend duty at the hospital but managed to swap duties with another consultant.

When Freddie had messaged Hannah that they were coming, Hannah's parents insisted the Wilde's stay with them, egged on by Hannah of course. The same was agreed between the Kaplan's and the Van Zyl family. The 'Four Teenagers of the Apocalypse' WhatsApp Group whirred with excited messages: reminders of what to bring; of what to say and what not to say in front of each other's parents; and warnings about their various eccentricities.

Since they numbered seven people between the two families, they agreed to travel in a convoy of two cars from Windhoek. They set off at sunrise on a Saturday to avoid travelling in the heat of the mid-day and travelled North from Windhoek on the B2 until they reached Karibib, where they had agreed to take a detour.

In order to maximise their trip, Ilana had suggested that they see the southern part of the Skeleton Coast - the Dorob

National Park and its famous seal colony - before heading south down the gravel, coastal road to Swakopmund.

They drove through the Namib, the oldest desert on Earth, which, because of the miraculous inventiveness of Nature, still managed to sustain extraordinary plants and wildlife.

They stopped at one point because Clara was 'bursting for the toilet' in her characteristically melodramatic way. A few minutes later, she ran back to the car screaming, which Anne immediately assumed was an animal encounter of the wrong kind.

'No, no come and look,' Clara pleaded, dragging her mother by the hand. The others followed, curious to see.

'Look!'

Where Clara had peed, the ground was alive with unfurling plants that were brightening into reds, oranges and vivid greens even as they watched.

'I am pretty sure these are the famous fields of lichen,' Ben said. 'They survive by taking moisture from the fogs and the humid air. When you water them they change colour.'

'It's a flower garden in the desert. I've got magic pee!' Clara danced a little triumph around the lichen.

Joe and Freddie meanwhile had wandered off, chattering away about school, and stumbled across, what looked like a giant, mangled cabbage. It was bigger than them both, and seemed to have been flattened by a truck.

'What the hell is that?' Freddie exclaimed.

'Let me look it up,' Joe suggested.

'What? In your two-thousand-page botanist's handbook that you just happened to slip into your rucksack before leaving home?' Freddie responded.

Joe dug him sharply in the ribs. He'd got used to Freddie's English sarcasm by now.

'No, I've got a plant app on my phone. Plant Snapp. It's extraordinary. Watch.'

Joe proceeded to photograph the giant, squashed cabbage with his phone, as Clara ran up and into Freddie's arms, babbling away about her magic pee.

'Whoagh!' she said, finally noticing the giant cabbage. 'What's that?'

'That's what we are about to find out, Pumpkin.'

Joe read out the description from his app. By now all four parents had joined them, equally struck by this plant that dwarfed them all.

'Welwitschia Mirabilis.'

'"Mirabilis" is the Latin for marvellous or wonderful,' Ralph interpreted, delighted that his GCSE Latin had finally proved of some value in his life.

Joe continued, editing out the dull bits.

'Named after the Austrian botanist who stumbled across it…. Blah, blah, blah. It's featured on the Namibian coat of arms and nicknamed the 'living fossil'. They can live for over sixteen hundred years. They can survive for years without water.'

'Extraordinary. Given the way our planet's going, that's the kind of adaptability we are going to have to learn,' Barbara said.

'Time has a different meaning in these landscapes,' Ben pondered out loud. 'This plant started to sprout in Roman times.'

'Everything seems so still here and yet it's not. It's alive,' Clara said quietly.

On the way to Uis, they passed a small cluster of mountains, including the Spitzkoppe which towered several hundred metres above the plains. It stood sentry over the Namib and was nicknamed the 'Matterhorn of Africa' because of its resemblance to the famous Swiss Alp.

The landscape flattened as they got closer to the sea, passing the vast Messum Crater, twenty-two kilometres across, visible from space and the site of an ancient volcano.

As they approached the Skeleton Coast, the famous early morning fog started to appear, descending with a silent menace. They stopped at a small roadside stall to have a rest and see if the fog would clear. It was selling marula juice and coffee and was on the banks of the Messum river: one of the several rivers that threaded its way from the highlands down to the icy sea. These rivers sometimes disappeared beneath the sand and then reappeared two hundred metres later.

As they sat chatting, a most unexpected sound arose from behind a small clump of trees. It was the sound of a slightly-out-of-tune piano playing a beautiful Beethoven sonata. It sounded very formal and European after the simple joy of African chants in the Boma.

'Is that a radio playing?' Anne asked the man running the stall.

He laughed revealing two rows of teeth more gap-toothed than even the landscape that surrounded him.

'No, ma'am. That's the real thing. Go and see. There's a little path through the scrub.'

They finished their drinks and made their way towards the cascade of notes. Ahead of them, through the trees, they could make out the figure of a man in a white T-shirt and khaki shorts, sitting bolt upright in that self-conscious manner of concert performers, at a piano. His sheet music was propped up in front of him. His 'stage' was a clearing in the scrub. Nearby stood a small and very simple church and they could only assume that the piano had been moved from there to sprinkle its blessings on the great outdoors.

As they entered the clearing, they fell silent on seeing a giant figure six to eight feet from the piano. It was an elephant, standing stock still, entranced by the melody. It swayed its trunk backwards and forwards in a gentle rhythm, its eyes half-closed, as if in a trance.

The pianist clearly didn't feel any sense of danger. The elephant only needed to take a few steps forward to crush the piano into matchsticks. He would stand no chance were it to charge. Yet, here they were, elephant and man, bonded in music and in trust.

The man, hearing them enter the clearing, turned towards them but carried on playing, lulling the elephant.

He said two simple words to them in the softest voice imaginable.

'It's blind!'

Then he turned back to his music and his loving, and loved, audience of one.

The reason they had deviated from the straightest route to Swakopmund was shrouded in a fog which slowed them to a snail's pace. Yet, they could smell it through the open car windows from several hundred metres away.

'Oh my God! What is that horrendous smell?' Freddie exclaimed.

Clara pretended to be sick.

'Clara, don't do that' Anne admonished. 'It's bad for your throat.'

'It's the seal colony. That's what we've come to see,' Ralph pointed out.

'Right,' Clara said. 'Well now we've smelt them, can we leave please!'

'I'm with Pumpkin on this one,' Freddie chimed in. 'Unless you've packed the gas masks!'

'This will be a unique experience,' Ralph said, trying to maintain his dignity amidst the mocking laughter and then finally succumbing with his own guffaw.

'Yes, well being eaten by piranhas is also a unique experience,' said Anne, 'but not one I would necessarily recommend.'

Ben signalled from the car in front that they should park.

'Welcome to Cape Cross Seal Reserve,' Ben said as they tumbled out.

'Welcome is not the word that my family have in mind, may I tell you,' Ralph retorted.

Ben refused to let his enthusiasm for wildlife be curtailed. 'Ah but...being highly organised as I am, I have the perfect accompaniment for this little outing.'

As they stretched the car journey out of their limbs, Ben opened the boot door of his jeep, fished around and pulled out a small, zipped bag. Inside were ten or so nose-clips with cotton-wool clamps to go over each nostril.

'Aromatherapists use these to take away your sense of smell. We sometimes use them when we're opening plague graves,' he explained, as he dished out the clips. 'I think you might find they make our little expedition more...palatable.'

They took a selfie in front of their cars, with their nose clips in place and posted it for the Swakopmund crowd to see. The photo was labelled 'Seven nasally-challenged explorers feeling sealy! Who "nose" what we might discover at Cape Cross?'

On the way to the seal colony, they stopped at the stone cross on the bleak and foggy headland, after which Cape Cross was named.

Ralph read out the Latin inscription, adding in his own observations as he did so.

'Right! So, it says "Since the creation of the world 6,684 years have passed." I think we now know it was a tad longer than that don't we?'

'6,684 sounds like a Jewish year,' Barbara offered up. 'So, who says the Jews weren't explorers?'

Ralph continued the translation: '"And since the birth of Christ 1,484 years ago…"'

'Although scholars now believe, of course, that Jesus was born between 4 and 6 BC, so that date is also wrong,' Ben observed.

'So that means that 2018 A.D. is not 2018, it's actually 2022, or even 2024,' Joe chipped in.

'So much for the exactness of maths, Joe.' Freddie couldn't resist.

'Nothing to do with math being wrong. It's humans not using math accurately,' Joe responded, punching him good-naturedly.

Clara pushed her way between the two of them.

'So, if nothing is when we think it is, we're all lost,' she said, looking at the fog that had still failed to clear.

Ralph exchanged knowing glances with Barbara who

smiled. 'The perils of having bright children, eh? Anyway, it basically says that in 1484 Diego Cao, a Portuguese navigator landed here.'

Several hundred metres later, Joe tripped over something and fell cursing, his ankle cut and bleeding.

'Goddam, what the hell was that?'

Barbara rushed forward. 'Joe, are you OK?'

He nodded but his face was screwed up in pain. Barbara always carried a small, first aid kit with her and started searching for an antiseptic wipe.

'Oh my God, this is it,' Ben exclaimed. 'Joe, you're a genius. You found this slate.'

'I tripped, Dad!' Joe responded, nursing his wound 'But of course that confirms my extraordinary detective skills!'

'Ah, but as Ubuntu might say, is any trip ever truly accidental?' Freddie said, managing to cheer Joe up.

Ben was too engrossed to notice his son's sarcasm. He knelt down and wiped the sand and dirt off a piece of ancient slate, half-buried in the ground. Anne knelt next to him, relieved that, for once, she was using her own detective skills on artefacts and not patients.

Ben continued with his explanation. 'A man called David Coulson describes this slate in his book called "Namib".'

Anne read it out. 'It's in English. It's dated 1838. "I am proceeding to a river sixty miles north, and should anyone find this and follow me, God will help him."'

'Who wrote it, Mummy?' Clara asked, tugging at her.

'There is no name darling!' Anne replied.

'That's what Coulson says,' Ben continued. 'No one knows who wrote the message or what became of them. I think it might be our friend, Captain Alexander.'

A slight chill passed through them all.

The sound of crying babies added to their disorientation.

'Seal pups,' said Ben.

A hundred feet further on, they stopped in their tracks. In front of them lay a vast army of seals. The fog had cleared enough for them to see there were countless thousands, and this was after the cull that kept the colony 'under control': an annual bloodbath, against which Ilana and many others had fiercely protested.

Some seals flopped, others swam; many lifted their head to the sky, honking as if at some invisible 'Sky God', asking for release. The colony looked like a religious festival, whose pilgrims ranged from the pious and ecstatic to the bored and listless.

The smell was so pungent that it couldn't entirely be stopped by their nose clips. The massive bulls honked and bit each other, fighting over territories. The pups cried like babies, some suckling from their mothers. Some cows dozed exhausted, enjoying a brief respite between demanding bulls and demanding pups.

As they looked more carefully, they could see that some of the pups were dead, and lay unburied. Some had drowned and been washed up on the shore. Others had lost their mothers and died forlorn. Worst of all were those who had simply been crushed by careless bulls rolling over on them. There was so much teeming life here, it could be killed without even noticing. Anne tried to distract Clara from the dead pups, but she was far too observant and started to sob, a little bit more than was believable.

There were boardwalks which enabled them to walk right into the midst of the colony. Joe felt as if he would drown in the noise and stench. It felt like being on another planet, a planet where life had dwindled to a single, surviving species, all diversity and beauty gone.

Then they saw her. At first, you couldn't be sure. Not from a distance. But the majesty of the walk betrayed her. A lioness was prowling the perimeter of the colony, but no more than thirty feet from where they stood. She must have walked the river valley from the desert to the sea. Who knows why? She was slimmer and slighter than most lions.

Perhaps food was scarce. Perhaps it was an accident, a loss of bearings. Perhaps, she was lured by the smells of the sea and the colony, certainly by the prospect of fresh and easy meat.

Now she was surveying her prize, mesmerised by the choice. Several prides of lions could feast on these seals for weeks, but only she had undergone the journey. She was alone but too proud to be lonely. She appeared to almost smile. She had all the time in the world but was damned if she was going to take it. Not now, after the achingly long walk, through the river-beds, that would have lasted days.

Seals started to shift and honk and barge each other as she rose like a flame from the ground. She moved slowly, sadistically. A pup wouldn't be enough. A bull might put up too much of a fight. So, a cow seemed perfect.

Instinctively, the two families all crouched together on the boardwalk, staying still and close together. Although they weren't the hunted, they felt they could be. Their breathing slowed. Everything sharpened its outlines, despite the lingering fog. Colours looked brighter; sounds were harsher.

Then she was off. The seals moved as best they could, pups scattering in her path. Cows reared and honked, protecting their young. The lioness chose and pounced. The cow, bitten in the neck, succumbed like a sacrifice, swooning into the lion's jaws and falling limp. She ritually gave herself up, as if dying for the colony. Several pups screeched like babies as she died. Bulls barked ferociously as if creating a wall of sound to shield the thousands. The lioness, dragged her prey, slowly but triumphantly, back to the rocks above the beach and proceeded to eat.

They all felt the same: the desire to be somewhere safe. They craved the oasis of the homes in Swakopmund. Even though they had never seen them, they could imagine their comforts.

Clara was the most disturbed by seeing the kill, but the adrenaline of it sang in all their veins for hours afterwards.

Once it was clear that they were safe and the lioness was dozing next to her prey, they carefully made their way back along the boardwalks back to the cars. Joe had a slight limp from his wound. They sat in momentary disbelief, and then set off on the gravel road to Swakopmund.

The young people wanted to be together and so Joe joined Freddie and Clara in the back of the Wilde's car.

'Are you all-right, Cluse?' Freddie asked his sister. He always used this nickname when he wanted to cheer her up, to remind her of simpler times when a game on the floor had absorbed them both for hours, lost in a miniature world.

'I thought lions lived in the jungle,' she said, her eyes still glazed.

'Lions used to roam the whole of the Old World,' Ralph

told her from the front of the car, looking in the rear-view mirror to check her reaction.

'I am glad we live in the New World then,' she replied.

'It says here that lionesses do most of the hunting,' Joe said.

'Just as with humans, Joe,' Anne replied with a twinkle in her eye and trading a cheeky glance with Ralph.

'Yeah sure!' Ralph replied. They were both relieved to be back in the safety of their car, with everyone inside, wearing their seat belts.

'You're not a lioness, Mummy,' Clara observed 'You're much nicer.'

'You haven't seen her at the hospital,' Ralph joked.

'Yes, I have,' Clara retorted. 'Stop being mean, Daddy!'

Joe turned to Freddie.

'Have you ever felt that way before?'

'What way?' Freddie asked.

'Hunted. Out in the open. You and the elements. No civilisation to fall back on. Just you and a predator,' Joe elaborated.

'Never. Terrifying… but thrilling. I feel alive.' Freddie said.

'Look at that!' Joe pointed to a shipwreck in the shallows of the ocean, buffeted by the South Atlantic waves.

'That's what I told you about,' Freddie said excitedly. 'Look, Mum, Dad, Clara, remember that first day and the shipwrecks? Sailing down this coast.'

'They don't look so scary now,' Clara observed.

She was right. Now that the fog had lifted under the heat of the mid-day sun, the shipwreck looked more like an abandoned bath toy than a demonic presence. This wreck was more modern than some: a large fishing trawler, whose carcass was largely intact. Birds nestled on its every rusted inch, using its height to view their ocean prey. Its lilt to one side gave the illusion of motion: of a downwards move in the waves, but one that never came back up, stuck in the freeze-frame of its disaster.

Soon they were passing the industrial saltworks on the outskirts of Swakopmund, and opposite, nestling by the beach, was a small complex of satellite dishes, pointing at the sky at various angles.

'Wow! A tracking station,' Joe exclaimed.

'I'm pretty sure that's the one belonging to the Chinese government,' Ralph responded. 'I was briefed on it the other day by my team. The Chinese use it to track the re-entry of their space vehicles.'

This description lit up Joe's head. Ever since he could remember, he'd loved space programmes. He'd watched recordings of the Apollo moon landings over and over. Ben and Barbara bought him a large telescope for his tenth birthday and had put it in pride of place by the picture window in the sitting-room. Every probe that set off to Mars or Saturn or the Sun, Joe tracked daily, marking its trajectory on graph paper.

After the trauma of the seal reserve, Swakop as it was often called, felt like civilisation. It had palm-lined, beautifully-clean streets, and German, colonial architecture. The Victorian buildings were painted in vibrant Caribbean colours as if to broadcast the town to passing ships. There were elegantly simple, Lutheran churches, well-kept parks and a stripy light-house like a stick of rock. It was all laid out in a neat, German grid system, parallel and at right angles to the sea.

'Gosh it's a real seaside town,' Anne exclaimed, 'in the middle of a desert!'

'Yes, someone called it Germany's most southerly Baltic resort,' Ralph chirruped, breaking into laughter. Ralph always liked his own humour, even when no-one else did.

The streets were bustling with people from Windhoek escaping the heat of the desert interior at the height of summer. There were open-air bars and cafes with frothy cappuccinos and artisan ice-creams being served by the trayful.

Both families stopped to get an ice-cream and bask in the sun, the temperature made comfortable by a cheery breeze off the ocean. Then they checked the driving instructions to their respective hosts on Google Maps, agreed when they would set off for the site the next morning and went their separate ways.

Joe was excited to see Selima's house for the first time. Sometimes people's houses are exactly as you expect them in your head: their personality in bricks and mortar. Sometimes they reveal what has been hidden.

Selima's house was modest but characterful, built in the 1970's by South African architects: during the Apartheid era and before Namibian independence. Darius had liked the fact that it was built by South Africans given his ancestry. He had immediately felt at home on entering its hallway for the first time. Ilana liked it because it was light and airy and from the second floor you had a clear view of the sea.

Darius had kept the outside of the house perfectly maintained. His practicality was one of the things that had first attracted Ilana to this rough-round-the-edges, bearded farmer's son. That and his blue eyes which always seemed to sparkle with the prospect of something new and glittering on the horizon.

It was years before she realised that most of what glittered was an illusion.

The house was as loveably chaotic and colourful as the Van Zyl's themselves. Shelves overflowed with Namibian pottery, jewellery, collections of rocks and gems. There were posters in loud colours advertising 'Darius's Unbeatable Sand Dune Tours', copies of which they had seen in town. They showed his Land Rover poised precariously on a ridge, tourists in the back screaming with nervy delight. Darius's tools seemed to nestle in every corner of the house, waiting to be used for some unfinished task. There were incomplete models of boats and cars dotted around and the architectural drawings of his parent's old farm.

Ilana's passions were also everywhere. Sepia and colour photographs of different Namibian tribes dotted the hallway and occupied one whole wall of the airy sitting-room. There were photographs of her leading tour groups across impossibly beautiful landscapes. A signed photograph with Nelson and Winnie Mandela, and another with the Namibian President Sam Nujoma, were, naturally, in pride of place. The fridge door was covered in vivid protest badges and flyers: some about the environment, others about protecting indigenous land rights.

'I have to say I'm very impressed with Swakopmund,' Ben said as they sat having cold drinks on the terrace. 'It's beautiful. Much more affluent than I expected.'

'It wasn't always that way I can tell you,' Darius responded. 'It was very run down for years and years, neglected, until the Rossing mine started in the seventies. Basically, the infrastructure of this place has grown to serve the mine.'

'Besides,' Ilana added, 'you've only seen the affluent part

of Swakop so far. Half the population live in the township: Mondesa. It was started during Apartheid.'

'And it still has the areas that they designated for ethnic groups,' Darius continued. 'The Ovambo, Nama and Herero: they all live in their own separate neighbourhoods.'

'We haven't washed Apartheid away yet, I'm afraid,' Ilana sighed.

'That's sad. But what we saw was very beautiful and clean,' Barbara said, trying to lighten the tone a little. She was very conscious that the last time she had met Ilana was in the confrontation over the hotel site and she was trying to tread carefully. 'In stark contrast, I might say, to the Seal Colony!' she added.

'Ah you went there, good,' Ilana said. 'That's why I suggested that route.'

There was an awkward pause.

'We saw a lioness make a kill,' Joe interjected.

This news shook Darius. 'A lion in the seal colony! My God that's rare. There used to be many more. Gosh, it would have been two days away from the rest of the pride. There must be a shortage of food inland.'

'It was amazing,' Joe said. 'I've never seen anything like it.'

'You're very lucky,' Darius observed.

'I'm not sure "luck" is the term I'd use,' Barbara replied. She still felt wary of Darius, despite the kind invitation to stay at his home. Why had he failed to tell Ilana that he was working with her on the hotel site? She looked at the two of them trying to detect what kind of marriage they had. Darius did seem jumpy, wary of the strong presence of his wife. He leaned back as much as she leaned forward.

'At least a lion only kills one seal… and in pursuit of its own survival. The annual cull is a disgrace,' Ilana commented.

'What's the cull?' Joe asked.

'The Government kill tens of thousands of seals every year and then sell the fur. It's a bloodbath. It's supposedly to stop the fish stocks getting too low and to raise money to protect the colony. It would really be far better to raise money through tourism. They should leave the size of the colony to Nature.'

'I am just going to show Joe the neighbourhood,' Selima interjected, fearing the conversation could slide ever further into one of her mother's moral lectures and keen to be alone with Joe.

They patrolled the quiet streets of Selima's suburb, alone and happy. Joe felt a contentment stealing over him. They aimlessly wheeled around corners and ambled along pavements, occasionally stopping for Selima to point out a specific house, or to cheekily pluck fragrant leaves from a neighbour's garden and put them under Joe's nose.

'So, how did you feel seeing a kill?' she asked.

'Look, I'm a city boy from Brooklyn, New York. To me lions are something you see at the Bronx Zoo when your folks can't figure out what to do on your birthday.'

'You haven't answered my question. Anyway, isn't New York a kind of jungle as well?'

'In its way! To be truthful, given my folks' lifestyle, I've spent more time away from New York than in it, but still… How did I feel? You want the truth? I felt like an electric fence watching the kill. I was buzzing but shocked.'

Joe never expressed things in the way others would. That was part of his appeal.

'In fact, ever since I arrived here,' he continued, 'I have felt more alive than I've ever felt in my life.'

'And is that just because of the landscape?' she asked, but without looking at him for fear of smiling too much.

'Perhaps,' he said, teasing her.

'How do you cope with the crowds in New York? From the movies I've seen it looks like the streets are always crawling with people.'

'I blank them. I literally air-brush them out.'

'I can't imagine that,' she responded.

'I couldn't imagine here. Until now…'

'Welcome to Swakop. Sounds like you've had rather too much of an adventure.' Li Chiang always liked to be ready on the doorstep when guests arrived and this was no exception, alerted by their texts.

'Hi, I'm Anne, and this is Ralph. You must be Li. Thank you so much for inviting us. This seems like a haven after the heat of Windhoek.'

Handshakes and polite kisses were exchanged, Sarah joining them, slightly flustered and taking off an apron dusted with flour.

'Please forgive me. I was just baking for tonight's supper.'

'No need to apologise at all. We're very honoured to be invited.' Ralph was always like silk in his manners, something for which Sarah was perpetually grateful. The oil of his voice could calm most things, both within the family and outside.

'Why are you all kissing when you don't know each other? And why isn't anyone kissing me?' Clara protested.

Anne was charmed. 'You must be Clara. Can I kiss you please?'

'Yes, thank you, that would be very nice!' Clara proffered her better cheek, the one she always turned towards the camera for photographs.

'Sorry about my younger sister,' Freddie said ruffling her hair affectionately as he did. 'She rarely makes a quiet entrance. I'm Freddie by the way.'

'Like father, like son,' Anne thought to herself... 'charming.'

Later, when supper was over and Clara had fallen asleep on the sofa, the six of them sat chatting at the dining-table. They had separated neatly, like a perfectly ripe fruit, into three segments: young people, mothers and fathers.

Ralph and Li were deep in diplomatic relations, politely circling each other to assess where they stood.

'I saw the Chinese Satellite tracking station as we came into town,' Ralph proffered.

'Yes, it was actually a collaboration between the Chinese and Namibian governments,' Li confirmed.

Ralph made a mental note for his next report to the Foreign Office.

'So, how important is space exploration for the Chinese?'

'Well, with 1.3 billion citizens, China has more incentive than most to find another colony out there in which to live.'

Ralph was struck by the term 'colony'.

'Gosh, I'd never thought about China's population as an incentive to explore space. How stupid of me. We'll all need to find another planet where we can live of course... if we carry on treating this one the way we have. Perhaps there's hope, now that we know there's water on Mars.'

'Yes, it's the size of Lake Windermere apparently,' Li laughed. 'Only the British could use the Lake District to describe space.'

Ralph felt slightly wounded, but was determined not to show it, something at which he had learned to excel. He took another sip of beer instead.

'When you come to a place like Namibia… so pristine, so unpopulated…it makes you realise how much we've ruined Earth already,' Ralph observed.

'And here I am plundering their minerals,' Li confessed. 'Yet if we are to save the planet, we need more nuclear energy and that requires uranium.'

'Not to mention for things like this,' Ralph said, lifting his mobile phone from the table.

'Well, we're not going to be mining much, at- the- moment,' Li said dolefully.

'Why?'

'Please treat it as confidential for now. We have discovered a mass grave at our test site.'

Everyone else's conversation stopped. Hannah looked slightly surprised that her father had shared this news. She was worried that this might make him vulnerable. She knew perfectly well that his employers would be secretive, just as she knew that her father was cut from another cloth.

'What kind of mass grave?' Anne asked. 'I mean, is it from a plague? Or radiation?' She thought of her burn victims.

'We have to wait for the Namibians to finish their tests. They're carbon-dating the skeletons. But the circumstances, the way the bones are piled, all points in one direction…' Li pronounced.

'Which is...?' Anne persisted.

'Genocide,' said Sarah. 'The genocide the Germans committed on the Herero and the Nama.'

Ralph had been doing his research. 'In October 1904, Lother von Trotha, under the instructions of the Kaiser, ordered the extermination of every Herero man, woman or child in the German Territory.'

'So, we've closed the mine and we're not sure we can continue. Meanwhile, the pressure builds from Shanghai for me to find another site.' Li had hoped to escape the pressures of his work at the weekend, but he knew this hope was forlorn.

'He's been having nightmares,' Hannah chipped in, not sure if she should, but wanting to share her worry about him. It was the first time she'd heard his wailing through the wall since her mother had miscarried.

'Man's inhumanity to man,' Sarah sighed. 'It's been very tough for Li.'

'Yes, but we have to carry on,' Li said stoically. 'We need nuclear power to save the world.'

'Or destroy it,' said Anne. 'I have an outbreak of patients in the hospital at the moment with unexplained burn marks. Some people are suggesting it's radiation leaks from the mines.'

'Very unlikely,' Li retorted defensively, feeling both under attack and worried.

After the parents had gone to bed, Hannah and Freddie stayed on the terrace talking, two tiny figures against the backdrop of a brilliant night sky. In the cities where they had both lived, the sky, if it was noticed at all, was squeezed between buildings and two-dimensional. Here the moon was a sphere not a disc and horizons lived up to their name.

'You can see so clearly here,' Freddie commented.

'No light pollution. Not much pollution full stop,' Hannah responded.

They both gazed at the carpet of stars.

'Is there somewhere out there to live?' Freddie asked

'Would we want it to, even if there were?' Hannah questioned.

'What, you'd rather die here?'

'I think so. I'd rather lie down on the warm grass I know and love, listen to one last bird and fall asleep. Look at that vastness out there. How would we find our bearings?'

'We are hurtling through space all the time, as we go around the sun.'

'Yes, I know but it's our home. We're travelling on our home.'

A shooting star shot across the sky. Another meteor reduced to a firework, seemingly for their pleasure alone.

7

The Dig, The Map

The site, thankfully, had been left untouched. The tarpaulin, anchored firmly by stones, was just as Darius had left it. For once, there had been no bribing of guards, no theft of artefacts. Ben put this down to fear. The impulse to steal was not as powerful as the risk of your soul being damned by disturbing a grave. The Elders would have held sway in this matter.

Sure enough, there was an expert from the National Anthropology Museum present to protect Namibia's interests in the find. Ben showed him his licence for the dig which he examined slowly with suitable gravitas, followed by a nod of mutual respect. The Museum Directors had been excited when the news first broke that Dr Kaplan from Columbia University, expert in African tribes, was going to spend a year in Namibia. Their dignity, however, prevented them from broadcasting the fact.

The Museum Director was accompanied by an anonymous civil servant who simply took notes on proceedings, whilst the Director made drawings, took measurements and intermittently snapped photographs with a digital SLR. Ben noted that the Museum must be well-equipped.

The families arranged some folding chairs and outdoor tables near the perimeter of the pit and laid down some ground sheets and tablecloths so that those who weren't digging could watch and support. They had packed a large alfresco lunch anticipating, correctly, that a dig would last a long time and make you hungry.

The Museum Director had been somewhat taken aback by the presence of four families and advised that no more than five people should be around the body, in the pit, at any one time. The parents all nodded sagely, but the younger ones wanted to be off the leash. Whilst Ben, Ilana and Darius, and two others by turns, got to work, the rest sat on the periphery of the dig, offering helpful and not-so-helpful suggestions.

Clara was over-excited and so they took it in turns to play cards with her, or to prowl through the nearby landscape looking for strange insects and small animals. She was especially taken with the ground squirrel that kept cool by keeping its back to the sun, using its tail as a sunshade.

Ben enjoyed taking charge and for once, not being alone, even if the other people's enthusiasm sometimes meant they got in the way. He had brought multiple prints of Victorian, military uniforms, gathered from on-line regimental archives. The Internet was a 'god-send' to anthropologists. He couldn't now remember a time without it.

He proceeded to lay the printed sheets in turn next to the body, looking for an exact match with the uniform on the skeleton. Joe was his second pair of eyes. After eleven attempted matches, he struck gold.

'That's it, Dad,' Joe said excitedly. 'Look at the epaulettes and the markings on the sash.'

Ben held the drawing next to the uniform itself.

'Fourteenth Regiment of the Foot, British Army. It's a Scottish Regiment.'

He checked in one of his many plastic folders.

'Yep, that was Alexander's regiment. It must be him then. All the evidence confirms it…the inscription on the watch, the uniform, even the travels he describes in the published journals and letters.'

There was a frisson of excitement in the families. Ralph, who had only reluctantly got involved in this whole enterprise, found himself thinking of his own ancestors and wondering whether any of them had been explorers. It would give meaning to his own wanderlust.

The next task was to thoroughly examine the uniform's pockets, being careful not to rip its already-decaying fabric. In an inside jacket pocket, there was a small pouch, containing an engagement ring. Anne and Sarah gathered round to examine. Its sparkle was untarnished, its facets seemingly glad to see the light again.

'Probably purchased in South Africa to give to his betrothed. Worn close to his heart,' Ben observed, touched by this affection.

'Think about that girl back home in the Highlands, waiting for a wedding that would never happen,' Anne added, looking dolefully at Sarah and Barbara.

'Did she die alone and unfulfilled, I wonder?' Sarah chimed.

Looking at the unfolding scene in front of her, Ilana regretted her initial, fierce reaction that the dig should have been left to local anthropologists. She was still proud that the Museum Director was there, as per her suggestion. Yet, she was also touched by Ben's delicacy and sensitivity when moving around the body. There was a cultural link with this fallen British explorer that no Namibian could feel. It struck her that this

Captain Alexander they had unearthed was a man much like Ben himself: fascinated by cultures, indeed the cultures of her own ancestors. Ben was effectively digging up his own future corpse.

After photographs and measurements had been taken, the local anthropologist and Ben carefully removed all items of clothing from the body and laid them, numbered and labelled, in crates.

Then a kind of stretcher was placed under the skeleton and four of them lifted the body as one and lowered it into a bare, wooden casket. It had all the gravitas of a second burial. After forensic examinations, the body would be shipped home to Scotland to any surviving relatives for a final burial in the Highlands.

Joe, Freddie, Hannah and Selima had felt like spare parts to this point, engrossed though they were in the intricacies of the procedures. Their turn to get involved had now arrived.

'Right guys, time for some serious digging.' Ben issued his call to arms whilst handing out shovels to all four of them.

He supervised them digging systematically in defined squares which he marked out with ropes stretched between tent poles that he hammered into the ground with a mallet.

'Good to see you lot at work,' Ralph called out affectionately. The four families already felt bonded by their common task.

'Thanks, Dad,' Freddie called back with cheery sarcasm, 'you just relax.'

'Can't I dig?' asked Clara, having bored, of her 'mini' excursions.

'No darling, it's too difficult for you,' Anne said.

Seeing Clara crestfallen, Ben called over to her.

'Clara, I've got a special task for you to do. Probably the most important. Do you think you can do it?'

'Of course, I can,' Clara said beaming and jumping into the pit. Anne and Ralph looked on in gratitude.

Ben gave her a small trowel and some protective gloves.

'Now, if you look, the others have got those huge, galumphing spades. This is delicate work and it requires your sensitive hands. I want you to start digging very carefully, just around where the skeleton was lying. Often, we find things close to the body and they can be easily damaged. So, go gently with this trowel. Do you understand?'

Clara nodded solemnly and set off with great passion and an exaggerated demeanour of extreme care.

Joe dug in neat rows in his square. As he dug, he tried to think through the physics of how he could apply maximum force for minimum effort. He was also trying to work out how much soil there might be for every century that passed.

Freddie took to the task with what he thought of as the relish of a British farm labourer. By so doing, he threatened to bury Clara, with his vigorously discarded soil, and had to be restrained.

Hannah tried to compete with Selima which proved hard. Selima had the advantage of having learnt how to dig Darius's Land Rover out of quicksand, on a number of occasions. Her technique, combined with her natural strength, meant that she had dug to twice the depth of Hannah in the same time.

It was thus a quietly satisfying moment when Hannah's spade hit something hard. She wanted to be certain and so she dug again a few inches across. There was a definite, metal sound, albeit softened by the soil, and when she tried a third time, a shockwave spread back up the spade, through her arms to her jaw. She had found something solid.

She nurtured the secret for a few moments, treasuring it, before she called out.

'I've hit something… something metal!'

Clara groaned that it wasn't her, and then dropped her trowel as everyone downed tools and ran to Hannah.

Ben took Hannah's spade, slightly to her annoyance, and quickly but carefully dug more earth away, then dropped it and dug into the soil with his bare hands. He felt his way along the object, trying to scope out its dimensions.

'It's metal and wood and it's big. I suspect it's a trunk of some kind.'

Ben proceeded to mark out an area, one foot wider and longer than the object he could feel, and arranged for them to dig on all sides, until there was a mud-encased rectangle in front of them, an altar of soil.

Then they used the trowels to carefully scrape the soil away.

'This is how a sculptor must feel,' Hannah said, 'as they chip away, and a figure emerges from the marble.'

'One, two, three…lift!'

Six of them lifted the emerging object from the pit and carried it across to the table at which Barbara had been working when she first met Ilana. Then came the painstaking exercise of wiping and removing dirt, until it stood clearly before them.

'It's an old steamer trunk,' Ralph declared, remembering his great-grandmother's that had been restored and kept in their entrance-hall as a child.

It was predominantly wood covered with, some kind, of

taut, protective skin that had helped to preserve it. It had wooden struts on all sides, and, also across the lid. There were enough bolts, locks and catches to have scuppered Houdini, the famous escapologist. It was clearly the trunk of someone distinguished and wealthy.

The same initials were imprinted on its side as on the watch: J.W.A.

The locks were a nightmare, jammed tight as they had been for almost two hundred years. They gathered around the trunk in a scene reminiscent of the crowd that gathers in an Italian street when someone gets locked out of their car. Everyone was screaming different suggestions as to how to crowbar the lock or drill or pick it.

Having frustrated all subtler attempts, Darius used the biggest crowbar and hammer he could muster and prised it apart. As the lid was flung open, a cloud of hot musty air spread over them. It was like entering an attic in the height of summer, the past brewing its heady stew beneath the rafters.

'This is where you thank your lucky stars that there is practically no humidity in Namibia,' the Museum Director commented. 'Everything is preserved by the sand and the heat.'

They gradually removed the objects inside, examining each one like a Christmas present. One of the first and heaviest objects to emerge was a Victorian sewing-machine. It was, as the Director had anticipated, in extraordinarily good condition. It was cast iron and japanned with black gold in intricate patterns. The words 'Arm and Platform' were inlaid into its top arm. It looked more like a lathe than a sewing-machine and had one large handle for turning the bobbin. The maker was one 'Edward Ward of Edinburgh.'

'Why would an explorer bring a sewing-machine from Scotland?' Joe asked.

'To help the Herero sow their dresses would be my guess,' Ilana said. 'You've seen how elaborate they are. The missionaries preferred them to look European.'

The trunk yielded much more: ostrich feathers and eggs; a rhino horn and some ivory tusks, both of which would now be illegal; precious stones and minerals; spears and axes, some pottery. There, lurking at the bottom, were two Bibles, four leather-bound journals, a sketchbook and, a number, of scrolls, bound tight with silk ribbons.

'This is the real prize,' Ben cried, holding them aloft.

An hour later, having divided the journals between them to read, they read out extracts, when struck by specific episodes, or descriptions by Captain Alexander.

'Listen to this…' Hannah said. 'Today, I went to Cape Cross Colony as suggested by a fellow-founder of the Royal Geographical Society. He had heard tale of extraordinary wild-life and sure enough I encountered a vast collection of seals. I was most struck by their ears which were visible and external to their bodies. This is unlike any other seals I have encountered.'

'I don't think we even noticed their ears, did we?' said Joe laughing.

'Aa ha, that's because you lack the trained eyes of a Victorian amateur biologist and botanist,' Anne chipped in. 'As a highly trained doctor, I, of course noticed them straightaway.'

'Oh yes, Mum, then how come you didn't say anything?' Clara piped up.

'I was distracted by a lion darling!'

'Also found the stone cross after which the Colony is named. It was erected in 1484 by Diego Cao, a Portuguese explorer. Set me thinking about the War of Two Brothers in which I fought in 1832.'

'He was clearly a seasoned soldier,' Ralph observed. 'Listen to this... "I am still exhausted from the Frontier War in South Africa. Looking back, I shouldered a huge burden as aide-de-camp to d'Urban. The weariness is very deep. I also feel very alone. There are Germans here and Afrikaners of course, but hardly any British. If not for Erastus, my translator, I would feel, unutterably, alone. Although he doesn't have my education, he is immensely kind and patient. He is also a fine storyteller. How I miss Margaret, my beloved. She writes often begging me to return to Scotland. The engagement has been planned for two years and she says the sound of wedding bells seems to be fading upon the wind."'

'So, Margaret is the one who was left behind,' Sarah observed.

'I hate to think of her pining away,' Anne said.

'Yes, it could have been years before she gave up on him being alive,' Ilana added. 'What foolish creatures we women are!' She shot a glance in Darius's direction but, happily, found him engrossed in Alexander's sketchbook.

Sensing her gaze, he looked up.

'His drawings are really rather good,' he said. 'It's interesting what struck him as important to capture. He's drawn Secretary Birds from every conceivable angle for example.'

'What's a Secretary Bird when it's at home... or at the office, come to that?' asked Freddie.

'It's a bird of prey,' Ilana answered. 'They are raptors... descended from dinosaurs and vicious.'

'Cool,' said Joe.

'Where can we see them?' asked Freddie.

'You'll see them soon enough,' Darius replied. 'They're used by farmers for killing pests. They kill snakes by jumping on their back and then breaking their necks. More effective than a mongoose.'

'Why are they called Secretary Birds?' Clara asked.

'Well, it's not because they can type,' Darius replied, but his humour was lost on Clara and so he continued. 'It's because they look as if they have quills behind their ears.'

'Quills?' Clara explained.

'Old-fashioned pens,' Hannah explained. 'But listen, he also mentions them here in one of the journals… "My friends the Secretary Birds appeared again today. In addition to their extraordinary ability to kill quickly and cleanly, at which one can only marvel, they also seem extraordinarily advanced. They are, by observation, totally faithful to one partner for their whole lives. They hunt on the ground by day, but, return to roost in the Acacia trees by night, to avoid being hunted. They seem highly intelligent and I am convinced that in some way they can help me find the burial site."'

'What burial site?' Joe asked. 'What was he looking for?'

'I don't know,' said Selima 'but I've found several mentions of it in this journal as well. Listen to this… "My anthropologist friends in London tell me there is increasing evidence that we are all descended from the San people here in Southern Africa. Which would make this corner of Africa our Eden. It is strange to think of Adam and Eve as African but if science is proved right then this surely must be the case.

The San impress me more each day. They are nomads and

see themselves as custodians of these vast lands which they call "Nores". Because they roam and hunt, they are expert trackers. I am convinced they could help me find the burial site. They also believe in one Supreme Being, which gives the missionaries hope that they are ripe for Christianity. I remain unconvinced."'

'He clearly loved the Herero as well,' said Ilana, 'judging by what he has written about them. A rare man for a colonialist. No wonder they buried him with garlands.'

'And took such care to bury his possessions with him,' Sarah added.

'We must pray for such people in our era,' Ralph said.

'Amen to that,' Ilana added.

'Why are you all sounding so religious? I don't understand adults,' Clara declared.

'Good,' said Anne kissing Clara on the nose. 'We are often not worth understanding.'

'Hold on. I think this might be important,' Sarah said, unravelling one of the scrolls and laying it flat. It was partly her understatement that drew them all round.

A very old and battered map lay open in front of her. She had pinned it down with rocks at the four corners. It looked crude like a child's drawing. Nothing seemed to be in proportion. There were very few words and even they were indecipherable, written in some African script. It was largely pictorial with symbols and animals. It looked more like an Egyptian papyrus with hieroglyphs than anything else. In the top right-hand corner, in faded writing, were two words underlined in English: 'Must decipher!

'This isn't his map,' Ben said, 'but that is almost certainly his comment. He clearly thought this particular map was important. It's African.'

'How can you tell?' Ralph asked.

'It's on animal skin for a start, which no European would use,' Ben answered.

'I recognise some of these symbols,' Ilana said. 'Many of them are used in rock paintings. Especially at Twyfelfontein.'

'Oh my God yes!' Hannah declared 'Isn't that the Lion Man? The lion with the tail that ends in a hand, that Ubuntu showed us!'

'Yes, it is!' said Selima. 'Mum, you and I have seen it a hundred times.'

Darius remained silent. There was something in the topography of the map that he recognised but he couldn't put his finger on it.

'I might be able to translate the language,' Anne offered. 'I would need some reference books though.'

'I'm sure that we can get you access to the language archives,' Ilana said.

'The University in Windhoek will help,' Ben added.

'The question is…' said Joe, 'what is this map and why did he consider it to be so important?'

They packed up the journals and maps. Ben and Ralph both signed the release forms that the Museum Director had provided for the artefacts.

Alexander's body and the rest of his possessions were crated up, numbered and taken to the Museum in Windhoek.

Exhausted, their minds on a torture rack of possibilities, the four families returned from the site to Swakop in late afternoon.

159

They desperately needed some normality and so they all walked to the Mole, the colonial, sea-wall on the ocean, and sat having dinner, overlooking Palm Beach. By the time they finished eating, it was dark and the Swakop lighthouse was casting its hypnotic beams across the ocean.

When they returned home, everyone except Hannah crashed into bed. She was haunted by Alexander's journals. She hadn't been as possessed by a book since the one she wrote for her stillborn sibling.

It must have been close to midnight when Freddie was woken violently by a pounding on his bedroom door. It wouldn't stop and he remembered that he had locked the door. He wasn't quite sure why.

Slowly, he dragged himself off the bed and unlocked the door. Hannah stood swaying in front of him like a hypnotised cobra, her eyes ablaze despite her obvious exhaustion.

'What the hell, Hannah…'

'You don't understand. I've been reading for almost three hours and I've found it.'

'Found what?'

'In his journal. Listen to this… "The San have given me a map. If I could decode its symbols, it will lead me to the burial site. More importantly, if I can find this site, then the secret of the Fairy Circles will be revealed. I am convinced of it."'

Just then an almighty crash seemed to envelop the house. Freddie thought the ceiling was about to cave in.

A thunderstorm had started overhead and was doing its best to clear the air.

8

Disturbance

It was Monday but The Augustineum had a Staff Training Day and so, happily, there was no school, extending Half Term by another day. The families had decided they would stay longer in Swakop to enjoy the cooler temperatures and sea air and return to Windhoek that night.

Li's mobile broke into his sleep like a burglar. Whatever ringtone he chose, it was only days before that new sound induced the same kind of dread as the previous one. This morning it sounded particularly grating.

'Turn it off, for God's sake,' Sarah grunted.

He picked it up and looked at the number that was ringing him.

'*+8621…*'

Damn. It was Shanghai. Why now on a Monday morning?

'I have to take this, Sarah, I'm sorry. It's work. Hello, Li Chiang.'

'Li, it's Huang'Fu here,' the voice said. 'What the hell's going on? How could you have let this happen?'

'Huang'Fu, we've started looking for alternative sites. You know these things take time.'

'I don't mean that. I'm talking about disturbing the bones.'

'Bones? What about the bones?' In his half-awake state, Li could only think about Captain Alexander's skeleton, about

161

which he had been dreaming a large part of the night. But then how did his boss know about their private dig?

Huang'Fu continued.

'Some of the bones from the Herero and Nama genocide that you found in the test mine have been moved up to the surface without the Namibians being consulted. The local people are up in arms. There's practically a riot at the site.'

'I don't understand. I haven't been at the site since Thursday. I left Shen Chi in charge.'

'Well, the bloody idiot has made a catastrophic error. Why didn't he check in with you before making such a major decision? Doesn't he understand that we are dealing with the victims of genocide here... revered ancestors?'

'I don't know what on earth possessed him,' Li responded. 'We have all been feeling the pressure. Perhaps he felt if the bones were moved to the surface, we could continue to explore the test site.'

'That may seem entirely logical, but we need to bring people with us. Now we've upset the Namibian Government, profoundly upset the local community on whose goodwill we rely, and, to add insult to injury, the Germans are furious because the genocide, for which they refuse to apologise, has reared its ugly head again. Hold on Li...'

Li could hear an urgent voice in the background.

'Oh great,' Huang'Fu continued, 'now I've got the Ministry of Foreign Affairs on the phone from Beijing. Got to go. Deal with it, Li!'

'I will, Huang'Fu. Rest assured.'

The call went dead before he'd even got to the end of his reassurance.

'What was all that about?' asked Sarah.

'There's a riot at the test site. They've moved the Herero bones we found to the surface, without consulting anyone,' Li informed Sarah.

'How stupid of them. Why didn't they ask you? You're going to get the blame for this, of course. They'll ask you to fall on your sword.'

'I'm driving to the mine.'

Ralph woke up early from a restless night. He had vague recollections of a thunderstorm. Despite travelling the world, he never slept well in a new bed.

He went downstairs, made himself a coffee and switched on the television to watch the morning news, rapidly reducing its volume with the remote control for fear of waking anyone.

Before he could change channels to BBC World, the local news caught his attention.

There were angry crowds chanting, and a scuffle between two Chinese men in hard hats and several protesters. He edged the volume up a little.

'Hundreds of protesters have gathered at a test mine in Damaraland operated by the Chinese Zjin Mining Company, after the bones of Herero and Nama people killed in the German genocide of 1904, were taken up to the surface without any consultation.'

Li entered the room, dressed for work and looking hassled. He nodded at Ralph.

'Morning, Li. Is this mine on the news anything to do with you?'

Li stopped in his tracks and looked at the screen, recognising some of his team. 'Oh God, don't tell me it's on the news already! That will not be helpful.'

'Looks like you've got a tough day ahead of you. Can I help in any way?'

'If you have any means of calming the Namibian Government, I would be most grateful. My deputy decided to move the bones, probably with the best of intents, but without consulting me.'

'I will see what I can do,' Ralph reassured.

Li nodded in gratitude, slammed the door and left.

Ralph's mobile started to vibrate. He picked it up. He knew it was the Foreign Office before he even looked at the number. They wouldn't miss breaking news like this.

Ralph braced himself. 'Ralph Wilde.'

'I've got the Minister for you, High Commissioner. Can you hold...?'

The Minister's voice was unexpectedly upbeat, contrary to expectation.

'Ralph, this is marvellous news. Two for the price of one. Tell me you had a hand in this, and I assure you your next post will be a major one.'

Ralph winced at the thought that Namibia was a minor post and tried to compose himself in the face of this onslaught.

'Good morning, Minister. Nice to hear you sounding so cheery. No, I'm glad to say I had nothing to do with the genocide controversy and I'm just watching it on BBC World now.'

'Well you're a recipient of good fortune then. Not only have the Germans been forced to re-acknowledge their dress-rehearsal for Hitler in Africa, the Chinese look like the new imperialists...which, by the way, they are. Even better, their

Governments are falling out with each other as well as with Namibia. Merkel apparently believes the Chinese have done it deliberately to scupper her own mining plans.'

'I happen to be staying with the man in charge of the test site: Li Chiang,' Ralph informed him.

'Why?'

'Our children go to school together. I thought we ought to try and calm things down a bit. It's a crass mistake but it is a genuine mistake. His deputy made a rash decision in his absence. He seems a very honourable man.'

'Look, Ralph, I have no sympathy for them, and I don't see any reason why you should, despite your personal connection. The Germans should have made proper reparations years ago.'

'Have we made reparations for all of our colonial misdeeds?'

'That's irrelevant. The Chinese certainly should know better than to put mining needs ahead of sensitivity to human suffering.'

Ralph couldn't disagree with the principle of what his superior was saying, but, the manner, in which he said it, stuck in his gullet. Long ago he'd abandoned the idea of the moral superiority of one nation over another. He'd seen too much.

With Li gone to the mine, and Ralph now embroiled in work emails, Anne and Sarah decided to take Freddie and Hannah and join the other families for breakfast. Ilana had invited them, partly under pressure from Selima who was desperate to get the Four Teenagers of the Apocalypse together.

Hannah had shared her discovery from Alexander's journal on WhatsApp with Joe and Selima soon after bursting into Freddie's room last night. The moment they were awake, they read it, triggering a flood of early morning messages and speculations as to the possible link between a burial site and the Fairy Circles.

'Mum, the map…' Hannah said across the breakfast table, 'when can you start to translate it?'

'Well, I do have a job, Hannah, as you may remember. Two, if you include being your mother.'

'But this is more important than any job could be.'

Ilana listened smiling as she made pancakes for everyone. They all sat around the scrubbed, wooden table in her kitchen. Darius was removing various tools, loose screws and rags from the table, under instruction from Ilana to 'make it look respectable, like a normal household.' Selima was dishing out plates and cutlery, delighted not to be sitting alone at breakfast for once.

'I know you're all very excited by these journals and maps, but you do need to calm down a little,' Barbara cautioned. 'This explorer – Captain Alexander – could be a crackpot for all we know.'

'Who's a crackpot?' Ben asked as he entered the kitchen. He usually found that this word, or something similar, was used of him.

'I am talking about your explorer, the corpse of the moment!' Barbara had grown weary of Ben's string of unearthed, ancient heroes. She felt their ghostly presence hanging over her like a third person in their marriage. They suppressed her husband's appetite for the present, for her. They tore his concentration out of their conversations. His obsessions were exhausting. She hadn't agreed to marry into burial sites.

'He's not a crackpot. You read some of his extracts and you

166

heard others. He was intelligent, caring, sane.'

'He was clearly obsessive,' Barbara pointed out, 'like someone else I know!'

'Sometimes we have good reason to be obsessive,' Ben retorted.

'And this might be that reason,' said Hannah, passing Ben the section of the journal she had struck upon. He read it avidly.

'Fascinating,' said Ben. 'I can't for the life of me see how a burial site would hold the clue to the Fairy Circles, but I'm intrigued to find out.'

'What are we doing today, Mummy?' Clara asked. Clara had always been like this as long as Anne could remember. She needed the scaffolding of her day to be built at its beginning.

'I am not sure darling. We have a day in Swakopmund ahead of us. I'm sure there are many things we could do.'

'Darius, are you going to tell them your idea?' Ilana prompted.

'Yes, I thought you guys might want to go quad biking on the sand dunes at Langstrand,' Darius suggested.

'Brilliant,' said Freddie.

'Yeah, Gucci!' added Joe. 'I've done it back home but never on sand dunes.'

'Hannah, you'll love it,' Selima added, sensing that Hannah was up for a day of researching rather than escapism. 'It's like sandboarding but on four wheels. Come on, you need a break. We all do.'

'Clara, we need to keep you to the flats and the Kiddies Track if you're on your own,' Darius said, 'but you can always ride the dunes with your mum or me.'

'You must all stick to the areas that Darius tells you,' said Ilana. 'We have strict zones marked out to stop any damage to the wildlife.'

'Are you joining us, Ilana?' Anne asked.

'I am afraid I have a tour group this morning, but I know you'll love it. You're in safe hands with Darius.' She felt the truth of her words as she said them and lingered momentarily on how she underestimated this vital quality in him.

'And I have an appointment at the Sam Cohen Library to research some Victorian newspapers,' Ben interjected. 'Which should prove useful in relation to you know who....'

It was settled: the sandboarding party set off in Darius's trusty Land Rover Defender and Ben and Barbara's somewhat less trusty 4x4.

The scene at the perimeter gate was chaos. As Li drove up, his car was mobbed by angry locals, Herero and Nama alike, appalled that their dead ancestors had been disturbed from their burial place.

They banged on every square inch of metal, spat on his windscreen and tried to rip his wing mirrors out of their sockets as if they were tiny, misshapen hands. Their eyes were ablaze. The local police made a token effort to restrain them but clearly sympathised with the Herero cause. Only the security guards hired by the mining company ensured his safe passage through the gates intact.

Once inside, Li tried to slow his breathing. As he approached the small cluster of Portakabins that made up their temporary offices, he saw a large, sprawling group of crates, draped in black. He assumed these held the remains from the mass grave.

They certainly hadn't been there when he left last Thursday night.

Shen Chi was waiting for him, looking pale and exhausted.

They stepped inside Li's cabin, the rising wind banging the door shut like an accusation.

'Let me first check what horrors await me,' Li said signalling for Shen to sit down.

Li entered his password on his desktop's home page and opened his emails. His inbox was flooded. The subject headings for each one said all he needed to know: 'PR Guidance'; 'Fwd: Chinese government expected to make an apology'; 'Phone me now'; 'Fwd: Is this the beginning of the end for Chinese mining in Africa?'; 'Think you ought to see this' and 'Strictly Confidential'.

He spent a few minutes reading the most important. Over the years he had perfected the art of speed reading, his eyes darting between paragraphs, seeking out significant phrases, like a heat-seeking missile. When he'd learned enough, he raised his gaze to his now-trembling deputy sitting in the corner of the cabin. He felt sick, for the Nama and Herero, for Shen and for himself.

'So, tell me, Shen. What happened?'

Shen Chi tried to settle himself before answering. He had rehearsed this moment over and over in his head since the scandal struck. Yet now the words seemed like disorderly letters in a Scrabble hand.

'It was a horrendous error and for that I beg your forgiveness.'

'I understand. Tell me what happened.'

'On Friday morning, Wang Lei made his usual visit. He

said that Shanghai were angry about the missed targets, that this unfortunate find of a mass grave couldn't have come at a worse time. He was angry you weren't there.'

'For God's sake, I went to Windhoek to see the Minister and try and find a solution to this appalling situation. I hope you explained that.'

'I tried. But he repeated that if you couldn't find a way to get exploration moving again, then perhaps I should.' Shen shifted uncomfortably in his seat and put both his hands under his buttocks.

'So, you decided to promote yourself and move the bodies?'

'I realised that there were sensitivities. But, I thought, that if we moved them carefully, respectfully, into crates and brought them to the surface, exploration could continue. I felt confident that you would be able to soothe the Ministry.'

'You felt confident, and yet you didn't ring me to ask how those meetings went, nor did you think to consult me as to whether you should bring up the bodies.'

'These people were killed over a hundred years ago and tipped into a mass grave. Their bones were all intertwined, inseparable. It's not as if they have living relatives waiting to identify them.'

'You don't understand their culture. To them, all relatives are living, however long they've been dead. They worship their ancestors. I've just been to a site where one Victorian, Scottish explorer was found and every item on his body, and around his body, was painstakingly removed, numbered and labelled. There are protocols for these things.'

'That's because the European tradition is that the death of an individual is important. To Africans it isn't,' Shen said confidently.

'You're wrong. That's a myth,' Li said, ashamed of his Deputy's lack of respect. 'To Africans each soul is sacred.'

'What do you want me to do?' Shen asked, already knowing the answer.

'I want you to publicly apologise and then resign, in front of the press, today…before any of this gets any worse.'

'But I was doing what I thought was best. If I lose my job, especially in these circumstances, my family will cut me off,' Shen pleaded.

'Shen, normally, I would simply ask you to take responsibility and apologise.' Li stared directly into Shen's eyes.

'But, in my emails just now, was one marked "Think you ought to see this". It forwarded an email that you had sent on Friday to Huang'Fu, implying that I was the reason there were delays in prospecting. You said I was cow-towing to local sensitivities. You then declared that, in my absence, you would deal with the bodies and hoped that this would be recognised in future promotions.'

Shen Chi bowed his head to his chest and stared at the floor silently. The door flew open with sudden force and a gust of sand and sickly, warm air invaded the cabin like bad breath.

As they drove along the narrow strip of Langstrand beach, in the direction of Walvis Bay, Darius noticed the tide whipping. The wind was rising. Nothing alarming yet, but he knew it needed to be watched. Every time he ventured out, he had to calculate the tides. The beach was never wider than sixty metres, and at high tide it disappeared completely, leaving you cut off in the dunes. So, all his trips had the backdrop of a tidal metronome clicking in his head.

171

Silas, his sidekick, had driven to Langstrand earlier with all the quad bikes on a trailer and set them up in the dunes ready to go, complete with helmets and visors. Everyone had their own bike apart from Clara who went with Anne.

'Follow me, guys,' Darius called after giving them the safety drill.

They practised on the flat, building up confidence and speed. Joe and Freddie started to weave in and out of each other's trails, laughing and trading insults. Selima stood up and beckoned to Hannah to do the same. This was the most alive Hannah had felt for ages, the wind buffeting her face, billowing her T-shirt, as she sped along the sand.

Clara clung on tight as Anne accelerated, whooping as she overtook Sarah, who immediately responded by opening, up, the throttle. Both mothers were building up confidence, loving the liberation. They all needed this. Soon there was a convoy of laughter spraying in the dunes.

Then came the dune-climbing, hurtling up the slopes - the 'stoss' side as Darius had informed them it was called - like a ship climbing a wave in a storm, reaching the ridge with its breath-taking view, and then hurtling down the lee side with a joyful abandonment to gravity.

No-one else was in sight. It was as if the whole planet was theirs. To cap it all, the moon appeared, its white pallor graceful amidst the reds and blues of the sand and sea.

It started slowly. Darius noticed little eddies at first. Then a thin, magic carpet of sand seemed to rise shimmering, hovering a few inches above the dunes. Their visors and goggles no longer blazed with sunlight. Ridges lost their sharpness. It was as if an optician had placed one of those blurring lenses in front of your eyes as part of an eye test. It became hard to judge where a slope ended and another started. The sky grew darker, and the air was smoking with sand. Before they knew it, they were in a full-blown sandstorm. It had risen like a cloud of locusts in a matter of minutes.

Ilana stood with her back to the sea waiting for the whole group to arrive. They settled.

'Ok, we're now standing on what is called the Mole. It's a sea wall built by the Germans. From here you can get a strong sense of the layout of Swakopmund.'

They all gazed back, at the neatly-arranged streets.

'Whoa!'

A strong gust of wind blew Ilana's hat off and sent her scurrying after it. Several of her group had to do the same. Their pursuit of their hats, stammering and skimming in the wind, bending low and constantly being foiled, hands snapping shut but empty, took on the appearance of a strange dance.

Hats finally gathered and dignity restored, Ilana re-started, but with one protective hand, held over her head.

'So, as I mentioned earlier, Walvis Bay, further down the coast, which was the region's only large, natural harbour, was under the control of the British and so the Germans decided to create their own harbour here…'

Ilana felt salt spray on the back of her legs and turned to find the ocean becoming frothier by the minute. She'd seen this in winter often enough, but never now at the height of the summer. She looked upwards. The sky was darkening. Then she looked across with alarm at Langstrand. It was swathed in a thick blanket of sand, which appeared to be heading for the city. The sea was now slapping the sea wall, rising and even breaching it. The sails of ships in the harbour started to billow and stretch. Their mast wires jerked like nerves, sending a harsh, metallic sound echoing round the harbour. The tourist group were getting anxious, like prey sensing a predator. Birds flew irrationally close to their heads and fluttered away like paint splodges thrown at the sky, feathers akimbo, seeking shelter.

'Ladies and gentlemen, we appear to be experiencing a sudden sandstorm. I need to stop the tour, I'm afraid. I would suggest that you quickly find your way back to hotel and stay there until the storm passes. Thank you.'

Just then, as the tourists scattered like breadcrumbs, her breast pocket burst into life, her mobile phone jangling. It was Darius.

'I've seen. I'm at the harbour,' she cried. 'I can't even see Long Beach the sandstorm's so thick. Is everyone OK?'

'It's madness here. We can barely see five feet,' Darius said, shouting in order to be heard above the storm. 'Never known anything like it. We've had to abandon the bikes. Everyone's OK but the kids are scared. Even Selima. I'm using the compass on my phone to head due west to the beach before the tides come in. I'm not sure I'll be able to locate the Land Rover, however. Is there any way you can bring the other four by four and drive down the beach with the headlights on?'

'Of course, I'll come now. When's high tide?'

'Less than two hours!'

She detected more than a little panic in his usually calm voice.

'Ben went to the Sam Cohen Library. It would be good to bring him with you if you can. Where's Ralph?'

'I left him at our house, furiously typing emails. Shall we all come? We need room for you in the car though.'

'He'll want to come, and Anne and the children need him. Look, I need to get them all on to the beach now. It's the only way we can be sure to orientate. Stay in touch.'

'Darius, wait… just stay calm.'

'You know me…'

'I love you. You know that, don't you?'

There was a pause at his end.

'Good to hear,' he said, the wind whipping across the phone and stealing his words.

Ilana had never been so thankful that someone answered their phone rather than go through to voicemail.

'Ben Kaplan.'

'Ben, thank God. It's Ilana. Are you still at the library?'

'I am. What the hell's happening? I can't even see the ocean. In fact, I can barely see across the street. Where are you?'

'I'm walking back from the sea wall. Listen, there's a freak sandstorm. I've never seen it anything like it. They've had to abandon the quad biking.'

'Oh my God, the children. I'd completely forgotten. I've been so engrossed in the archives. Are they OK?'

'They're fine, but they've had to abandon the bikes in the dunes and they're walking towards the beach. The problem is that the tide is coming in. If we don't get to them in the next ninety minutes, they'll be cut off.'

The line went silent.

'Hello. Ben, can you hear me?'

'Yes, I can hear you.'

'Stay at the library. I'm getting our back-up Land Rover from the house and picking up Ralph. I should be with you in about ten minutes. Please be ready. Look out for the car.'

'I will, I will.'

Her phone rang again. She glanced at the Caller ID.

'Hi, Ralph. No time to talk. They're OK but we need to move fast. I'm running to the house now.'

Shen Chi steadied himself. Every light imaginable was thrown on to his face. He looked shockingly pale, almost a mirage in front of the darkening horizon.

He cast a glance in the direction of Li, who acknowledged his gaze with a nod. He signalled for Shen to be calm, by lowering both his outstretched hands in the manner of a conductor steadying his orchestra for the opening bar.

Cameras were quietly whirring; boom mikes were held aloft just out of frame and notepads were twitched open. Li reckoned there must be thirty journalists, maybe more. For once, the spotlight was on Namibia but for all the wrong reasons.

Shen coughed, then spoke. Cameras clicked and whirred.

'Ladies and gentlemen, I wish to make a statement about recent events here at the Zjin Mining Company in Namibia. A week ago, whilst excavating here in Damaraland, looking for uranium deposits, we discovered a mass grave of several hundred people. Carbon dating has now confirmed that they perished in the first few years of the twentieth century.'

Some of the journalists gasped, all of them scribbled. Shen continued.

'Analysis of their skeletons, and some of the possessions found scattered amongst their bones, has confirmed that

176

these were people from the Herero and Nama tribes. These findings, along with many historical accounts, have led us to the conclusion that these are the victims of the genocide perpetrated by the German soldiers during their rule in this country.'

He paused to let the historical significance sink in and to sip from a glass of water. His throat felt like a desert. Cameras whirred again and flashbulbs splashed. The tension rose several notches.

'Last Friday, when I was in charge of this site, I took the decision to move the remains of these tragic victims of genocide to the surface and place them in protective crates.'

There was a slight gasp at the frankness of the admission.

'This was done with the utmost care and respect for the bodies and their possessions. My decision to do this, in which I must stress I acted alone, was taken because I feared for the preservation of these bodies with our heavy machinery so close. I was especially aware that pump failure would cause the mine shaft to flood. In making this decision, I failed to consult either with the Namibian authorities, or, more importantly, with the local Herero or Nama Elders. In doing so, I fear I have caused great offence for which I sincerely and humbly apologise. Because of my poor judgement, I have decided to… tender my resignation, to the Zjin Mining Company, and will be returning to China immediately. Thank you.'

Li slumped back in his seat with exhaustion. He was too tired to feel relief and there was still too much to do that evening. Nevertheless, he was pleased there was some sort of closure, at least for now. Sarah had made the decision not to tell him that she and Hannah were in danger, having calculated that this might push him over the edge, given everything else he was dealing with.

Ilana exited the track on to the beach. It was a race against the incoming sea. Long Beach already felt narrow. Their visibility was ten to fifteen feet at best. She had switched on every light conceivable: headlights, sidelights, and fog lights; plus, a special spotlight mounted on the roof that Darius only used to find nesting turtles or whale carcasses at night, or in emergencies such as these. From a distance, their jeep looked like a lighthouse on wheels.

Ben and Ralph wore their eyes out, scanning every inch of the beach and dunes ahead. They had all donned goggles and were breathing through headscarves that Ilana had handed out.

'How much longer before high tide?' Ralph asked, voice muffled by the scarf.

'Less than an hour,' Ilana replied. 'If we don't find them soon, we'll have to turn back. Otherwise, we'll be trapped. Though to be honest, the idea of turning back makes me feel ill. If they are going to have to survive a night on the dunes, then I want to do the same.'

'Agreed,' chimed Ben. 'Presumably, if we have to, we can drive this thing inland far enough to get off the beach, cover it and hope the morning brings clear light.'

The windscreen wipers weren't designed for sand. Not even on a Defender. They scraped and squealed, threatening to give up. Ilana tried full beam again. The light from the headlights just bounced back from the storm, threatening to blind them.

Darius wasn't sure how much longer he could go on. He'd carried Clara a few miles now, feet sinking into the sand, until his back ached. Everyone was shattered and on the edge of giving up. They could hear the sea pounding ever closer but could barely see it. They knew they had to walk North parallel to the ocean.

They kept their helmets on and visors down to protect their faces from the abrasion of the storm and to help them breathe. If you wanted to speak, you had to lift your visor briefly and talk through a scarf to keep the grit out of your teeth.

Hannah felt like an astronaut on Mars, walking in slow-motion. It felt as if her feet were being grabbed by thousands of invisible hands. Selima saw her starting to stumble and ran to prop her up. Freddie marched next to Darius holding Clara's hand. Joe walked slightly ahead of Barbara, trying to act as a windbreaker.

The temptation to just sink into the sand and just let it absorb you was beginning to feel overwhelming. They dreaded seeing the sand darken under the incoming tide.

Sarah lifted her visor to shout out.

'What's that ahead?'

'Please, not another mirage,' Anne muttered to herself.

'No, look, look,' screamed Joe. 'The lights are coming closer.'

Ilana saw them emerge from the storm as if from the haze of battle, eight figures visibly slumping forward with exhaustion.

'There they are!' Ilana screamed. 'Thank God.' Her eyes streamed with tears which mixed with the on-blowing sand to form tiny rivulets of paste. She wiped them away with the back of her hand, which sand-papered her skin.

She stopped the car and all three of them leapt out.

They ran forward, opening visors to talk and kiss.

Ben lifted Joe clean off the ground and smothered Barbara in kisses. Ralph took Clara from Darius and she clung to him crying. He then hugged Freddie and Anne and helped them to the car.

'Thank God, you're here,' Darius said as Ilana, he and Selima hugged.

'Look we're running out of time,' Ilana screamed. 'The tide is coming in fast. Get in. Find wherever you can to sit or perch. Kids on parent's laps. We need to use every available inch.'

Ilana turned the car around and twelve of them tumbled over each other. The sea was racing in, but with everyone now on board she screamed 'Hold tight!' and set off at a pace, the tyres spinning in the surf.

It was 9.30 in the evening before Li finished answering all his emails. Sarah called.

'I didn't want to add to your worries. We were all caught in a sandstorm on the dunes. Ilana, Ralph and Ben had to come and rescue us. It was terrifying.'

'Oh my God, you should have phoned me. How is Hannah?'

'She slept for an hour when we got home. The others have set off back to Windhoek. They're taking Hannah back to the school with Joe and Freddie.'

'The skies went dark here as well.'

'Are you feeling under siege?'

'Yes. But Shen Chi has publicly apologised and resigned.'

'I heard that on the news. Was that the right thing? I worry for him.'

'He acted alone. He must take the responsibility.'

Sarah rarely heard Li be so definite, so cold towards a colleague. He was normally very protective of his team.

'Be careful driving home.'

'I will.'

Li switched his desktop off. He felt a sense of relief as the screen died to black. All he wanted to do now was sleep. Thank God, Sarah and Hannah were safe. He would call Hannah tomorrow. Too late now.

He shut and padlocked the door to his Portakabin.

The moon was low in the sky and blood-red. It looked more like Mars.

As he approached the perimeter fence, he saw to his relief that the crowd had thinned to a few stragglers. The journalists had all fled to Swakop to email their stories. He wound down his window to thank the security guards for keeping him safe.

A mile or so down the gravel track that led to the main road, he saw a group of about thirty people a short distance off the road. They were gathered round a pyramid of fire made from a wigwam of thick, round logs. He switched off his engine and the car lights and watched. They seemed too engrossed to notice him.

The women were dressed in full-length, flowing dresses with puff sleeves and skirts billowed by layers of petticoats. Their rich colours were lit to a brilliance by the fire. They wore hats with 'cow horns' made from bright fabric, which splayed and pointed, as if to the furthest horizons.

Some of the men were dressed like 'Sapeurs' in suits of yellow and peacock blue. A few wore military uniform with three distinct bands of red: a red, flat-topped, military cap; a red waistband that erupted into the shape of flames; and finally, red spats covering the ankles.

The whole scene was bizarre. It was as if a fully-fledged Victorian ball had been transported from a European salon into the heart of the Namib desert. In the process it had shed its formal manners but gained in intensity.

They danced slowly, arms interlinked, and sang in harmonies that rose high into the desert air, like the flames that lit them. The dignity of their singing, and the swelling of its passion, carried its magic far into the night.

Li knew enough about the Herero to know that this was a sacred fire and that they were praying to the Supreme Being for their ancestors, who had been so cruelly killed, and whose bones had now been disturbed.

Somehow, he found himself standing outside his car, by the roadside, sobbing uncontrollably. All the tension of the day ran out of his eyes and his shoulders slumped forward. His eye was caught by a strange movement.

From amongst the dancers a priest rose up, dressed in skins and pelts, his head-dress made of feathers, his wild hair streaming over his shoulders. In one hand he held a staff and in the other a carved, wooden doll. He danced ever more trance-like around the fire, picking up speed until he was whirling like a dervish. Then he stopped, put down the staff and doll, and pointed his face upwards to the heavens. The eldest woman present approached him and solemnly placed a wooden bowl in his upturned hands. He continued to face upwards to the heavens, holding, but not looking at, the bowl, muttering a mantra.

The singing intensified. He turned his face to the crowd and then he poured the contents of the bowl on to the Earth.

Li could see that it was viscous. Then he realised it was blood. It seeped slowly into the Earth. The priest swayed and lowered his huge frame to the ground. He kissed the blooded ground with his lips, as if the ground itself could be healed.

Ralph and Anne, Ben and Barbara, had never been so grateful to see the gentle hills of Windhoek. Its clean and well-ordered streets, its office buildings and embassies, seemed the epitome of civilisation after the trauma of the sandstorm.

A thunderstorm was raging overhead, its cracks and blasts echoing round the hills. They felt safe and cosy inside their cars, their convoy of two. Not even the thunder could wake them.

They had phoned ahead to the Augustineum to explain why they were returning so late. The caretaker had agreed to let them in, and Ubuntu had been informed.

On the way to the school, they passed the Alte Feste where Joe had spent time with his father in half-term. As they passed the Independence Memorial, a bolt of lightning struck between the male and female slave. It was if the bolt had split open their shackles. The figures appeared to jump at the shock. Then the rain started, softly at first, pattering on the car roof like a cat. Soon, it gathered force until it was shaking the drainpipes of the buildings.

Shen Yue woke up not knowing what time it was. Her digital alarm said 02:36 in green, angular numerals. She turned over expecting to find Chi fast asleep snoring, as was his habit. She felt for him, but her hand only glided over an empty sheet. She sat upright yawning. No doubt he'd gone downstairs to watch something on the television and fallen asleep.

She got up, went over to the bedroom window and looked outside. The air had cleared after the storm and Swakopmund looked back to normal. Its lights twinkled in the reflecting sea. Only the moon seemed strange: low and red.

She switched the light on in the hall and found her way down the stairs. Sure enough, the television was on, playing some very second-rate movie but no Chi asleep on the sofa. She fished out the remote control from between the sofa cushions and turned it off.

'Chi?' she called. The kitchen was empty, but the bread board was out with a half-finished loaf on it. She looked out of the kitchen window on to the driveway. His car was still there.

She walked into the downstairs toilet, desperately needing a pee now that gravity had worked its force on her bladder. She noticed that the laundry light was on and the door slightly ajar. As she pushed the laundry door it felt heavy. She struggled to open it and ventured in. It was only when she turned her back on the washing-machine that she saw him.

Shen Chi's soul had fled, but his body was hanging by a strap on the back of the laundry door.

9

Science Project

Joe, Freddie and Hannah all threatened to oversleep on Tuesday. The morning bell could barely penetrate their fatigue. Hannah pulled back the curtain, encouraging the Sun to work its magic and wake her brain. She wanted to burrow back into the warmth of her dreams.

She half-opened her eyes and gazed into the garden. Basarwa was busying himself around the baobab tree, planting. She found his presence comforting, the simple and patient movement of his hands. This set her thinking about how many people there were in the periphery of your life who were essential to you feeling safe, but who never knew it.

Things were no less philosophical in the boys' dorm.

'Joe, what do you reckon the probability is of a sandstorm blowing up that quickly?' Freddie asked.

'I don't have the data,' Joe said. 'I imagine it's rare.'

'You don't think it might be linked to the bodies being moved from the mine?'

'You mean that the spirits of the ancestors were angry…and they created some sort of force that made the weather extreme?' Joe said incredulously. He knew that Freddie was susceptible to such ideas but couldn't pretend to dignify them.

'Something like that,' Freddie said defensively. 'Don't you believe in spirits?'

'Someone once suggested that a plane only flies because of the collective will-power of all its passengers egging it aloft,' Joe offered. 'Do I believe it? No. Am I fascinated by it as an idea? Yes.'

'What is the maths of life? Of all its intersections and forces?' Freddie asked.

'I don't know, but the math of breakfast is that it finishes in seven minutes.'

Jericho Andjaba was a brilliant science teacher. He brought science alive.

'My great sadness,' he used to say, at least once in most lessons, 'is that there are no distinguished Namibian scientists… yet!'

Joe had once asked him why this made him so sad.

'Because Science, Mr Kaplan, as you know as a mathematician, is everything. Great art might inspire us. Music might lift our souls. But Science enables us. Look at this country. If Namibia is ever to grow, we need to use solar energy better. We need to desalinate water and learn how to make the deserts bloom. We need to link the country better through non-polluting transport. We need to stop cybercrime. We need to find new ways to stop corruption. We need something to prevent the spread of the AIDS virus which afflicts a quarter of our population. Science is the key to all of this.'

Today was the start of the Science Project.

'I want you to work in pairs or three's,' Andjaba said. 'You need to pick a topic that needs unravelling. Think of something that needs some research but also some original thinking. This can't just be a cut and paste from the Internet.'

Joe, Freddie and Hannah took all of ten seconds to choose the Fairy Circles. Surely Science could unlock their secrets.

Jericho Andjaba wasn't convinced.

'I would really prefer you to tackle something other than bare patches in grassland. Why not choose something medical? Hannah, your mother is a doctor. Surely that must interest you. Joe, what about new eco materials to build your mother's hotels?'

'Sir, supposing there is something about the circles that can revolutionise agriculture or irrigation, make the desert bloom as you suggested?' Joe asked.

Joe was always adept at finding and pushing the right buttons.

Jericho looked at their pleading faces and couldn't resist.

'OK, but do you know where to start?'

'Yes, sir.'

Within three weeks, they had unearthed a huge amount of knowledge, printed it and pinned it to an A1-sized board. The board was mounted like a landscape on the Science classroom wall. It was awash with charts, data, satellite photographs, local mythology, drawings, formulae, maps and newspaper articles. It was an impressive assembly of their individual skills and a declaration of their joint obsession.

Such was their excitement that they had asked Mr Andjaba if he would give them an hour after school one day. This he duly granted, delighted to find pupils who wanted to give extra time to his beloved subjects.

'OK, you three tell me what you've discovered so far.'

Freddie kicked off, pointing to a map and some aerial

187

photographs that showed Mother Earth with freckles.

'OK, sir, so the Fairy Circles exist about a hundred miles inland and they stretch about fifteen hundred miles from here to here. They occur in the arid desert and grasslands. They vary typically between two and fifteen metres wide, although there are reports of circles up to twenty-five metres wide. They are circular patches of barren land often encircled by a ring of grass.'

'Have they been found anywhere else in the world?' Andjaba asked.

Freddie moved along to another map.

'Yes, in 2014 they were discovered here in Pilbara, Western Australia. They exist nowhere else on Earth.'

Hannah took over.

'Professor van Rooyen undertook a long-term project in 1978, hammering metal stakes into the centre of numerous circles. He returned to the test circles twenty-two years later and found that they hadn't moved an inch.'

'Was this what you'd expect?' Andjaba stabbed. He was energised by their keen, young minds but determined to make their neural pathways zing even more.

'Probably not, because two of the theories suggest animals as the cause of the circles and animals tend to move,' Hannah replied. 'One idea was that the circles were formed by ostriches or zebras giving themselves dry baths in the sand. The much more common idea, though, was sand or harvest termites.'

'OK, good we will come back to that,' he said, peeling open a packet of mints and handing them round to help sharpen the mind and share the joy.

'What they did discover, however, is that the circles have a life cycle,' Freddie added.

'Excellent,' Andjaba cried 'In other words they are dynamic in another way. What is the lifecycle?'

'It differs between the smaller and larger circles, sir,' Hannah continued, 'but they are born, mature and die on average in forty-five to sixty years. They…'

He put up his hand to stop Hannah continuing and looked around at all three of them.

'What occurs to you about that fact, gentlemen and lady?'

Joe piped up.

'They have roughly the same lifespan as human-beings, sir.'

'Exactly. Many of the Namibian tribespeople believe that each circle is the soul of an ancestor, or of someone slaughtered by foreign invaders,' Jericho elaborated.

Joe looked at him quizzically. 'But you don't believe that, sir, do you? Not as a scientist.'

'What I believe is that there may be a link. Do any of you know what I am driving at?'

Freddie raised his hand somewhat hesitantly.

'You don't need to raise your hand, Mr Wilde. We're not in the classroom now. We're in something far more precious.'

'I think what you might be suggesting, sir,' Freddie answered, 'is that if the tribesmen observed that the circles grow and die with the same lifespan as humans, this might have then encouraged their view that each one is controlled by a human soul.'

'Precisely. Myths don't necessarily ignore facts. Sometimes they are built from them,' Andjaba summarised.

'Extraordinary,' Joe muttered. No teacher had ever inspired him in this way before.

'So, Mr Kaplan, as you seem hot to trot, what theories have

been given to explain the circles, and how much credence can we give them?' Andjaba asked.

'Well, there are two common explanations. The first is that sand termites create the ring by consuming the vegetation and burrowing in the soil to create the ring. The barren circle allows water to percolate down through the sandy soil, keeping the soil moist and allowing grasses to grow which the termites then eat. As they progressively eat the grasses at the perimeter, the circles get wider. Radar studies have confirmed that there is this moist layer of soil just beneath the surface, in the middle of the circles.'

'So, job done, right? You have cracked the secret of the fairy circles! It's termites. Can I go home now?' Andjaba said, pretending to leave.

'No, sir,' Joe called out.

'No. Why?' Andjaba was delighted with Joe's certainty.

'Because the geographical spread of the fairy circles is much wider than that of the termite species,' Joe answered. 'Moreover, Tschinkel, a biologist from Florida, who was the man who discovered that the circles had a lifecycle, says that when he and his wife excavated a number of circles, they found no termites.'

'And the other common theory, Miss Chiang, tell me about that.'

'The other theory,' Hannah responded, 'is that the circles are a result of plants organising themselves into territories, to maximise their access to scarce resources. Plants effectively use the centre of the circles as a water and nutrient trap from which they feed themselves around the edges. They keep away from other plants doing the same with their own circles. They have organised themselves to share scant resources.'

'How sensible. If only humans did the same, we might have fewer wars,' Jericho observed. 'So, we've cracked it again. It's competition for resources that Nature has resolved.'

'No, sir. Because other scientists have replaced the soil inside the circles with soil outside the circles and it didn't cause the vegetation to grow back, suggesting that there is no lack of nutrients in the bare soil of the circles. Samples tested in Pretoria also showed no lack of nutrients.'

'So, where do we stand, fellow scientists?' Andjaba asked them all.

Joe piped up. 'There is no single, or even multiple theory that yet explains why there are 1,500 miles of circles that are broadly organised in hexagonal patterns like a honeycomb.'

'And the myths? I see you have them here.' Andjaba signalled to a section of their board.

Freddie ran his hands over each of them in turn as he spoke.

'Myth Number One…the rings have magical powers. Number Two…they are the footsteps of the gods. Three… they represent the grave of every bushman killed by a foreigner. Four…Mukuru, the Himba's Supreme Being, made them. Five…they are from the poisoned breath of a dragon. Six… they are created by meteorite showers.'

'At least the last has some link back to logic as Namibia has had frequent meteorite showers,' Andjaba noted. 'But of course, meteorites are a nonsense when you look at the millions of circles and their regularity of pattern. So, what do we do? We are at a familiar place for scientists. We have the available facts, the prior theories, the superstitions, but we don't have the answers.'

They stared into the abyss of ignorance, silent and thoughtful.

'This is the real challenge. How do we move forward?' Andjaba asked.

Still, silence.

'You have done an excellent job. You have collated, sifted, categorised and explained. I am very proud of you. You are standing on the threshold. Now you need the spark, the crazy thought that isn't actually crazy.'

That night, for the first time in weeks, the Four Teenagers of the Apocalypse WhatsApp group was silent. Apart that is, from one post. It was from Selima. 'Hi guys, is anyone there? Hello?'

An air of gloom had descended over their dorms.

A week later, Jacob Ubuntu was explaining in African Studies, how people had created a system of writing down, in symbols as well as with letters, the clicking languages.

'The Khoisan languages are the languages we all used to speak. Some have as many as forty-eight click consonants. But there are agreed to be four main types of click. There is the dental click, represented by a vertical line that sounds at the back of your teeth, like this…'

He drew a single, vertical line on the board.

'There is a click like the popping of a cork that is represented like this…'

He drew an exclamation mark on the board.

'There is a lateral click like the one you make to urge on a horse…'

He drew two vertical lines.

'And finally, there is a palatal click, like someone clicking their fingers…'

He drew a vertical line, crossed by two short horizontal lines.

'Before we had language as we know it and before we had alphabets, we had clicks.'

A voice rose from the back.

'Oh my God! Oh my God,' Joe rose up from his seat. 'Of course, that's it, sir. That's it.'

Jacob Ubuntu was not sure whether he should be angry or delighted that his exposition on the beginnings of language should apparently cause a Eureka moment in one of his pupils.

'I'm sorry, sir. I've just realised something. We need to use computer modelling sir.'

'On languages, Kaplan?'

'No, sir, on the fairy circles. We need satellite photos and we need massive computing power. Hannah?'

Hannah, was as alarmed as anyone at Joe's apparent madness, but nodded silently in acknowledgement of his manic gaze.

'We need to speak to your father.'

10

Mapping

'Hi, Baba, how are things? Has the scandal died down?' Hannah was on the phone to her father.

She was sure he was still under a lot of stress and couldn't help but resent Joe piling further pressure on him by asking his help with computer modelling. On the other hand, she was as determined as Joe and Freddie to find out if anything new could be detected about the pattern of the Fairy Circles. She had found herself fantasising in the last few days about viewing Namibia from the International Space Station and being able to detect something extraordinary from on high. She'd even Googled whether people were able to put in requests to NASA.

'Lovely to hear from you, Baobei. Nicest thing that's happened to me for days,' Li answered.

Hannah immediately felt guilty, knowing that her motives were not purely altruistic and that he would soon detect this and then feel hurt. He was always very sensitive to motive.

'Are things any easier?' she asked.

'The scandal has died down, but not the after-effects. I'm haunted by that poor man's death.'

'Your Deputy?'

'Shen Chi, yes. I've seen his wife twice and she looks devastated. I looked into her eyes and I could see nothing, Hannah, nothing. It's like her soul's in retreat. I should never have asked him to resign.'

'It's not your fault, Dad. I said that to you at the time and I'm sure Mum has. You did what you felt was right. How could you have possibly known he'd kill himself?'

'He told me that he wouldn't be able to face his family. There is too much fear of disgrace in our culture Hannah. I've said this to you before. This is what it can lead to.'

Hannah, always felt glad but uncomfortable when he assumed she understood 'our Chinese culture.' In truth, she often felt caught in a limbo between the two cultures of her parents. She often didn't know what a typical Chinese reaction was, or an English one either.

'Look, Dad, he made a terrible mistake. He was also trying to stab you in the back. Mum told me.'

'I know, but I was also an ambitious young man once…'

'Dad, you would never have done this to your boss. Not in a million years. It's not in your character.'

Li felt healed by his daughter's certainty, her belief in his good character.

'I love you Hannah and I do miss you. I keep thinking I hear you in the house.'

'I miss you, Dad. I'm coming home next weekend.' Hannah had already agreed this with her mother. They were both worried sick about him; that this whole episode would make him depressed, ill, even.

'That's wonderful, I didn't realise.'

She could hear the smile in his voice. He continued more cheerfully.

'Look, we'll get through this. Our company's name is mud in

Namibia and that isn't going to change quickly, but I am determined we'll set things right. I'm hunting down alternative sites.'

'I am sure it will get better,' she reassured. She was feeling increasingly anxious about asking him the favour. This was made worse by Joe hovering in the background, like a bird following a boat, hoping for fish. She signalled to him to be patient and to stop pacing.

'How's your Science Project going?' Li asked, wanting to escape from the current horrors of his life to the hopefulness of hers. 'It sounded as if your teacher was delighted with your progress.'

'He is. Dad, you would adore him. His name is Jericho Andjaba. Listen, I'm glad you mentioned the Science Project because Joe's just appeared, and he wants to ask you a favour. Would you mind if I put him on?'

Joe was frantically signalling that he didn't want to get on the phone, but Hannah felt positively self-righteous that she deserved a dignified exit at this point in the call.

'No, of course not,' Li answered.

Hannah muted the phone and whispered to Joe. 'It's your bloody idea, you ask.'

Joe took the phone, unmuted it and adopted his most studious tone.

'Mr Chiang, good evening. I was so sorry to hear the news about your colleague.'

'Thank you, Joe, that's very thoughtful of you. I hope your parents are well. I hope to see them soon.'

'Yes sir, hopefully not on a quad bike or in a seal colony.'

Hannah was impressed by Joe's diplomatic skills. He rarely used them on her.

'How can I help?' Li asked, laughing at Joe's remark.

Joe cleared his throat.

'We've been looking at the Fairy Circles for our Science Project as I'm sure Hannah's told you. We need to do some pattern analysis to test out a theory. The school computer has, well … strong limitations shall we say. So, I wondered if we could possibly process the data on your company's computers. I imagine they must be pretty powerful…for a mining company.'

'Well I would love to help, Joe, but it's quite a difficult time. You don't feel you can ask Freddie's father about using the High Commission's computers?'

'I have sir and there's a confidentiality problem using Government computers.'

'Yes, I suppose there must be. Well, look I'm always happy to help my daughter… and her friends of course. Let me ask our IT guys. I can always say it's to help our prospecting. Is the data ready?'

'Thank you, Mr Chiang, so much. Yes, I can send you the data and the brief for the analytics. They're big files so perhaps I should send them via We Transfer to you… if your IT people say it's OK. I'll get your email address from Hannah.'

'Sounds like a plan. Can I ask you a favour in return, Joe?'

'Of course.'

'Would you give Hannah some extra maths lessons? Don't tell her they're lessons… her pride wouldn't allow it. Just offer to explain a few things when there's homework. It's so important and I worry that no-one has inspired her about maths. I suspect you can.'

'Of course,' Joe said, flushed with honour, 'I would be delighted. Here she is…'

Joe handed Hannah back her mobile, as she gave him a quizzical look about what might 'delight' him.

'Baba, thank you so much. It will really help us,' she cooed.

Li wanted to ask her if that was the only reason she'd called. But he didn't want to hurt her and deep in his heart he knew it wasn't. Not the only reason anyway.

'Anything to help my Hannah. I'll expect a namecheck in your project report of course.'

'Naturally!' she laughed.

Barbara was beginning to tire of the journey. The Land Rover was bumpy. She looked down at the map to validate her choice.

She had scoured Namibia for a new site for the hotel for weeks: ever since the burial site of Captain Alexander had put a stop to her first choice. She ran through the options in her head again. At the moment, Fish River Canyon was unique, and not well-served with accommodation. Something on the rim would be spectacular of course. There was only Fish River Lodge, but, there were too many restrictions on building inside the National Park, and it was a long way south, which made it difficult to combine with other tourist itineraries.

In the North, Victoria Falls was spectacular, pouring forth the fury of its waters at the edge of four countries, but there was far too much competition. The Caprivi Strip was more of an appendage than a destination. Anyway, there had been a history of trouble there.

No, Damaraland was a good choice, she was convinced of it. It was a comfortable distance from Windhoek and Swakop. It had the unique attraction of the Twyfelfontein caves. It was close to the Skeleton Coast and easy to combine with safaris in

Etosha National Park. For those with an eye for the spectacular, there were the Spitzkoppe Mountains and the moon-like craters of Doros and Messum.

The map stopped vibrating on her lap. The Defender had come to a halt.

'We've arrived,' Darius announced from the front. Selima looked up from her book and Barbara from her map.

'Thank God for that,' Barbara replied.

She had never forgotten Darius's courage and clarity in saving them from the sandstorm. He broke his back carrying Clara. He had understood Joe perfectly, his mixture of brilliance and insecurity, and he'd kept everyone calm and together as a group. The whole episode also seemed to have changed him. He appeared more confident in himself and less morose. However, Barbara couldn't help speculating what the effect would have been if they hadn't escaped the storm. It could have crushed someone like Darius.

Darius got out of the Land Rover, mopped his brow and took a heavy swig from his water bottle. He looked ahead intently, stock still. Everything seemed frozen for a moment. Then Selima opened her door and walked round the front of the jeep to be with him. She hadn't thought of him as vulnerable for a long while, not since the sandstorm, but he looked it now. She hugged him. Barbara was cross-referencing something on her map and hadn't shifted since the car stopped.

'Dad? Are you OK?' Selima asked, slipping her arm through his.

He turned to her with a half-sad smile and vaguely nodded.

'Why did you ask me to take the afternoon off school?'

'You didn't have to,' he responded, sounding wounded.

'I wanted to. You know I always want to come on outings with you. They've been some of my happiest times.'

He beamed at her.

'Do you remember this place at all?' he asked.

She looked around but couldn't remember anything. It was beautiful, remote but not unlike many places in Namibia that she loved.

'I brought you here when you were five, held you in my arms and told you all about it.'

Barbara got out of the car just in time to hear the tail-end of their conversation.

They seemed so intimate, father and daughter, that she hesitated to interrupt. It felt like an invasion.

'Is that the farm?' she asked pointing to some buildings in the near distance.

Something clicked in Selima's mind. She could smell African lilies.

'Wait. It's not Grandpa and Grandma's farm! Is it?'

He turned to her smiling, his eyes wet with remembrance and nodded.

Barbara wasn't sure whether to feel touched or puzzled and then worked out that she felt both. 'So, Darius, this is the farm your parents owned?'

'Yes,' he replied simply.

'And you think we could build a hotel here? On the farm?'

'I can't see why not. It's beautiful isn't it? Or is that just my sentimental eyes deceiving me?'

Barbara felt she owed him a proper answer, one that dignified his question. So, she scanned the scene carefully. The farm was too distant at this point to judge it in any detail, but it was pretty and ordered and she guessed about a hundred years old. It was a cattle farm, an oasis of green amongst the flaxen grasses. It could almost be European. You could see the Brandberg Massif and the Spitzkoppe mountains in the distance. It felt peaceful.

'It could be perfect,' she said, glad to validate both him and the two generations before him who had chosen it as the place to build their life. 'Wouldn't you feel odd though? Your family farm becoming a hotel?'

'If it can't be my shrine, it may as well be shared with as many others as can appreciate it,' he responded. 'Besides which, I don't want those bastards who forcibly took it from my parents to keep it.'

'How do you know they'll sell it, Dad?' Selima asked, taking the question out of Barbara's mouth and relieving her of the need to ask herself.

Darius turned to Barbara. 'If your company has the kind of money I assume it has, then they won't be able to resist.'

She smiled nervously, anticipating a bumpy and stubborn set of negotiations ahead.

'Well, it certainly ticks all the boxes. We'd have to keep your family's name completely out of the negotiations of course,' she responded.

'I have three small requests if I help you acquire it,' he said, fixing her in his gaze.

'Go on,' she responded.

'One is that you leave the main farmhouse intact, if you can integrate it into your design somehow. The second is that you build it to standards that Ilana would approve of… in terms of sustainability, I mean.'

'And the third?'

'The third is that our family have visiting rights.'

'I'll go you one better than that,' Barbara replied, increasingly intoxicated with the landscape in front of her. 'If we buy this property, I might help you build a small lodge on the boundaries.'

Whilst Barbara and Darius were talking, Selima had got her father's ever-trusted binoculars from the dashboard of the Defender and started scanning the farm. She was curious to pick out more details, even spot the current occupants if she could, get a sense of them.

As she slowly prowled the landscape with her eyes, something caught her eye in the trees. She returned to it and adjusted the focus. She couldn't be sure, but it appeared to be a leopard. It was lying still in the afternoon heat, except for its head which twitched slightly to remove the flies. It was staring intently in one direction. She followed the line of its sight and found a sleepy herd of cattle.

'Dad look at this,' she said, handing him the binoculars. 'I think it's a leopard.'

Darius took the binoculars, hanging the straps around his neck.

'At four o'clock,' she said. He had trained her in the language of directions.

'Got it. That's very bizarre,' he exclaimed. 'It looks like a leopard but there are no rosettes, no spots at all. It's as bare as a lioness, but slighter, thinner. I've never seen anything like it.'

'Perhaps it's a good omen,' Barbara said.

'The Golden Leopard,' Selima said quietly.

The baby had survived for several days but now lay silent. Anne looked at it, heart quietly breaking.

The mother had willed it to stay alive. Anne had seen her constantly looking into the bassinette; her finger placed in its tiny palm, around which it closed like a flower. She sang to it singing low and soft. The baby barely moved. Yet, it surely must have sensed the looming presence of this large, loving being, her mother, stooped over her. At least, Anne hoped so. It must have smelt her; felt the warm air around her breasts and hands and face as she held it close. The mother had tried to entice this small soul into the stream of life. But, the body was too weak, and the soul had ebbed away.

Anne had lost count of the number of babies who had succumbed to AIDS in the months since she'd been there. She did the same for this mother as she had done with all the others. She closed the baby's eyes, held the mother's hands in her own and told her 'You couldn't have done any more.' This had the benefit of being true, but she would have said it anyway.

Yet again, she made the solemn walk, back to the staffroom, to fill in the paperwork.

'Will it ever get better?' the ward sister asked her, knowing from Anne's demeanour that another baby had died.

'Yes, it will. The drugs are getting better. If the education can keep up, we'll make significant progress,' Anne replied defiantly.

'I wish we could solve the mystery of these burn marks,' Sister observed.

'I agree. I was trying to think. Is there anything in particular, that links the victims? Their age? Their diet? Previous illnesses?'

Anne asked, mentally filing through the faces of those she could remember.

The ward sister tried to think about them systematically.

'Working age mainly. Many of them live outside the city. More agricultural workers than city workers, I would say. I haven't seen any from east of Windhoek either.'

Anne looked up from her form-filling. 'Say that again!'

'All of it?'

'No, the last bit.'

'None have come from east of the city.'

'Of course. Why didn't I think of that before? We can map all the burn victims, where they live. Then if it is radiation of some kind, we pinpoint where it's coming from. Have we got all the patient addresses?'

'Of course.'

'Collect them for me, will you?' said Anne, suddenly hanging her white coat on the back of the door and grabbing her handbag.

'With pleasure. Where are you going?'

'I am going to buy the largest scale map I can find.'

Every month, Ralph had a meeting with his opposite number in the Department of Foreign Affairs. He enjoyed the chance to probe, to get the official perspective. He felt he almost understood Namibia better as a private citizen than as a public official and was keen to understand other perspectives.

Sam Nashandi was tall, elegantly dressed and clearly ambitious. He appeared in the pages of 'The Namibian' newspaper more often than the Prime Minister. This didn't go unnoticed amongst his superiors. Indeed, it was just one of the many ways in which he caused resentment. Ralph understood his ambition, disliked his arrogance, but found him extremely charismatic. He was sure that he was a future President. Nashandi found Ralph as polished and urbane as his predecessors but much less stuffy which he welcomed.

'I hear you got caught in that freak sandstorm in Swakop,' Nashandi said as he offered Ralph a seat opposite him. Nashandi sat behind his desk rather than at his meeting-table. It was a declaration of power and distance.

'I did indeed,' Ralph replied. 'It was like a swarm of locusts… rather Biblical in fact.'

'Yes, well there was a lot of nonsense linking it to the unearthing of those genocide bodies. This country will never progress until it stops being yoked to superstition.'

'All countries have their superstitions. How are relations with the German government? Are you any closer to getting your apology…or even, dare I say, reparations?'

Nashandi laughed.

'We can go fish for our reparations. I don't see those ever happening. You clearly haven't heard the latest. The Germans claim that the mine shaft was too far west to have contained the victims of the 1904 genocide. They have compiled, as only they can, an 80-page report with detailed maps, reproducing every journal entry made, and telegram sent, by von Trotha. It all concludes with a detailed map of all German troop movements made that year.'

'Ah, the use and abuse of maps… how many wars has that started? It sounds very Germanic. It also sounds pointless, insulting. All the evidence, including the carbon dating of the skeletons, points to 1904.'

Nashandi lifted a dossier from his desk and opened it on a page, much of Ralph could see he had angrily highlighted in yellow and red. The colour had seeped through to the back of the page, making it bulge with indignation.

'According to them, carbon dating is inaccurate enough to be out by ten years. The worse thing is that they have described Namibia at the time, and I quote… "as being awash with inter-tribal warfare and massacres in the 1900's, as typifies Africa to this day." Nothing makes me angrier than this condescending….'

Nashandi searched for expletives in both his head and his mouth.

'Pap!' he finally exploded, which was not the word Ralph was expecting. 'This rubbish that is spouted about Africa as 'The Dark Continent'. The place from which civilisation set out, but to which it has never returned. For a start, lumping us all together is as insulting as saying Britain is identical to Luxembourg. Secondly, Namibia is a modern democracy and that should be respected.'

'What will you do?' Ralph asked, absorbing Nashandi's rage. 'I mean, even if they're right about the carbon dating, there is no doubt that the genocide took place.'

'We will do nothing. Other than write a polite and firm diplomatic response. Which is exactly what we will do with the Chinese government who did not respect our sacred ancestors.'

'Well, one Chinese individual acting alone. I know the man who was in charge at the mine. He was absent when the decision was taken.'

'Li Chiang? Yes, he's a good man, He's been in here to explain and apologise. We are a tiny country, Ralph. A 'David' between two 'Goliaths', with no sling. So, we'll "suck it up" as the Americans so charmingly say.'

Ralph remembered the Minister's request to stir up trouble about the Chinese in order to move Britain's place forward in the uranium queue. The most he was prepared to do, however, was push Britain's friendship and 'integrity'.

'Well, if there's anything that the British Government can do to help, we'd be delighted,' Ralph offered. 'We're a friend to Namibia as I hope you know. Influencing the Germans behind the scenes, that sort of thing.'

Nashandi put down the dossier, got up from his chair, walked round to Ralph's side of the desk and half-sat across its corner keeping one leg on the ground. The height difference between them now felt uncomfortable, almost threatening.

'The problem, Ralph, is that Britain no longer has any influence over Germany. Brexit has put pay to that. And you never had any influence over China. Our main trade is with the EU, and the biggest economy in the EU is Germany. You may have more than 25 times our population, but Britain, my dear friend, in the new world we find ourselves in, is just another small country.'

Nashandi smiled and Ralph shifted uncomfortably in his seat, hoping to change the conversation.

Clara was entranced. How could she not be?

She was standing at the Post Street Mall in Windhoek, with her school class, looking at meteorites. Rather strangely, they were displayed in a very ordinary shopping mall, almost as if they weren't from outer space at all, but a shop just around the corner. Mounted on steel pedestals of different heights, you could view them from different angles, and get a sense of their striking, organic shapes. Some of them looked to Clara like metal brains. Each meteorite fragment was suspended on small steel tendrils and so they floated at their various heights as if still showering the Earth.

Their Geography teacher continued, standing in front of the display, holding aloft a large-scale map that Clara guessed had been used many times. It had a battered appearance, slightly torn along its folds.

'The Gibeon meteorite shower is the most extensive meteorite shower known on Earth,' she explained.

Clara's mouth fell open, until she worried she might swallow an insect, and shut it tight.

'The meteorites fell across a large area which I have marked here. It measures two hundred and seventy-five by one hundred kilometres. That's bigger than many islands. Most fragments fell just southeast of Gibeon, the town after which they were named. So far, a hundred and twenty meteorites with a weight between them of almost twenty-five tons have been found.'

Clara's hand shot up, unprompted but irresistible to her teacher. One day, she would teach a whole class of Clara's.

'If there were a hundred and twenty, Miss, where are the rest of them?'

'That's a very good question, Clara. Well sadly, some of them have been stolen.'

Some of the class burst out laughing and Dinari, one of her friends and the class joker, added 'But how would you fit one in your pocket, Miss!?'

'Well, Dinari, the last one to be smuggled out, weighed a ton and went to America. So, you'd need the pockets of a giant.'

'Or metal trousers,' Clara suggested.

Once the giggling subsided, which including their teacher's, she continued.

'A lot of them have been sent around the world to be studied. In 1838, a British explorer called Captain Alexander sent some samples to a chemist in London who confirmed that they were meteors.'

'Miss, did you say Captain Alexander?'

'Yes, do you know him, Clara?' the teacher teased.

'I feel as if I do, yes, Miss,' said Clara.

'I see,' said the teacher, dismissing it as one of Clara's fantasies. Clara made a mental note to message Freddie as soon as she could.

'Since then, samples have been sent all over the world. Now, I want you to imagine what it would have been like to see these meteors arrive. Something the size of a double-decker bus entered the Earth's atmosphere travelling at tens of thousands of miles per hour. Yes Grace?'

'Miss, is that faster than Usain Bolt?'

'Yes, it is, Grace. Thousands of times faster. It came in at a low angle and it fragmented high up in the atmosphere, breaking into many parts, all of them glowing like fireballs or like shooting stars. We know from their shapes that they travelled through intense heat for a long time.'

'Wow!' Clara mouthed to herself.

'Shooting stars are not in fact stars at all. That's just a name. They are dust and rocks like these meteorites, falling to Earth. Most of them are burned up completely in our atmosphere. It's our shield. Now, who has seen a shooting star?' the teacher asked.

All the hands in the class shot up except for Clara's.

'Well, I am not surprised. It's the best free fireworks show on Earth and you can see it every night, over Windhoek.'

'I think this is mad,' Joe said, out of breath at the top of the final staircase.

'We know you do,' Hannah said, 'but you have to keep an open mind.'

'Most seances have been fakes,' Joe said. 'Anyway, it's dangerous to meddle with the spirit world.'

'You can't have it both ways,' Freddie protested. 'If seances are fakes, then people aren't contacting the spirit world, are they?'

This wasn't the first time that Freddie had exposed Joe's lack of logic and Joe couldn't help resenting it. Sometimes, he felt it might be better to have less perceptive friends.

They had climbed up to the attic floor of the boarding-house. The low ceilings made it feel claustrophobic and added to their nervousness. There was a small room under the eaves that was occasionally used for private study, or homework supervision, but which had largely fallen into disuse. They felt reasonably sure they wouldn't be found or interrupted.

One of the cooks had lent them two candles stored in the kitchens in case of a power-cut. They'd claimed it was for a science experiment they were conducting in the gardens.

'Don't for heaven's sake, light these anywhere other than outside,' she'd said, handing them over. 'If you light them in here, and one of them catches a curtain, this whole place could go up. I am trusting you.'

They had nodded, looked suitably serious, and felt guilty as hell underneath.

They had decided to hold a séance to see if they could contact the spirit of Captain Alexander, to extract his secrets from beyond the grave. Hannah had made an improvised Ouija board by writing all the letters of the alphabet, the numbers 1 to 10, and the words 'Yes', 'No', 'Hello' and 'Good-bye' on individual pieces of card. Joe had sneaked a water glass, into his rucksack, at dinner.

There was no light shining out from under the closed door of the room, but to be sure, they knocked lightly and waited to hear if anyone was inside. After a few seconds there was a knock back. Hannah jumped with fright.

'Oh my God,' she said, clinging to both the boys, 'let's not do this.'

'Don't be ridiculous,' Joe said, 'that came from downstairs. There's a bathroom below us, remember. It's from one of the pipes.'

Joe opened the door, peered in and switched on the light. 'All clear,' he said.

The room looked as if hadn't been cleaned for weeks. Freddie ran his finger over the surface of the round table that occupied the centre of the room. His finger left a slug-like trail.

'No wonder no-one uses this space. It's positively spooky,' Joe said.

'At least it's quiet,' Freddie observed.

'I'm sure Selima wouldn't approve of us doing this,' Hannah said, 'It's basically witchcraft.'

'Probably. Look, if we're going to do it, let's just get on with it,' Joe said impatiently.

They dusted down three chairs and the table and laid out the cards in a semi-circular arc on the table. Freddie placed the water glass upside down, whilst Hannah lit the candles and placed them on a side-table. Joe switched off the light.

They all sat next to each other on one side of the table, the arc of cards sprayed in front of them. Lit by the candles, their silhouettes flickered on the wall like a shadow puppet play.

'How do we do this?' Joe asked.

'We each put a finger on top of the up-turned glass,' Hannah explained, 'but gently. Then one of us asks the questions of … the spirit. We wait to see if the glass moves. If it does, it will move to each letter or number in turn, spelling out the answer.'

'Why are we using the candles?' Joe asked.

'Spirits hate harsh light,' Hannah answered.

'Honestly, Joe, I'm amazed you had to ask that,' Freddie said giggling.

Joe caught the giggle like an infection.

'Stop it you two,' Hannah pleaded. 'Nothing will happen if you don't believe. Freddie, did you bring the picture?'

Freddie cast his mind back and then remembered it was in his trouser pocket. He fished out and smoothed down a creased black and white photocopy of a painting of Captain Alexander, placing it in front of them.

'It's supposed to help… to look at the image of the person who are trying to contact,' she explained.

They each put a finger gently on the cold glass.

'Captain James William Alexander,' Hannah intoned gravely, 'we want to speak with you.'

They waited, staring at the glass. It didn't move.

Hannah repeated herself and they each stared intently into the dark eyes of Alexander's portrait. One of the candles flickered, stirred by a current of air from the window, bending their shadows on the wall.

They sat silently for two minutes, their arms slightly trembling with the effort of holding their fingers on the glass.

The glass edged slowly sideways to the word 'Hello', making a slight scraping noise as it did.

'You're moving it,' Joe accused Freddie, 'I can see your arm twitching.'

'I swear I am not. It's twitching from the effort of holding my finger up.'

They could both tell from his indignance that Freddie was telling the truth. Joe looked at Hannah inquiringly, implying the same question of her. She shook her head.

The room felt colder.

'Will you talk to us about the burial site?' Hannah asked.

The glass moved to 'Yes'.

They all had the same queasy feeling. The glass was moving as if it had a definite force behind it. Yet it also felt too smooth to be pushed by any of their arched and aching arms. This oddly smooth motion left them hovering between scepticism and belief.

The glass now moved between letters. Hannah said the letters out loud as it touched each one and confirmed the words after each one.

'I W-I-S-H-E-D I H-A-D N-O-T F-O-U-N-D T-H-E B-O-D-I-E-S. I S-H-O-U-L-D H-A-V-E L-E-F-T T-H-E-M I-N P-E-A-C-E'

They stared at each other, still wondering if this was real.

Hannah decided to continue.

'Can you tell us where they are buried?'

213

Two minutes passed without the glass moving.

'Perhaps, we shouldn't ask any more questions,' Freddie suggested.

Before his sentence had even finished, the glass jolted and started to move between the letters, as if it were hovering on a tiny bed of air.

'Y-O-U K-N-O-W W-H-E-R-E T-H-E B-O-D-I-E-S A-R-E.'

'He thinks we have already deciphered the map,' Freddie said in a whisper that rasped his throat in frustration.

'We cannot decipher your map. Can you help us?' Hannah pleaded.

The glass stuttered along the table as if it were an extreme effort to push it

'T-E-L-L M-Y W-I-F-E I A-M S-O-R-R-Y'

They looked at each other baffled.

'But he never married,' Joe said, 'at least according to his journals.'

'Perhaps, there was another wife,' Hannah suggested.

'It makes no sense,' Freddie added.

They all sat, forefingers resting on the glass, pointed and aching like God's fingers reaching out to Adam on the ceiling of the Sistine Chapel.

'Perhaps, this is not the same Captain Alexander,' Joe suggested.

'When did you die?' Hannah asked.

The glass moved slowly, as if in pain.

'L-A-S-T W-E-E-K'

They looked at each other in a mixture of astonishment and frustration.

'What is your name?' Hannah asked, when she had regained some composure.

The glass sat stubbornly still, as if glued to the table.

Freddie decided to see if he could move it, and to his amazement, found it resisted his finger. He gazed at Joe's finger with its cracked and dirty nail, and Hannah's soft and manicured, and then back up their bare forearms, trying to detect if there was any sign of a muscle twitching or contracting. There was none.

Suddenly, the glass flew around the table at an alarming speed, dragging their arms with it.

What it spelt out, froze their blood.

'S-H-E-N C-H-I'

Then the glass flew off the table and smashed against the wall, shattering and splintering as it fell to the floor.

'Who is Shen Chi?' Joe asked.

'My father's deputy,' Hannah said. 'He hung himself on the back of the laundry door.'

Freddie's mobile rang insistently on his dormitory bed. He ran but just missed it. He looked at the screen. Drops spattered onto the screen from his wet hair. Five missed calls from his mother.

He delved into 'Recents' and pressed her number.

'Mum? Sorry, I was in the shower. Is everything all-right?'

There were a few moments of silence, during which Freddie though he detected a rasping sound.

'Freddie, has Clara been in touch with you?'

'No, why?'

He heard her mouth go dry and her tongue stick.

215

'She's disappeared, Freddie.'

His breathing stopped. Every protective moment, every anxiety he'd ever felt about Clara seemed rolled up into one, all-consuming panic.

'What do you mean she's disappeared? When? How?'

'Dad and I hosted a drinks reception at the High Commission…'

'You didn't leave her alone,' he said.

'Of course, we didn't. Erva was babysitting. She was doing some ironing…'

'How could she?'

'What do you mean, Freddie? She's our housekeeper and Clara was happily watching a film in the next room.'

'Except she wasn't!'

'Erva thought she heard a noise. She stopped ironing and came in to find Clara gone. The patio doors were open.'

'My God, she might have been kidnapped. Have you called the police?'

'Dad's speaking to them now in the dining room. They came almost immediately. Of course, she hasn't been kidnapped.'

'Mum, how can you say that? She's the daughter of the British High Commissioner. These things happen to diplomats. You know that!'

This awful possibility had already been injected into Anne's mind and had started to spread like a virus. She wasn't, however, going to admit that to Freddie. She knew how suggestible he was, a victim of his own vivid imagination.

'Freddie, please check your phone to see if she's been in touch.'

Freddie checked his WhatsApp. Clara had been desperately

upset that they had not included her on the 'Four Teenagers of the Apocalypse' group. They told her that there weren't 'Five Teenagers of the Apocalypse'. The real reason though was obvious to all: that she was simply too young, and too prone to leaking stuff to Mum and Dad. So, Freddie had set up a two-person group for Clara and himself, called the 'World Wilde Web', in tribute to their name. He told her it was 'much more exclusive', which she had grudgingly accepted.

The number five appeared in white out of a blue circle next to their Group. He'd never been so pleased to see a number there. Normally, rising numbers felt like FOMO or a pressure to reply.

He opened it and put Anne on speakerphone.

'Mum, there is something.'

'Oh, thank God. What does she say?'

Freddie speed-read her long, excited paragraphs.

'She says that she went to an amazing display of meteorites with their Geography teacher today. Blah, blah. Meteorite the size of a bus entered our atmosphere. Etcetera, etcetera… Captain Alexander was the first person to have them examined and isn't that amazing as a coincidence? Blah! She ends by saying that she's desperate to see shooting stars and that she's the only one in her class who hasn't seen them yet.'

'None of that really helps,' Anne replied despondently.

'It does, Mum. She'll have gone out somewhere to try to see them. I know Clara. That's exactly what she's done.'

'The question is where though Freddie. WHERE!!!!???'

Anne couldn't be the well-mannered diplomat's wife, or the sanguine doctor, anymore. She could only at this moment, be defined as the mother of a lost child and she needed to scream.

Freddie stared in despair at his phone. The sound of his mother's pain went through him like a blade. He suddenly had a brainwave. He switched the speaker off on his phone and put it to his ear.

'Mum listen to me, I know how to find her. Did you put her 'i-phone' on Family Sharing?'

'What do you mean?' Anne said trying to disentangle her thoughts.

'The 'Find my i-phone' app. Did you register Clara's mobile on it?'

'Yes, yes I did,' Anne shouted in gratitude at Freddie throwing her a lifebuoy. 'For once, I do want her to have taken her bloody phone!'

When they found Clara, she was sitting, oblivious to all panic, on the lawns at Zoo Park, gazing hopefully up at the skies.

It was only nine-thirty in the evening when they found her. To Clara it seemed like seven o'clock and still not her bedtime. It felt the darkest hour before dawn to everyone else. Ubuntu had found Freddie sobbing in his dorm and drove him to join his parents at the park where the mapping app had located her to within ten feet.

The police were soon dispatched with warm thanks and handshakes and went back to the station in an unexpected mood of happiness. Rarely did missing child episodes end well.

Clara was overwhelmed as the tearful members of her family embraced her, telling her to never leave the house again like that.

She looked into Anne's face beaming and said 'I've seen four of them, Mummy. Four shooting stars in one night.'

11
Hunting

It was around the table by the fireplace of the Reading Room that so much had happened between the three of them. It felt like hallowed ground. Secrets had been traded; summary judgements made on teachers and fellow pupils; Instagram's created and shared. They had played Poker, Pontoon and Bridge with matchsticks borrowed from the kitchens as betting chips. It was here that 'Namib' had been created, their own language including signs and clicks. The last of these often ended in hysterical laughter at their tongue-twisted nonsense.

Sometimes, other boarders would try to lay claim to their territory. Standing over them, spraying sarcastic or threatening remarks would usually move them on. If they were younger of course, they could be shooed away like flies. Yet, occasionally, older boarders would settle down with a misjudged sense of entitlement. Then the strategy would be to draw up chairs alongside them and talk about the time a rat had scurried down the chimney and up their trouser leg. Bribery with items from the tuck-shop also worked. As a last resort, Hannah would offer to help with an English essay or Joe with an algebra challenge.

They had abandoned the fireplace more recently in favour of the Science Lab where, piece by piece, they filled up their noticeboard with the results of their investigations. Tonight, Joe and Hannah reclaimed their hallowed spot to meet with Sarah and Ben, who were coming to discuss the trip to Twyfelfontein.

Sarah had spent the afternoon meeting her opposite number at the Augustineum: to exchange notes and ideas on their special-needs students. So, they had seized on the opportunity to meet. Ben, tipped up, predictably late, from the University. Normally, parents were only allowed to visit at weekends, but they had special dispensation from the Headmaster to help with the Science Project. Besides which, anything to do with his beloved Twyfelfontein always bewitched Ubuntu.

'Did you bring the cake?' Hannah asked Sarah, as if her life depended on it.

'Yes, coffee and walnut as requested,' Sarah answered, laughing at her daughter's intensity and handing over the tin.

Hannah grabbed the tin, lifted the lid and inhaled the smell of home baking with a satisfied sigh.

'Did you bring anything, Dad?' Joe asked, knowing the answer before it was delivered.

'No, I'm sorry, Joe. I forgot. Next time, next time...' Ben muttered, looking down at his empty hands.

Joe nodded in that sad way that young people greet repeated failings in their parents.

'So, when do we head for the caves?' Hannah asked, filling the tense silence that threatened to balloon.

'Twyfelfontein,' Ben intoned reverently.

'Dubious or doubtful spring?' Sarah enquired. Her German was decidedly rusty. She looked to Ben for certainty on the translation.

'"Doubtful" is probably closer,' Ben replied.

'The story is that it was named after a German farmer who bought the land and was constantly worried about the water supply failing,' Joe explained. Ben smiled quietly to himself at being relieved of his duties.

'I've been researching it since we spotted the link with the map,' Joe added.

'Apparently, there are over 5,000 engravings,' Hannah added. 'So, how on earth are we going to find Alexander's clues?'

'If I always thought about the odds, I wouldn't embark on most of my digs,' Ben answered. 'We can start by discarding those engravings that are graffiti, copies or too faint to distinguish. Also, there are two or three different periods of engravings. The earliest were done by the hunter-gatherers five or six thousand years ago. They are mainly of animals.'

'Aren't some of those part-human?' Hannah asked.

'Yes…' Ben answered, admiring her quiet self-possession and the kind of curiosity he had always encouraged in his sons. He cast a glance over at Joe who was also looking at her admiringly. He wondered if anything more than friendship was growing between them. Joe stared back at his father, defying scrutiny.

'Yes, what?' Sarah asked, breaking into Ben's silent enquiry.

'For a long time, it's been assumed that, somehow, they were just keeping records of animals, or using the drawings to teach their children how to hunt.'

'And now?' Joe asked.

'Now it's thought that many of the more fantastical animals are taken from dreams…dreams that the priests had when they entered the spirit world.'

'There's something else of course…' a voice boomed out, echoing around the fireplace. Jacob Ubuntu had been drawn to the tight and intense group in the corner of the Reading Room, especially as, unusually, it included two parents. Parents were always a magnet for him, both for his own stimulation, and to protect the income of the school.

On seeing the Headmaster, they all stood up. He was warmed by their respect.

'Please, please sit down,' he said, shaking Sarah and Ben's hands. 'Would you mind if I joined you?'

'Of course not, we'd be honoured,' Sarah smiled. Joe and Hannah didn't feel as comfortable. Somehow Ubuntu's presence felt like control.

Ubuntu continued, his strong arms resting on the table, gently but emphatically, like a Sphinx.

'Hunter gathering has been misunderstood. Mr Kaplan, I would be interested to know if you concur. The animals were never just food. It wasn't just about eating to survive. There was a bond between the hunter and the animal. The animals sacrificed themselves to pass on the blood and energy of their life. This is why the engravings and paintings in the caves are not just representation. They are a kind of worship of the animals that gave their lives.'

A silence fell over the other four as Ubuntu's words drew new wisdom in their minds. Hannah and Joe were too daunted by the presence of both parents and their Headmaster to respond.

Ben was feeling slightly displaced, and even a little shallow, in the presence of Ubuntu, a sapling next to an oak. He felt the need to grow a little.

'The later drawings are by herdsmen and they were often not of animals,' Ben added. 'Many of them are geometric patterns. We think these might depict the position of herds. But no one knows.'

Joe's interest was sparked by the mention of patterns just as Hannah's spluttered out, like a candle at the end of its wick.

'What kind of patterns?' Joe asked.

'Patterns that no one has deciphered. That's part of the reason I wanted your help Sarah. You've studied hieroglyphics and semiotics. Perhaps, there's some detectable pattern, some symbolism in the shapes, that you could help me decode.'

Sarah who had been leaning back in her chair enjoying the role of audience member, leaned forward and joined them in the front row of their enthusiasm.

'Something did occur to me the other day,' she responded. 'I noticed that when people write Khoisan languages down, they represent the clicking noises with strokes and symbols.'

'We do indeed,' Ubuntu said. 'I explained this very thing to your children recently.'

'Supposing then, these shapes and symbols on the cave walls are a kind of language, an alphabet.'

'Do you have any photographs of them, Dad?' Joe asked with feverish excitement.

'I have some, yes,' Ben replied. 'I wanted to show you, Sarah. They may not be the best, but…'

He opened a plastic folder and flicked through a selection of images.

'Here…' He pushed two or three across the table towards Sarah and Joe.

Ubuntu remained respectfully silent, diplomatically knowing when to take a back seat whilst parents drove a conversation.

'What are you thinking, Joe?' Hannah asked.

'I am wondering,' he replied, 'if the cave engravers were trying to crack the same problem as us, and how long ago that might be.'

'Which problem?' Sarah asked.

'Trying to decipher a series of circles in extraordinary patterns…'

Ubuntu believed that all his pupils should visit the townships and villages around Windhoek: to see how most Namibians lived. He felt it gave them a vivid understanding of poverty and hardship and a yardstick by which to measure their own privilege.

Joe, Hannah and Freddie's year visited one such township. They started at the local quarry where people laboured with not much more than their hands for tools, in the full sun, for less than a dollar a day.

Their backs ached in sympathy, their minds couldn't conceive of the soul-sapping tedium of these chores. They would have felt guiltier if they hadn't been so shocked.

A woman of eighty sat, legs stretched out in front of her, her feet wrapped in rags to protect them. She hammered rocks on a rusted, metal pedestal that acted as a makeshift anvil. She embraced her task with a weary familiarity and a certain pride at her skill. Her look seemed to say 'What else would I do? What else do I know?' without it ever being said. Her patient smile, haunted Hannah for many nights afterwards.

Later, they moved to a market which assaulted every sense in their bodies and a few more they didn't even know they had. On the fresh fish stalls, the women waved shredded cloths at the end of stubby, wooden handles: they used them

224

as swats to keep the flies off. Their hands moved erratically, without being looked at, almost as if they were not part of their bodies.

On the dried fish counters, the carcasses stretched out far and wide, their backs arched with desiccation, their mouths open as if still trying to take one last breath. The stench was indescribable.

The Augustineum pupils shuffled along in disbelief. There were dishes piled high with caterpillars and grubs of various colours and textures, interspersed with tiny, dried anchovies that looked insect-like by association. Rock salt dotted the stalls like punctuation marks.

Jericho Andjaba, who had been assigned this field trip, enjoyed their horrified looks.

'This is one of our staple diets. Caterpillars and grubs are first class protein. The future of our planet may rely on them. Anyone want to try?'

'You've got to be joking, sir,' Joe responded.

'And please don't tell us they taste like chicken,' Freddie added.

'No, sir, that's what they always say about anything revolting,' Hannah chimed.

'No-one want to try? OK, then I will,' Jericho said relishing the challenge and knowing the ashy texture would soon be washed away by his soda.

There were howls of protest.

'No, sir, please don't.'

'They're disgusting, sir!'

But before their words had even faded on the air, Andjaba had popped two caterpillars into his mouth. He chewed hesitantly at first, then munched vigorously with comic exaggeration, making his eyes bulge.

Everyone fell about laughing and then howled in disgust as the twitch of his Adam's Apple indicated a swallow.

They continued to patrol the market. There were so many carcasses of fish and animals that even the vegetables seemed to take on animal forms. Sun-dried tomatoes lay on their backs like severed crab claws. Cabbages lolled on to each other like brains. Small, round onions popped out from under lettuces like eyeballs.

'You see these?' Andjaba asked, picking up a dusty, plastic bag with milky-white slabs that resembled 'Turkish Delight' frosted with icing sugar. 'These are actually, pebbles. Now, why would anyone buy these?'

'They don't, by the looks of it, sir,' Freddie said. 'That's why there are so many, left.'

'Very funny, Wilde. Ever the class jester.'

'I aim to please sir!'

'These pebbles are bought by pregnant women. They suck them for the iron. Very important for the baby's health.'

Hannah had a flashback to the small, dark-red iron tablets her mother had taken when pregnant with her sister. They seemed so synthetic and sophisticated by comparison to these white stones. In the end, of course, they had proved useless.

They left the market, picking up the bikes they had used to get to the village from school. As they cycled around a corner, a group of children surrounded them. They were aged from about five to ten, overflowing with excitement. They swamped them like the sea racing up a beach. Some, of them sat on their crossbar's without being asked, some rang their bells, giggling.

226

Many were desperate to have their photos taken by the pupils' mobile phones, demanding to see the pictures immediately afterwards.

'They're too poor to have mirrors,' Andjaba explained. 'That's why they are so desperate to see themselves. They are people without reflections, except in puddles.'

This set Hannah thinking about whether life was better without mirrors. Perhaps you could feel happier about yourself if you could only judge your appearance by the way people reacted to you. On the other hand, this might make you more vulnerable. It might be better to at least have some reality from the mirror on which to peg your self-esteem.

All the children were dressed in second-hand, Western clothes: T-shirts and sweatshirts with the over-designed names and clever slogans of American and British fashion brands: products for whom they were an unwitting poster, but with which they otherwise had no connection.

'They call them "Dead Man's White Clothes,"' Andjaba said, noticing them read the labels. 'We get tons and tons of donated clothes from America and Europe.'

Some of the children wanted to tell them their names. They asked their names back in return, giggling at the strangeness of them. Many of them touched the foreigners' pale white skin as if it were mother-of-pearl. Hannah, Freddie and Joe had never felt exotic before. They smiled at each other. They felt both special and ashamed. Their worries seemed so indulgent in the face of such poverty. The noise of laughter and surprise rose to a crescendo, like a flock of birds gathering for a migration.

Joe's attention was distracted by two children playing a game at the side of the road. They started with twenty or so round rocks of roughly equal size, arranged in a pile. On a count of 'one, two, three!' they ran and picked up five rocks.

Then they raced to arrange their rocks into patterns. Then, they ran back to the pile, picked up more rocks and raced to the other person's side this time, building on the pattern their opponent had created.

'Mr Andjaba,' Joe called. 'What are they doing?'

'It's a pattern game. It's called Dabra. You build up a picture of something recognisable with the stones. To make it more difficult, you work on each other's patterns, building on what they have done.'

'Two people then act as judges, guessing what the picture intended. The first picture to be guessed correctly is the winner.'

'This could be good for learning maths: pattern recognition,' Joe observed.

'I'm sure. It's centuries old,' Andjaba said, proud of the tradition, now that it was so admired by an outsider. 'Bushmen use something similar, to teach hunting. They show people how to draw different animal tracks.'

'A game after my own heart,' Joe thought to himself.

'Wondergat! Taotatide! Bergsig! Grootberg! Another in Bergsig!'

Ralph struggled with some of the pronunciations but was determined to be as accurate as possible, as befitted his civil service training. He was reading out the towns and villages from the list of patients with burn marks that the ward sister had prepared for Anne.

Anne sat at the dining-table, feeding the names into her laptop. Freddie had loaded the right software to turn the addresses into a map. Joe had helped, but Freddie was keen to take all the credit.

Clara was busy on the floor, trying to pin flags for each person on to her own physical map at the same time.

'Mummy, I'm finding it hard to fit all of them on,' she complained.

'Never mind, darling, it doesn't matter,' Anne replied casting a glance at Clara's crowded arrangement of cocktail sticks on the noticeboard taken down from her bedroom wall. 'It's just to get a pattern. Any more, Ralph?'

Clara had been somewhat subdued since the shooting-star episode and Anne felt warmed to see her so enthusiastic again.

'Three in Huab. That seems to be it,' Ralph said, turning the pages to double-check.

'OK, let's see if your software can work its magic, Freddie,' Anne said, vacating her seat for him.

Freddie took his place at the laptop, somewhat nervously. He hoped he would remember what Joe had told him about the modelling and was cursing himself for not having written it down.

He tapped away feverishly.

Clara joined him at the table, leaning into him. He pushed her away, irritated by her closeness which felt invasive.

'Hey!' she protested. 'It's only going to show you what my map does already.'

'Yes, but this one's likely to be more accurate,' he observed.

'So? Mine's three-dimensional,' she retorted.

'Now you two,' Ralph admonished.

A few minutes later, Freddie turned the laptop screen triumphantly towards his parents.

'Here. They're all within a 50-mile radius….in Damaraland, not far from Twyfelfontein.'

They all moved closer to look properly.

'So, why are all my patients with skin problems coming from such a small area?' Anne asked, excited about the diagnosis but worried about the cure.

'Some kind of pollution, in the local water supply?' Freddie suggested.

'Unlikely, they look like burns or scorch marks.' Anne said.

'Are you sure it's not some sort of infectious skin disease?' Ralph asked.

'Well, if it is, it's not one I've ever seen. Look…'

Anne handled Ralph a couple of photos she'd taken on the ward. She was careful to keep them anonymous. Freddie left the computer to look.

'Not you Clara,' Anne said. 'I don't want you having nightmares.'

'Don't be silly, Mummy, I saw them on the wards, remember?'

'What?' Ralph exclaimed, staring wide-eyed at Anne.

'She followed behind me without my knowing,' Anne explained.

'It must be some kind of radiation,' Ralph suggested. 'The uranium mines?'

'No. It's unlikely to affect anyone other than the miners themselves, according to Li anyway,' Anne said.

'Nonetheless, why don't we just ask Li to check his company records?' Ralph suggested 'Can you print this for me, Freddie?'

'Sure,' Freddie replied, flushed with pride at being the trusted guardian of the software.

'Print two copies could you, darling?' Anne added 'One with names. I need to notify the Department of Health.'

'Can you leave notifying them for a few days?' Ralph asked her.

'Why? It's a public health hazard. I must notify them. You, above all people, should realise that.'

'This could be politically sensitive. Iran are trying to get hold of uranium for their nuclear programme. If this is them… or the Russians, botching it by bringing uranium up to the surface unprotected, it needs to be dealt with in the right way.'

'Dad, protecting people's health must come first surely,' Freddie pleaded. He could see his mother was taken aback at Ralph's response. Freddie always jumped in to protect her. It was like an automatic response of his nervous system and had been since he was tiny.

'The health of international relations is also critical Freddie. Please don't challenge me,' Ralph admonished.

'Freddie, please do, always challenge your father. And me… everyone in fact,' Anne counselled, her eyes burning with indignation at her husband.

'What do you think?' Ralph asked as Li examined the printed map of burns victims laid out amidst the unwashed coffee cups on his desk.

They were in Li's make-shift office in the industrial zone of Walvis Bay. It was functional, rough, the walls lined with whiteboards crammed with schedules and drilling diagrams: a world apart from the polished desks and delicate crockery of the High Commission.

Li gazed up from the map.

'Look, Ralph, radiation is often misunderstood. I don't

know how much you know…I don't want to teach grandma how to suck eggs.'

Ralph signalled for him to continue, given his ignorance on the subject.

'Radiation is everywhere. It's in the soil, in rocks, in the air, in our homes, our workplaces. It's like a constant shadow. It comes from outer space and from solar flares. Flying in a plane for ten hours exposes us to as much radiation as an X-ray.'

'Remind me to cut back on my air travel,' Ralph interjected.

'Uranium mining involves relatively little exposure to radiation. We've had forty years to monitor and deal with it.'

'Even if, say, uranium was brought to the surface and left unprotected?'

'The product of mining is uranium oxide concentrate. It's shipped from the mines in two-hundred-litre drums and is barely radio-active. It's no more toxic than lead.'

'So, these burns can't be because of that,' Ralph half-asked and half-stated.

'The kind of reaction you're talking about, over an area this big, is different. It's very unusual. Perhaps radiation from a hole in the ozone layer?'

Ralph walked round to Li's side of the desk, putting down the undrinkable mug of coffee Li had made him. He pointed to the centre of the map.

'What about the concentration of cases here?'

'I agree. There seems to be an epicentre. It does suggest a source. But, as I say, that source is not a mine.'

'Is there anything about the area that strikes you? Is it…I don't know… near a tectonic plate or anything?'

'Only the coincidence!'

'What coincidence?'

'It's very near where Barbara is planning to build the new hotel… on Darius's father's old farm.'

Jacob Ubuntu's office was a tribute to his passions. There was a mahogany and glass cabinet full of the school's cups, trophies and shields, brightly polished and awaiting the inscriptions of next year's winners. There were the yearly school photographs, panoramic stretches of hopeful faces yet to be weathered by the world. The older photos were starting to fade in the sunlight that powered through his study windows. You could see enough detail, even from where they sat, to know that the pupils had become more diverse with time, as the school had taken on more Asian and African students.

The Namibian flag was stretched and framed proudly on the wall next to a signed photograph of the current President. Next to that were various certificates of excellence awarded by the Department of Education. Joe found himself disturbed by their lack of symmetry. He wanted to get up and re-arrange them.

There were two bookshelves even taller than Ubuntu himself, heaving with books, some slotted in sideways like vagrants.

His pride, and joy, was a display case, with embroidered covers laid over it to protect the objects from sunlight. Inside lay clay pots, weapons, utensils, drawings, land deeds, photographs and items of clothing arranged by tribe: Herero, Himba, San, Damara, Caprivian, Kavango, Nama and Ovambo.

On Ubuntu's desk were stacked piles of exercise books to

mark; textbooks; a Victorian letter-writing box; Secretary Bird quills in a pot and ostrich eggs in a wooden, oval bowl.

Ubuntu stared at the three of them.

'So, when are you planning to go?' Ubuntu asked.

'At the weekend, sir,' Hannah answered.

They had agreed that she should be their spokesperson as she was clearly his favourite.

'You realise that there are up to five thousand engravings at Twyfelfontein. Many of them are closed to the public.'

Joe piped up.

'My father has been given a special licence by the Department of Culture sir. I think it gives him access to all the drawings sir.'

'Yes of course, I'd forgotten. He is a professional in these matters. Which begs the question why you need me to come at all.'

Hannah looked at Freddie, egging him on to speak. He took the cue.

'Headmaster, you were the one who inspired us about Twyfelfontein in the first place. It was your talk in African Studies. You know a lot about the engravings. We hoped you might be able to help.'

Ubuntu paused before answering. A breeze rustled the trees outside the open window behind him.

'Don't get me wrong. A study of the engravings could not be more fascinating or worthwhile. What I can't quite fathom is the reason why you are so obsessed by them.'

They looked at each other. They agreed that were he to ask, they would have to divulge the whole story.

Hannah took a deep breath.

'Sir, Joe's mother is planning to build a hotel here.'

'Yes, I am aware of that,' Ubuntu said disapprovingly.

Joe shifted uncomfortably in his seat.

Ubuntu could see that Joe felt his mother's integrity had been questioned and gave him a healing smile.

Hannah continued.

'In the process of digging some test foundations for the hotel, a body was found. It has been identified as Captain Alexander, a Victorian soldier and explorer.'

'Yes, I have read something of him. He befriended the Herero and Himba tribes I believe.'

'Sir, the tomb shows that they buried him with honour. There were garlands,' Freddie added, conscious that this would warm Ubuntu to the cause which indeed it did.

'Go on,' he said, leaning forward, his arms resting on the desk.

'We found a trunk next to him,' Joe continued.

'You were at the dig?' Ubuntu exclaimed.

'Yes sir. My father led it.'

Hannah stepped in.

'In his trunk were several journals and a map.'

'What do the journals tell us?' Ubuntu enquired.

'They tell us that he became obsessed with a burial ground. Not the one in which he was found, but one that the Bushmen, or other tribes, wouldn't go near.'

Ubuntu nodded vigorously.

'As I have taught you, there is always reverence for the burial places of our ancestors.'

'That is exactly what fascinated us, sir,' Freddie said emboldened. 'Alexander wrote that this burial ground held the clue to the Fairy Circles.'

235

The room went silent. Ubuntu pushed his chair back. It was decorated with African beading which glinted in the sun as he vacated it. The scrape of the chair was like the whelp of an animal.

'Now it makes sense,' he boomed. 'This is all linked to your obsession with the circles.'

They returned his stare, suddenly guilty prisoners in the dock.

'I should have known. So, all our sacred places are a glorified treasure hunt for you.'

They were shocked by his sudden pivot into anger.

'No, sir,' Joe said 'not at all. We've fallen in love with Namibia, sir.'

'Have you?' Ubuntu challenged. 'Think about your words carefully. Have you fallen in love with this country? Or are we just a stopping-off point in your international lives? Another curiosity to play with?'

Ubuntu paused by the window, aware that his own anger was getting the better of him and could lead him in a dangerous direction. Looking at their hurt and curious faces, he had never felt so keenly the tension between seeing his pupils as future ambassadors for his country, and invading, foreign brats who condescended to him.

He walked over to his prized display case and tore off the covers.

'These tribes,' he said signalling to the objects inside 'were not just surviving, but painting, potting, engraving, thousands of years before your civilisations even spluttered into life.'

'With respect, sir, the Chinese had mastered…' Hannah started.

'Do not interrupt me please, Miss Chiang. I am aware that you all come from cultures with long and great histories. The point is, that... so... do...I.'

These last three words were said individually and staccato like a knife stabbing the air.

'Sometimes, it is best we let secrets stay in the soil with the dead,' Ubuntu concluded.

'But, Headmaster,' said Freddie, trembling with indignation and passion, 'you have taught us to be inquisitive and to pursue knowledge. Surely, you can't feel that what we are doing is wrong.'

'The Fairy Circles are almost certainly caused by termites or plant competition. One day soon, doubtless, the scientists will prove it beyond doubt. You will not find any new secrets in an ancient burial ground. You must respect the traditions and fears of my people and not prise open a scared place. Every foreigner seems to feel it is their God-given right to dig up our country... for minerals, for gold, for... hotel foundations and, yes, for anthropology. But I do not want my country's heritage to be a wing of the British Museum or the Smithsonian.'

He looked at them all in the eyes with an intensity that felt like a shock wave.

'Stop digging!'

'It's here,' Hannah said, carrying a large package from the post room to the Reading Room.

Joe and Freddie barely responded. They were still in a state of shock form Ubuntu's animated rant. It was still difficult to fathom.

'He's accusing us of raiding his country,' Freddie said.

'It probably doesn't help that my mum is planning to build hotels here,' Joe admitted.

'But what's wrong with that?' Hannah asked 'Especially if it's done respectfully. It will bring money into the country. It certainly doesn't help that my dad is mining uranium.'

'Then they need to build their own mining industry,' Freddie retorted.

'Maybe he's right and the Fairy Circles are just down to natural causes,' Joe said despondently.

'We've been through this. The science doesn't add up yet. Why, for example, don't the circles exist anywhere else apart from here and Pilbara?' Hannah asked.

'This might help anyway,' she continued, opening the end of a poster tube and removing its innards as if she was foraging inside a crab claw for meat.

'What is that?' Joe asked, suddenly clocking the package for the first time.

'The analysis from my dad's company… of your data!'

The penny dropped and suddenly Joe kicked into life, grabbing the tightly-curled sheets of paper from her.

Hannah and Freddie gathered round it as he thumbed through the data.

'They've done an amazing job,' he muttered. 'They've analysed several hundred square miles of satellite and Google Earth imagery.'

'And?' Freddie asked.

Joe didn't answer for several minutes. When he did, there was no hiding his disappointment.

'There don't seem to be any clear patterns. They've tried analysing it by taking squares, rectangles, circles and pyramids of circles.'

'It was always a long shot,' Hannah observed.

'What about the different types of circle?' Freddie asked. 'Did they get to a number?'

Joe checked the tables.

'Twenty-eight.'

'So, they could be an alphabet?' Freddie speculated.

Joe rushed round the table, and hugged and kissed Freddie, like a Russian.

'You're a genius. Why didn't I think of that?'

'We could allocate twenty-eight letters - one to each circle type - and see if it creates repeating words,' Freddie added. 'This is the Enigma code all over again. I could get my mum to help. This is where her translation skills would be brilliant.'

'There is one difference between this and the Enigma code,' Hannah said quietly. 'We knew it was German being coded. How do we know what these repeating words mean even if we find them?'

'Surely, we could run them against every world language to look for patterns?' Joe suggested.

'You're assuming the Circles were made by humans,' Hannah said.

12
Revelation at Ui Ais

'Will it eat me?' Clara cried.

'No, it's a rock,' Freddie replied.

'That's the famous Lion's Mouth rock formation,' Ilana said. 'It guards the whole valley.'

The rocks protruded like jaws over the landscape.

The four families clambered over the rocks behind her. They had set off at sunrise, to avoid the heat, and to maximise the daylight hours for finding clues amongst the Aladdin's cave of engravings.

Soon they arrived at an overhang.

'OK, this is it, folks,' Ilana announced. 'Although it is often called Twyfelfontein – the Afrikaans name – we prefer to call it by the original name "Ui Ais."'

Ilana was partly in tour-guide mode and part in family friend mode, hovering uncertainly between the two.

The four families stood in front of a vast array of engravings. They were everywhere: on large sandstone slabs, on the walls and underneath cliff overhangs. They had this magical place entirely to themselves. The public wouldn't be let in for another couple of hours. The tiredness already aching in their eyeballs was almost worth it.

'What does it mean?' Joe asked.

'It means "jumping waterhole" in the Damara language.

This site has been inhabited for six thousand years,' Ilana explained.

Clara put up her hand as if she were in class.

'Yes, Clara,' Ilana said responding in teacher mode.

'Why? There's nothing here!'

The parents all smiled.

'Now that's a very good question, Clara. The answer is water…precious water on the edge of the Kalahari Desert. And the water attracted animals. So, what did the animals attract?'

'Fleas?' replied Clara.

Everyone laughed and no-one more so than Ilana.

'That is probably true. But what I meant was, hunters, bushmen to be precise, the ancient San. They carved into the rocks exposing a lighter layer underneath. Then, perhaps two thousand, five hundred years ago, we find a different kind of art, from the Khakhoi, who were herders.'

'The hunters and the herders,' Ben muttered.

Anne found herself thinking that the world still basically divided into those two types.

They gazed at the jumble of ochre, yellow and white drawings, protected by the arid heat and the patina of the rocks. They tried hard to imagine ancestors scraping, carving, daubing, transplanting forms from their eyes and heads, through the magic of their hands, to the rocks. You could almost hear the sounds, feel the concentration, six thousand years later.

The animals were sometimes drawn realistically, but often not. Giraffes had necks that were even more exaggerated than in real life. Eland and antelopes had pregnant bodies unfeasibly supported by stick-thin legs. There was a dancing kudu, half-beast and half-man like the archer Sagittarius. Hannah, Joe

241

and Freddie smiled in recognition of the lion man with his human feet.

'Why are, so many of the animals, half-human?' Hannah asked.

Ben jumped in before Ilana could answer, keen to re-assert himself.

'The San believe that all animals were once human,' he explained. 'It's Darwin in reverse…their creation myth.'

'Imagine how differently the world would be, if we thought of animals as evolved from humans, and not the other way round,' Hannah said quietly.

'What about these?' Freddie asked, gesturing behind them.

He was pointing at figures that stalked like shadow puppets across the face of the rocks. They were ochre-red, darker than the paler orange of the rocks on which they were daubed. Some figures hunted, some sat cross-legged as if in storytelling mode. Others were on their knees possibly in prayer. The figures that were simply walking, were graceful and slim, with the same straight-backed look as Egyptian pharaohs.

Anne noted, with a doctor's eye, that our posture has got worse and worse through time, by becoming desk-bound.

'What about these three?' Hannah asked.

The three figures were dancing, their right arms raised, their left legs extended. They teetered on a knife-edge between being sacred and comical, knowing and naïve. They could almost be dancers from the Moulin Rouge.

'Hey, what's happening to this poor antelope?' asked Clara, spotting its plight as if it were her own.

'They often led an eland to a hilltop and sacrificed it to

bring on the rains,' Ben explained. 'That's where the Israelites got it from,' he added.

'Freddie, Hannah, Selima, Clara! Come here!' Joe's voice rang out like metal.

He was above them, directly under a large overhang of rock. They scrambled up to him, their minds already a muddle of myths and symbols. The caves were often painted in a trance and looking at them made you feel the same, as if you were hallucinating.

'Look at these. I've read about them,' Joe said.

Next to his jabbing fingers they saw engravings of circles, many of them double circles, one inside the other.

'They look like breasts!'

Selima merely voiced what they were all thinking. Clara giggled. Hannah nodded, smiling.

In between the circles were stick-like figures. Some were walking. Others appeared to be squatting next to the circles.

'These must be fairy circles surely,' Joe said feverishly, taking more photos with his i-phone than he could ever possibly use.

'I think you'll need to increase your data allowance, Joe,' Freddie jibed.

'Already done it,' Joe replied grinning. 'I've downloaded more data in the last month than I have done in the previous year. Dad will go ballistic when he sees the bill.'

'All in a good cause!' Selima soothed.

'Look, tell me I'm wrong,' Joe started.

'You're wrong!' Freddie proffered.

Joe continued unabated…

'These drawings suggest the circles were around a long time ago. The rock painters were as intrigued by them as we are.'

'They could be fake,' Selima pointed out. 'Mum?' she called.

Ilana left the parents and joined the others on the upper ledge.

'What are you lot up to now?' she asked affectionately, touched by their excited huddle.

'How old are these engravings, Mum? Do you know?'

'I'm not sure. Joe, your dad is much more likely to know than I am.'

A minute later, Ben was poring over the drawings, using a fine brush to remove any dust and gazing through a magnifying glass like a restorer at a canvas.

'These are Victorian drawings of the Fairy Circles.'

Ralph approached them, holding the face of his watch towards them as he did so.

'I hate to be the voice of focus,' he said, 'but we only have a few hours before the site opens to the public. Shouldn't we be trying to decode the map?'

'Absolutely, we should,' Ben said.

Minutes later, they had gathered around the Victorian explorer's map. It was laid out on a picnic table that Sarah, with her usual forward planning, had brought with her, along with enough folding chairs to seat the adults. The younger ones stood around the wise council of their parents.

It was impossible to know what scale the map was drawn to. Or even if it was drawn in proportion to distance, as opposed to imagination. The most striking elements of the map were symbols, drawn in a similarly crude style to the cave engravings.

In the middle of the map were the beautifully etched words 'Ui Ais.' So, they were sitting at its epicentre. In the bottom right there were three seals with fat bellies and exaggerated whiskers. Diagonally above them were two or three huge craters in the ground, one with two concentric circles around it. They were drawn in crude cross-section with chambers underneath the ground.

'One of these must be the burial chamber surely,' said Joe, pointing at them.

'They certainly look that way. But, why two of them?' quizzed Ben.

'Perhaps he found two,' Hannah suggested.

'Perhaps there are two different entrances to the same chamber,' Freddie proffered.

On the bottom right-hand side of the map was a harbour. Directly above that was a boy standing on a mountain.

'The mountain is clear enough. That must be Spitzkoppe surely,' Ilana said,

'But why the boy? Is he symbolic?' Anne asked.

Ben was keen to shine a light in the fog, if only for himself. He did this, as so often, by talking out loud and following the trail of his own thoughts like breadcrumbs.

'Look, the most prominent writing on the map is "Ui Ais" which is here. That surely suggests that he meant people seeing the map to come here. He must have either taken these symbols from these caves. Or he has carved his own symbols as clues to be discovered here. Let's fan out and try to find them.'

They split into pairs and began to search the caves for clues. All except Joe who couldn't be wrested away from the circles and patterns, amongst which he was determined to find a code.

After twenty minutes a cry went up from one corner of the cave, finding a faint echo in the Hueb valley below.

Everyone rushed to the spot.

'We've found the seals,' Hannah yelled, eyes ablaze.

'So, let's think about this,' Selima said. 'The sea is a hundred kilometres from here. So, it's very unlikely the San would draw a creature so far away. Perhaps, Alexander did.'

'Are any of his other symbols nearby? The boy on the mountain? The craters?' Ben asked as he scoured the walls. There were none to be found.

'The sea might have been a lot closer when these were drawn,' Darius observed. 'The coastline has moved as the dunes have built up.'

'And anyway, the nomads could easily have wandered here from the coast,' Ben said.

Half an hour later, the puzzle was no closer to being solved. No symbols had been found and an air of despondency had fallen over the group like a cloud. What had been a hive of worker bees in the honeycomb of the rocks was now like a pack of drones drugged on smoke.

Ralph called over to Ilana, pointing half-heartedly at an engraving.

'Could this be the boy or girl on the mountain, Ilana?'

'Say that again' Ilana replied.

'What? Boy or girl on the mountain?'

Ilana struck her own forehead in frustration.

'Oh my God, I've been so stupid. The "White Lady of Brandberg" of course.'

Ralph looked at her stupefied.

'It sounds like a Gothic novel!' he exclaimed.

'Have you got a map with you?' she asked.

'Always,' he replied, 'It's in my rucksack.'

'Is it, large scale?'

'Reasonably, I think.'

'Great, can you fetch it…quickly. Ben, I think I'm on to something.'

Although only Ralph had been asked to bring the map, and only Ben called as fellow detective, the news of a breakthrough spread like a virus of optimism. Everyone hastened to the picnic table, gathered like a pack of conspirators about to hatch a plot.

The two maps were laid out side-by-side on the table: the tattered and symbol-strewn, Victorian map next to the clean, thin, colour coded lines and topography of the Ordnance Survey map that Ralph had retrieved.

Ilana was almost dancing with excitement. It took all her energy to stay rooted to the spot and explain.

'The boy on the mountain - here - is actually know as a lady. And this mountain is not the Spitzkoppe, it's the Brandberg.'

'Of course,' chimed Ben. 'There is a famous rock painting called "The White Lady of Brandberg." She is walking in a procession, surrounded by people and animals. In her right hand is a flower or an ostrich egg cup. In her left is a bow and arrow.'

'I thought you said a boy,' Sarah intervened.

'Scholars now think that it is a boy undergoing an initiation ceremony of some sort. He is painted in white from the chest downwards, giving the impression of a dress. Hence the confusion.'

'But what about the other symbols?' Anne asked.

Ilana danced around the two maps, pointing out the modern-day names that corresponded to the Victorian symbols.

'Look at the map here, on the left-hand side. Seals.'

'The Cape Cross Seal Colony,' Freddie yelled out, remembering the smell of their adventure.

'Exactly,' Ilana responded. 'And if we follow the line up here, we come to the two craters. You can see here on the modern map, they are called Messum and Doros - the remnants of two vast volcanoes.'

'So, if those are volcanic chambers, they probably aren't the burial chamber,' Hannah surmised.

Ben leapt up.

'If you take a straight line up from the seals and through the craters, you get to where we are now,' he said, drawing the line with his index finger.

'What about the right-hand side of the map?' Joe called out having finally prised himself away from the patterns on the upper ledge. 'The harbour? Wait, wait…'

He pushed to the front and grabbed the modern map examining it close up.

'Of course, it's Walvis Bay. Does anyone have a tape measure or a ruler? Anything with a sharp edge?'

Pockets and rucksacks were rummaged, but nothing found.

'Use Alexander's notebook,' Freddie suggested.

It seemed singularly appropriate and so Joe placed the explorer's notebook on the map. He pulled a pencil from behind his ear, where he'd kept it whilst making notes. He drew a straight line from Walvis Bay on the coast, through the Brandberg mountain and up to Ui Ais.

Then he drew a second line, already traced roughly by his finger, from Cape Cross seal colony through the craters and up.

'Where these two lines meet, is probably the site of the chamber,' he said. And they don't meet here. They go up further.'

He finished the two lines until they intersected. Everyone leaned forward.

'OK, let's just check the co-ordinates,' Ben said, 'and I'll look on Google Maps.'

A moment later he'd pinpointed it on his tablet screen and showed it round.

'Anyone recognise it?'

'I do,' said Darius 'it's just north of my father's old farm.'

'My hotel site,' Barbara added, feeling the triviality of it as she did so. She couldn't quite determine whether her sites were cursed or blessed.

There was a moment of silence as they all absorbed the discovery.

'So Ui Ais is only written on the map as a point near the intersection?' Ralph asked of himself but out loud.

'That doesn't make sense,' Sarah said. 'It's so prominent, it has to hold some other significance.'

Sarah had felt largely inadequate for the last few hours. She had found herself an expert in words, in an environment in which only images were relevant. Ben had thought she might be invaluable in decoding symbols. Yet this rock art contained nothing like hieroglyphics. It wasn't logical, but she felt she'd let everyone down. She continued…

'He must have wanted to direct whoever found the map to come here. There has to be a clue here… we just haven't found it.'

'That's because you've been looking in the wrong place.'

The familiar voice boomed form behind them, causing them to turn as one.

Jacob Ubuntu was almost unrecognisable in khaki,

complete with shorts, belt with a bowie knife and a rucksack. Perched on his head was an unlit head-torch. He looked ten years younger as he stood between them and the valley. The lion's mouth rock was visible in the distance and seemed to match his spirit.

'Headmaster, you came,' Hannah cried, feeling the emotion in her voice.

Li felt momentarily displaced as her father.

Joe, Freddie and Hannah all rushed to Ubuntu. They would have hugged him at this point, but he signalled a high five, and they returned it with vigour in quick succession. Selima joined them, clasping Hannah's hand in hers.

'I thought you weren't coming,' Joe said half plaintively and half accusingly.

'I was determined not to, but then realised the error of my ways,' Ubuntu replied. 'I must apologise. I got into a ridiculous state and wanted to get out of it but couldn't. I just didn't want you to treat my culture as some sort of giant crossword puzzle, there to be solved for your sport.'

Ralph stepped towards Ubuntu, ever the diplomat.

'Headmaster, I can totally understand your concerns. We as parents…'

He gazed round at the others to check their camaraderie and found it.

'We have also been worried about their obsession with the Fairy Circles,' he continued.

The five of them shifted uneasily recognising this portrait of themselves.

'But we also love their curiosity. And their obsession is not disrespectful of your culture. Quite the opposite in fact.

Namibia has triggered something magical in all of them… a kind of love.'

Ubuntu was silent, choked with hearing his country spoken of in this way.

'Might I also add,' said Ben 'that the study of the tribes in southern Africa has been a significant part of my life's work. Not to win some sort of academic glory, but to find the truth, to unearth the nobility of your past, Headmaster, which is, of course our common past. I am just as passionate as you to rid the world of its outdated, Western views of Africa.'

Barbara found herself regretting her statement that she hadn't intended to marry archaeological digs and burial sites. She had a strange feeling of knowing her husband for the first time, here in a cave in Africa.

'I am touched,' Ubuntu responded. 'Perhaps our countries can start to understand each other at last. Let's hope so.'

He looked at the five eager faces.

'Anyway, who could resist the curiosity of these infuriatingly bright youngsters?'

They all laughed.

'To be honest,' Ubuntu continued, 'I have also been obsessed by the circles for many years. One often reacts badly to what one sees in one's self. I, of course, respect the views of my countrymen that each circle is the soul of a dead ancestor. Yet, I am also too much of a rationalist to believe it.'

'You said we were looking in the wrong place,' Ben prompted.

'Yes, we need to go deeper, into the cave proper,' Ubuntu advised.

They carefully folded up the maps and followed Ubuntu

along the rocks and boulders that were already starting to radiate heat, to the concealed entrance of a cave.

'Does everyone have a head-torch? Or, some kind of a torch, anyway?' Ubuntu asked. 'It will be cold in here as well, so you might want another layer.'

They had to unhook a chain to enter. A sign which read 'No public admission. Approved guides only.' was put to one side.

The beams of their head-torches criss-crossed the cave and at different heights: from Clara's darting four foot and ten inches to Ubuntu's measured and stately six-foot three.

'This is just a hunch,' Ubuntu admitted 'but the Victorians often liked the earliest engravings which are in here... also the paintings of which there are very few. If Captain Alexander were to paint or engrave anything himself, it might well be in here or the adjoining cave.'

At Darius's suggestion, they split the cave between the four families, each one taking a different section of wall and ceiling. They assumed that a Victorian painting would look fresher and have more varied colours than the subdued ochres and whites of the San's.

Sometimes they encountered a name or initials alongside a date: 'ABJT: 1861'; 'Pinkerton: 1903'; 'The Boer Constrictor: 1971'. The Victorian dates made their hearts flutter with hope and their eyes keenly scoured its vicinity.

After an hour of patient searching, they had covered the first cave between them. Necks aching and eyes adjusting, they sat in the sun of the cave entrance, sipping hot chocolate and milky coffee from Thermos flasks. The chill of the cave penetrated your bones after an hour.

Fleeces were donned for the second cave which was significantly colder than the first being further underground. After ten minutes Ben called to Sarah.

'Sarah, your moment has come.'

She felt flattered but anxious in case he had exaggerated her knowledge and skill in his mind.

Fortunately, what greeted her gaze were hieroglyphs. Her eyes settled, her brain whirred.

'Well, they're Egyptian, as I'm sure you can tell.'

'Alexander had a fascination with Egyptology,' Ben noted excitedly. 'Those earlier journals show that he had visited the Valley of the Kings. He made copious notes and drawings.'

Sarah pressed her face closer to the wall. She brushed some dust away with her fingertips.

'These are a slightly cod version, whether deliberate or not.'

'You mean an amateur has painted them?' Ben asked.

'Exactly. But they're clear enough, despite the mistakes, to pick up the meaning.'

She started to translate, and Ben took notes.

'From the cave of paintings…'

'That must be here,' Selima said.

'Head towards the place of the elephants and rhinos.'

'That must be Etosha,' Ilana suggested. 'It would make sense because it's north-east of here.'

'Heading towards the point of the intersection,' Joe added.

Sarah continued.

'Keep the valley…'

'The Huab,' Darius suggested.

'… and the mountains at your back.'

'The Brandberg and Spitzkoppe,' Ilana confirmed.

'Then, this next section is unclear…. Something about three rivers?'

'Three rivers meet just north of my father's farm,' Darius confirmed.

As Sarah's torch moved slowly along, it found every archae-ologist's worst nightmare: a missing section, a gouge taken out of the rock.

'It's been vandalised,' Ben sighed. 'It looks deliberate. It's too deep for water damage.'

'Was someone else on the same trail as us?' Freddie speculated.

'Impossible to know,' Ben responded. 'It seems unlikely, as we have what we assume to be the only copy of his map.'

'He might have told someone where to look before he died,' Joe suggested.

'Or he could have sent a copy of the map back to his spon-sors at the Royal Geographical Society who then sent another expedition,' Ben added.

They all suddenly felt a competitor at their back, adding to their sense of urgency.

'Look further along the wall,' Li suggested.

They inched systematically along for several feet but found nothing.

'Below,' Freddie suggested.

The floor lit up as they dropped their heads together, as if in prayer. Nothing met their gaze.

'Where do you look when you want to be inspired?' asked Ubuntu, not much louder than a whisper. In the light reflected from the floor he'd already seen what they had missed.

They raised their eyes to the ceiling as one. There looking

down at them was a painting of the Golden Leopard.

'Not a single rosette!' Selima noted.

13

Hunting the Golden Leopard

Freddie had been awake a large part of the night. First, there was the cooing of a woodpigeon, which was curiously British and soothing. This was followed by a sound like a tiny anvil being struck by the most delicate of hammers. It came in very uneven intervals, thus causing maximum alertness. No metronomes in Nature. Finally, came the whooping of the hyenas.

They were camping near the banks of a river and he was convinced he could hear the splash of crocodiles, emerging from the water, followed by the slither of their bellies across the coarse, lush grass. Irritatingly, Joe had seemed oblivious to it all, breathing heavily and rhythmically.

Then, the low growl of a lion fired up Josh's adrenaline like a car battery at the turn of a key.

Finally, just as he was drifting back to sleep under the influence of Joe's breathing, there had been the sound of something heavy but soft, like a giant walking with felt shoes. The snapping of twigs played treble to the bass of the padding feet. Then, the back wall of the tent started to bulge and darken. He sat bolt upright and shook his sleeping friend.

'Joe!' he whispered.

'What?'

'There's an elephant outside the tent.'

'Sure, and I'm the forty-fifth President of the United States!'

'You've forgotten, we're sleeping out in the bush.'

Joe suddenly came to, with a jolt.

'OMG!' Joe said seeing the bulge in the tent wall. 'What if it decides to sit down?'

Freddie had started to giggle at this point.

'When did you ever see an elephant sit down?'

'At a circus!' Joe answered mildly hurt. 'And in Dumbo…'

This last comment sent Freddie into uncontrollable, suppressed giggles.

Just then, the corner of the tent squeezed in, which made his throat convulse in a different way.

'Just be quiet for God's sake,' Joe said in the kind of angry whisper that's triggered by fear.

'I want to see if it really is an elephant,' Freddie said, starting to get out of bed.

'Don't be mad!' Joe exclaimed in a whisper rasping with rage. 'People have been trampled to death!'

Once the bulge had gone, and the noises retreated, they decided to look. They carefully rolled up one window cover and hooked it up. Through the mosquito mesh they could see two elephants chewing the grasses at the edge of the river. They seemed a deathly grey in the moonlight, like giant ghosts. Their breathing slowed now the danger had passed, and stories from Kipling came flooding into their heads.

'God, this place is magical,' Freddie said.

It was almost an hour before they returned to a haunted sleep.

'Come on guys, wake up! Glorious morning!'

'Wakey, wakey! Rise and shine!'

The unmistakeable voices of the two fathers penetrated the tents. Ben's was a call to action in the enthusiastic, American tradition of 'fresh morning, fresh energy'. Ralph's was English, firm, almost military.

It felt more like the middle of the night than even the middle of the night had felt.

Selima felt for her torch, but instead found Hannah's face.

'Hey!' Hannah complained.

'Sorry, I was looking for a head torch rather than a head.'

'What time is it?'

'5.45.'

'What? I'm suing under the UN Charter for Young People's Rights!'

Selima burst out laughing.

'Hannah, how on earth can you think of such things this early in the morning? You're crazy!'

'It came with the family. DNA doesn't lie!'

'Can you girls cut the banter please?' Joe called from the next-door tent. 'We're trying to get some sleep in here.'

'You need to get up,' Selima called. 'It's 5.48.'

'Is that the time or an isotope?' Joe asked.

'Only from a geek's mouth,' Freddie cried, for which he got a pillow in the face.

'Who else was freezing in the night?' Hannah called, still protecting her body in a foetal position, for fear of contact with the early morning chill.

A couple of 'Me's' responded through the canvas walls.

'You, wimps!' Selima cried. 'You've clearly never camped out in Africa before.'

Hannah put on her walking shoes and exited the tent. The moon was still up and the colour of wax. The sun was a blood-red disc barely visible above the treeline. Then, gradually, after playing hide-and-seek amongst the thickets, it rose, calling the landscape to life. Shadows and animals stretched and so did Hannah.

The river was flat and silent. The air felt like the purest drinking water.

'Come out, guys!' she called to the other three. 'The sun's just up and it's incredible. However tired you are…'

Selima felt pride at the thrill in Hannah's voice. This was Selima's country, her landscape.

Darius, practised in the art of living out in the bush, was already re-kindling the fire. He placed the ends of three hard-wood logs on top of each other, reviving the coals from the previous night that lay smouldering underneath. The fire was small, but darting, like the tongue of a priest.

Selima emerged from her tent and watched her father move at ease between his chores. He was always happiest outdoors.

'Dad, how long have you been up?'

'Almost an hour. You know me. Listen, you and your friends need to get up sharpish. If we want to find that leopard, we need to leave in less than thirty minutes before it starts to warm up.'

Ralph had been taught how to drive jeeps over rough terrain when he was a teenager: by his father, off-road on various military bases. So, it was decided that he and Darius would drive the open-sided Land Rovers.

The five rode together in Darius and Ilana's jeep, whilst Ralph drove behind and took the remaining adults.

259

Before they set off, Darius issued some safety instructions. By now, the sun had set the sky ablaze with crimson and the smell of wild basil was already rising from the bush.

'Keep your hands and feet inside the jeeps at all times. When we do find animals, no standing up and no sudden movements.'

'Why no standing up?' Clara asked.

'Animals use silhouettes to hunt. In the jeep we blend into the shape of the vehicle. They don't pick you out as an individual. If you stand up, they can identify you as prey!'

'Prey?!' Clara gulped.

Freddie put his arm round her.

'It's all-right. I'll stay close, pumpkin.'

They sat in three rows in the open-sided jeeps.

The moon-white gravel road was bumpy and jolted their spines.

'This is what we call a free African massage!' Darius yelled.

They all smiled, even Selima, who'd heard it a thousand times before.

'Hold tight!' he called as they turned off the road and into the bush.

The jeep rocked like a cradle, tilting and lurching.

'This is like being drunk,' Joe called out.

'How would you know, Joe?' Ilana asked, turning around to him with an amused smile.

Joe went silent. That one evening, raiding the drinks cabinet in their Brooklyn apartment with his brother, had not ended well. He never wanted to look at a crème de menthe again.

'Here,' Selima said, handing out binoculars.

'Mine don't work!' Clara said distraught, as everyone else seemed lost deep in the landscape.

'That's because you need to take the lens caps off first,' said Joe, removing them for her.

She wasn't used to brotherly attention from anyone other than Freddie and decided she rather liked it.

Looking through the binoculars only exaggerated the jeep's bumps and so she strung them round her neck for now.

The cold morning air chastened them all into blankets, but it was intoxicating: their eyes on patrol, the cold air refrigerating their face, the horizon bouncing and ever-changing. The adventure sang in their blood.

'So, this, is why people hunt,' Freddie said.

'I guess it's what we're hard-wired to do,' Joe observed. 'We've been doing it for thousands of years.'

'We've also spent thousands of years looking after animals, not hunting them,' Hannah pointed out, wanting to tell a different narrative.

'But we still kill them,' Joe pointed out.

'Sometimes we need to kill to cull,' Darius intervened. 'There are too many elephants in Botswana for example. They're destroying the landscape.'

'There are seven billion of us and we're destroying the planet,' Ilana barked. 'Who's culling us?'

'Disease? War?' Joe offered.

'You Augustineum kids are too bloody smart by half,' Darius said snatching at the clutch and jerking their necks in the process.

'If we ate less meat, the world would be a healthier place in every sense of the term,' Hannah said.

'Well said, Hannah,' Ilana cheered. 'Selima, you could take a leaf out of Hannah's book.'

'Thanks, Mum!' Selima said sarcastically. Like her father, she was too in love with meat to give it up. The smell of it cooking was enough to intoxicate her.

They continued in silence for a while.

'Narnia trees!' Clara exclaimed as they passed bushes like Christmas trees, shrouded in white by the wind-blown sand.

'How likely is that we'll find the Golden Leopard, Darius?' Hannah asked.

'Leopards are crepuscular,' Darius explained.

'Is that like a pancake?' Clara asked.

'No, it means that they are active at dawn and at dusk, when it's cooler, but not in between,' Darius replied.

'Are we out early enough?' Joe asked.

'Yes, but this is needle-in-a-haystack stuff,' Darius replied. 'Leopards hunt alone for a start. They're also the shyest big cats and good at camouflage. Finding any leopard is a minor miracle. Finding the rare, and possibly mythical, Golden Leopard is even harder.'

'It's not mythical, Dad,' Selima said firmly 'We both saw it at Grandpa's farm.'

'And that's why we're here, Sel. But it was a long way in the distance, and we can't be sure. Perhaps it was a young lioness.'

'You were certain at the time,' Selima protested.

Suddenly, Darius stopped the jeep. Ralph, who was still not fully awake, and struggling with the gears, almost crashed into him but slammed on the brakes just in time.

'Ralph!' Anne screamed. 'Be careful. You're looking decidedly uncomfortable. Perhaps Ben should drive.'

'Sure, I don't mind,' Ben called out from behind. 'I drove four-by-fours in Afghanistan.'

'I'm fine,' said Ralph, finding Ben's confidence about everything rather grating. 'I just need to get familiar with this clutch that's all.'

He flashed Anne a thunderous look and she decided to back off. Ralph could quickly flare when undermined. Barely suppressed anger often lies beneath the gentle surface of a diplomat, as she had learned to her cost.

Darius switched off the engine, opened the jeep door and leaned down to examine some tracks.

'This is where we could do with a Bushman,' he said. 'They're expert trackers. But there's definitely a leopard foot-print here.'

'How can you tell?' asked Joe, leaning out and taking a photo with his phone.

'Four toes and a paw pad: looks like an upside-down, molar tooth. Three bumps at the back. Narrower than a lion, wider than a cheetah.'

'How do you know all this?' Freddie asked.

'Darius trained as a guide,' Ilana said proudly. She always appreciated him most in times of danger.

'They're quite fresh tracks. Heading in the direction we're heading,' Darius said. 'This is bizarre though…'

He jumped down from the jeep having checked his safety first with a three-hundred-and-sixty-degree scan.

'What is it?' Ilana asked, leaning over to see what he was doing.

'There seem to be cheetah tracks as well. Just as fresh and walking in parallel.'

'Why is that so strange?' Freddie probed.

'Leopards and cheetahs don't hunt together. They're in fierce competition.'

'Perhaps scarcity of food has made them collaborate,' Ralph suggested from the jeep behind.

'Never,' said Darius. 'They are sworn enemies. Cheetahs may be the fastest animals on Earth, but they are also the weakest of the big cats. Leopards often steal their prey. They both keep to their territories and defend them at all costs.'

They drove on. The sun had risen enough to bless their skin. As so often in Africa, trees were the architecture of the landscape. Some had fallen, reduced from majesty to perches for birds and back-scratchers for elephants. Others were bolt upright but bare, like a forked lightning of wood. Some held their canopy of leaves up proudly, like an offering to be blessed by the sun. Individually, the trees could be anywhere. Collectively, they could only be in Africa.

The front jeep broke through some seemingly impassable bracken and a large bull-elephant was revealed, fifteen feet in front of them. Darius slammed on the brakes with Ralph following in a jolting chain-reaction. They all lurched forward on to the inner bars of the Land Rover that ran like sentinels in front of their seats.

'Stay absolutely still,' Darius, whispered. 'Don't talk!'

The elephant stared, seemingly inscrutable and unblinking. Its eyes threaded with Darius's. Its trunk had been draped across one tusk to rest. Anne thought it looked strangely like hanging out the washing to dry on the line. On seeing them though, the trunk quickly returned to its probing state. Its giant ears twitched.

Darius spoke over his shoulder, quietly but with an exaggerated firmness.

'Whoever is right at the back needs to tell Ralph to start reversing slowly but calmly.'

The word went back. Ralph crashed the gears with a horrible grating sound. Darius winced.

The elephant started to lower its head: the first sign of a mock-charge.

Ralph tried to engage reverse for the second and third times, Anne trying to steady him. Finally, the gear engaged. Rarely had metal slotting into metal sounded so sweet.

'He's threatening to charge,' Darius observed. 'Tell Ralph to bloody well reverse now.'

'Dad!' Freddie called from the back of their jeep, 'it's going to charge unless you reverse.'

Instructing the others to be his wing-mirrors, Ralph reversed along the cratered track.

The elephant lowered its head, held its tusks to the sky and moved one foot forward shifting its enormous weight forward through its shoulders.

Both vehicles reversed, edging back from the confrontation zone, keen to shed their predator status.

'Turn around and drive away but calmly,' Darius instructed. Ralph, composure somewhat regained, obliged.

As Darius reversed, the jeep got caught in a rut.

'Dad, get out of here!' Selima screamed losing her usual, automatic trust of him. Their hands seized the roll-bars, and seatbacks, their knuckles white and bony like ivory.

Darius grated the gears, changed the angle of the front tyres, rocked forward and back, and then rammed the clutch

265

down and re-engaged in first.

The elephant started to move as they took off at speed.

They looked behind. The elephant had slowed with their retreat and now stood still and proud in its victory. It shook its head as if at their folly.

'Thank God for that!' Freddie spoke for all of them.

They continued, nerves now jangling. Their brains constantly re-interpreted their eyes. Every tree now seemed to wear a face. Every fallen branch undulated like a snake. The grasses moved as if they had limbs.

Then Selima saw it. She could scan like a bushman. Her eyes which made thickets of words, penetrated landscapes like a laser.

'Leopard!' she called. 'Can't see it now. You need to reverse a little.'

Reversing now triggered an automatic nervous system response in all of them as Darius pulled up alongside the other jeep.

'Between the two thickets. See where the heron is. Look to the left,' she advised.

They raised their binoculars, like a crowd at a racecourse.

'Do you see it?' Selima asked.

Sitting with slim majesty on a fallen tree, surveying the landscape for prey, was a beautiful leopard. Its shapes were pure grace. The shoulders flowed into the back; the back into the haunches, the haunches into the tail; the tail into the ground.

'Not a single marking,' Ben exclaimed.

'Who says a leopard can't shed its spots?' Freddie couldn't resist.

'I told you it existed,' cried Selima in triumph.

'It's the creature they told the story about at the Boma,' Hannah exclaimed. 'The one that shook off its spots as it ran, making the Fairy Circles.'

'I don't know about mythical. It's a freak of nature,' Anne suggested. 'An albino, or a genetic defect of some kind.'

'No, it's not, Mummy,' Clara protested. 'It's beautiful.'

'The strange thing is that the spots are for camouflage,' Darius observed. 'Not having them is an evolutionary disadvantage. Being plain makes it easier to be seen and harder for it to hunt.'

'You don't need to hunt if you're immortal,' Freddie pronounced.

'It's slimmer than I thought,' Hannah noted.

'Strong though. Look at those shoulders,' Ilana corrected. 'Imagine the strength it takes to haul a carcass up a tree.'

'Look into those golden-green eyes,' Darius said, binoculars to his eyes. 'No wonder the Bushmen believe it's sacred.'

'My Pa used to shoot them from the terrace in India.' Ralph's comment opened the door on to another era.

'That's so cruel!' Clara cried in protest.

'Yes, it is!' Ralph responded, now rethinking what he'd accepted as a child.

The leopard faced them and seemed to be taking in each of their faces by turn. It then leapt off the fallen tree and prowled away, its long, sinewy back unzipping the tall grasses.

'We must follow it,' Clara cried, jumping from the Land Rover and starting to walk in the direction of the leopard.

Ralph leapt out of the jeep after her.

'Clara, stop immediately. We don't want another shooting star episode. Get back in the jeep now. You could be killed.'

267

He caught her in his arms and hauled her back into the jeep. The Land Rover ignitions fired up like clearing throats and the pursuit was on.

Tracking the leopard proved as hard as predicted. It was slim and lithe and seemed well-camouflaged despite the absence of markings. It disappeared into thickets, forcing them to loop round in front of it, hoping it would continue in the same direction and exit the other side. This it obligingly did, but it was picking up speed.

As the jeeps lurched up and down the tracks, they all felt in danger of being thrown out. They held on for dear life, putting their heads out a little, like periscopes, when they could. They often had to lean inwards as branches thwacked against the metal uprights of the jeep and then sprang back, whipping their arms. The jeeps' canvas roofs snapped against their metal frames with cracks like gun shots.

'There it is,' Freddie cried. 'Ten o'clock!'

It was off again before they could focus. They chased it for ten to fifteen minutes, straining their eyes, shredding the tyres, until it disappeared.

'Damn!' Hannah spoke for all their frustrations. 'Down the rabbit hole like Alice.'

'How can it just disappear?' Clara asked in frustration.

'I thought it would lead us to the burial ground,' Joe said.

'We have to be more cunning trackers or decode that map more accurately,' Darius concluded.

The switched off the jeeps and sat, parked side by side, as the disappointment soaked into them like rain. They were quiet, each decoding the last hour.

Darius gazed across the landscape. He thought he could see

sunlight flashing from a window in the distance.

'I wonder if it happened here,' he muttered to himself.

'Wonder if what happened, Darius?' Ralph asked.

'This Northern edge of the farm was always difficult. Many of the farm workers said it was sacred land and refused to work it. So, my father often worked here alone. One day, he came back to the farmhouse, pale as a ghost. When my mother asked him what was wrong, he didn't reply. He went out to one of the barns and got the biggest length of rope he could find and some crampons. He pulled on his climbing boots, kissed us both on the forehead and left, heading North.'

He paused, his throat closing with emotion.

'What happened?' Sarah asked.

'We don't know. He never returned. His body was never found. We buried an empty casket in his honour… under his favourite tree.'

'How far did you search?' Li asked, trying to contemplate the desperation that must have ensued.

'Further and wider than you can imagine. I even took a couple of Bushmen, figuring that if anyone could find him, they could. But as soon as we got to the perimeter of the farm, they refused to go on. They were shaking with fear, which for a bushman is rare. I kept thinking "If only I had two Maasai with me. They are afraid of nothing."'

'What happened to Grandpa?' Selima asked.

'We'll never know, Sel.'

'You've never told anyone else except me before now,' Ilana said. She wondered, whether telling others would be therapeutic, or re-imprison him in the same truth.

'No,' he said quietly.

Darius trusted these new friends in his life. He felt sad but unburdened. Now seemed right. The revelation should fit the moment and the moment do it justice.

'He talked about the Golden Leopard… about following it. But we dismissed it as fantasy. Worse still, we thought he was hallucinating.'

'Now you know he wasn't,' Ilana said threading her arm through his.

'How long ago was this?' Li asked.

'Twenty-five years ago. I was sixteen,' Darius replied.

'Leopards only live twelve to fifteen years,' Joe observed.

'So, this can't be the same leopard,' Hannah completed.

'Unless it's immortal,' Freddie added.

'But this could be its cub,' Selima said.

'Perhaps your father found the burial ground,' Freddie suggested.

'Perhaps it's near us now,' Hannah said.' Or even beneath us.'

'If he went out with climbing boots, rope and crampons, he was clearly going to either climb up or climb down,' Joe deduced.

'Exactly,' said Darius, 'and the mountains are too far away.'

'The intersection of Alexander's line is probably accurate to within two to three square miles,' Joe calculated. 'The only way we can find it is to scour the area systematically.'

'The trouble is that it's probably a concealed entrance. Captain Alexander would have covered it,' Ben conjectured.

'We could persuade some Bushmen to come with us and track the leopard on foot,' Ilana suggested.

'You're assuming the leopard will lead you to the burial ground,' Joe pointed out.

'You're also assuming, that you will persuade Bushmen to come with you,' Ben pointed out.

'It seems from his accounts that they abandoned Captain Alexander, just as they abandoned my father,' Darius said.

'There is one person who might be able to persuade them,' Hannah suggested. Ubuntu sprang into all their minds.

'I'm afraid we have another issue to contend with,' Li interjected.

He pulled a thin, black Geiger counter from his belt. Its LCD screen was glowing.

'Radiation.'

14

Preparing the Expedition

Basarwa wanted to fold himself into nothing. He was a humble gardener and he was sitting in Jacob Ubuntu's study. This was the chamber of a great man, a famous Namibian and Headmaster. He had barely been in the room since Ubuntu originally offered him the job.

'Have I done something wrong, Headmaster?' Basarwa asked with characteristic humility.

'Absolutely not. Your work is immaculate, as it always has been. Our gardens are our pride and joy.'

Basarwa felt a glow inside. He allowed his presence in the room to expand a little.

'I know you are a member of that noble tribe, the San,' Ubuntu said respectfully.

'I am, sir, yes.'

'And correct me if I'm wrong, but I sense that you have adapted well to life in Windhoek. Whereas, many San have found city life hard, unnatural.'

Basarwa felt understood and raised his eyes to meet Ubuntu's, with a smile.

'I work with Nature, Headmaster. That keeps me calm, connected to the soil.'

To others 'connected' may have sounded a strange term but to Ubuntu it made perfect sense and he nodded emphatically.

'The San have been treated disgracefully. Not just here, but, all over southern Africa. Black farmers and white farmers alike have carved up the land, displacing your people who were there first, who had roamed it as their own.'

'That is true. I heard that in India, they have a tribe called the "Untouchables",' Basarwa said solemnly. 'I think we are the "Untouchables" of Africa.'

'Ah yes, the dreadful caste system,' Ubuntu said. 'As bad as apartheid in its way.'

Ubuntu pushed his chair back from his desk and walked over to one of his two looming bookshelves, towers of knowledge and the backbone of his study. He ran his fingers along the book spines, until he found the volume for which he was searching.

'You see this book?' Ubuntu asked. 'In fact, all of the books on this shelf?'

Basarwa nodded, his eyes scanning the volumes.

'These books are the studies of how language evolved. You speak one of the clicking languages, don't you?'

'Yes. In fact, I find it difficult to speak English without clicks. It feels as if something is missing,' Basarwa admitted.

'As indeed it is, because linguists now believe that clicking languages are the world's most complex and expressive. Put simply, you play with a bigger orchestra, Basarwa!'

Basarwa laughed.

'To be precise, a bigger percussion. Of the world's twenty language groups, four are different and all of them African. The San or Khoisan languages are one group of them.'

'Has it served us well to be different?' Basarwa asked, searching himself for the answer.

'Good question. Probably not,' Ubuntu replied honestly. 'The point is that human language started with your ancestors and finds its richest expression in your very throat and tongue.'

'I am not a man of words.'

Ubuntu found himself profoundly moved by Basarwa's modesty.

'The point I am making is that you come from a tribe that should never have become an underclass, that is misunderstood and denigrated too often.'

'Now, they come from outside Africa to make films about us,' Basarwa observed.

'Yes, that's true. You have become a "cause celebre". Filmmakers and anthropologists have been queueing up to make you the new "noble savages". You are the hunter-gatherers in touch with the life most of humanity has left behind. You are pure and untainted.'

'It's a joke,' Basarwa responded. 'Our ancient ways have almost gone. My mother and father were forced into the city. He became an alcoholic and beat us. Where is the film about that?'

'I agree with you totally.'

Ubuntu walked back from the bookcase to take a chair opposite Basarwa.

'Basarwa, I want to ask you to help me in the true, the noble tradition of the San.'

'You know I would do anything for you, Headmaster. You saved me from the streets.'

'I need you, and perhaps one of your brothers, to help me track an animal,' Ubuntu said, looking directly into Basarwa's almond-shaped eyes and enjoying their keenness.

Basarwa paused before responding.

'It's a while since I tracked in the bush,' he replied.

'Yes, but these skills are deeply embedded. You can conjure them in a moment I'm sure. You just need the landscape to awake them.'

Basarwa got up from his chair, feeling Ubuntu uncomfortably close and wishing to back away, retreat from his intensity.

'What kind of animal are talking about?'

'A rare one. Possibly unique.'

'And that is…?'

'A Golden Leopard!'

Basarwa froze inside but tried to maintain some composure.

'There is no such creature,' he said emphatically.

'There is.'

'You've seen it?'

'I haven't but friends whom I trust, have. So have three of our pupils.'

'Where?'

'On a farm north-east of Ui Ais.'

'When?'

'Last week. They were tracking it in a jeep, but it escaped into the bush.'

'You have to track an animal like that on foot.'

'Precisely!'

'Clearly there is something important in finding this animal. Not to kill it as a trophy I hope.'

Ubuntu stood up, indignant.

'Would I ask you to do anything so crass?'

Basarwa moved over to Ubuntu and put his hand on his arm.

'I didn't mean to offend you, Headmaster, I'm sorry.'

Ubuntu turned full on to Basarwa and, grasping both of his forearms in his hands, stared deeply into his countryman's eyes.

'I am not going to lie to you. They believe, rightly or wrongly, that this leopard will lead them to a burial chamber. A burial chamber that a Victorian explorer unearthed and which he believed would unlock the secret of the Fairy Circles.'

There it was, said. A paragraph and it was done.

What Ubuntu had practised many times in his head in the last few days, had been released into the ears of its receiver and was settling like magic dust in the depths of his brain.

For a minute or more, they stood, arms interlocked, like a statue of Ancient clasping Modern Africa.

Ubuntu released Basarwa's arms and turned away, felling his cause to be hopeless and worried that he was bullying.

'Have you asked any other San?'

'No, and I shouldn't have asked you.'

Seeing Basarwa trembling in tension between his duty and his fears made him feel ashamed.

'I trust you and I'll do it,' Basarwa announced, much to Ubuntu's surprise. 'But I want to ask a reward.'

'Name it!'

'I would like a sponsored place to be offered every year at the Augustineum for a San child.'

'Nothing could give me greater pleasure. And if I needed further proof that you are the perfect guide, you have just provided it.'

'We don't know what we are going to encounter and so we need to allow for anything and everything,' Darius suggested.

'Sounds like my average working day,' Li chimed.

The four families had gathered at the Wilde's house to plan their expedition.

Various maps had been spread, stained with the snack-smeared hands of those poring over them.

'Can everyone please be careful with the maps,' Anne barked. 'They're getting oily. You need to make sure your hands are clean.'

Tabs were ripped on beer cans and soft drinks; wine was poured with a glug like a stream. Ralph was so excited that he was offering to make cocktails, to everyone's amusement.

'Ralph, darling, this isn't an Embassy party!' Anne admonished.

'No, thank God,' he replied. 'It's far more interesting!'

Selima, Joe, Freddie and Hannah were drawing route maps on random pieces of paper. Clara was putting the final touches to her painting of the burial chamber as she imagined it. It was an interesting hybrid between a Pharaoh's tomb, a beehive, and a large toy store. She trundled it round to all the parents, at various stages of its artistic evolution, picking up praise, suggestions and a large number of toffees.

The parents assembled around the dining-table to agree the practicalities.

'Let's start with the logistics,' said the ever-practical Li.

'Ubuntu has talked to the San guides who say we must track on foot,' Ben confirmed.

The teenagers of the Apocalypse were in their own huddle but eavesdropping.

'You know who the San guide is don't you?' Hannah asked.

'No,' the others chimed.

'Basarwa, the gardener from school. Apparently, he used to be the most skilled tracker in Namibia.'

'I always said there was something special about him,' Joe bragged.

'Oh yeah, right,' Selima jibed.

'I can't believe he's guiding us,' Freddie said. 'Don't you remember that warning he gave us, when you tripped over him at the beginning of term.'

Ben piped up.

'Listen everyone, we'll have to drive to the outskirts of the farm and pitch camp overnight, followed by an early start.'

'Yay! I love tents,' Clara called out without even looking up from her model.

'Listen, Clara, you're going to have to behave,' Anne warned her. 'No wandering off, you hear?'

'When do I ever disobey you?' Clara said, cheekily raking up her own indignation.

'How long have you got?' Ralph responded.

'We'll need five tents,' Darius calculated.

'The San will bring their own,' Ben reminded him.

'We still need five,' Li pointed out. 'One for all the equipment.'

'We'll need to start early again. Five thirty at the latest,' Darius said.

'Because leopards are very muscular,' Clara said proudly.

'Crepuscular,' Freddie corrected.

'Food?' Ralph asked, as he busied himself, topping up drinks.

'Sorted,' Barbara replied. 'I'm organising the groceries, but everyone needs to help with the cooking.'

'The four of us want to make the meal,' Hannah offered.

'Five,' Clara corrected.

'Great,' Barbara said. 'I'll believe it when I taste it!'

'You won't, Mum, that's the whole point,' Joe protested. We're talking gourmet here.'

It warmed her heart to see him so animated by friends.

'Li, what about the radiation?' Ben asked.

'I've managed to get radiation suits from work. Standard issue for uranium mines. I'll also bring more sensitive Geiger counters. We need to keep measuring.'

'I have ropes,' Darius said. 'Plus, two rope ladders and a winch for lowering equipment…or people if necessary. If the entrance is deep, we'll need them.'

'The children aren't going anywhere deep,' Anne said. 'I'll bring a full medical kit but I'm not packing splints and Plaster of Paris for broken limbs.'

'Now you mention it, don't you think it might be wise?' Ilana asked.

'Ok fine,' Anne said, resigning herself to the group neurosis that had now gripped them.

'Mum, is there a cure for Golden Leopard fever?' Freddie asked, reading her thoughts.

'If there were, Freddie, I would have administered the antidote by now, believe me,' Anne responded with a loving smile.

'Who wants to stop this madness?' Selima asked, intoxicated by the whole adventure. 'If it's a fever, bring it on!'

'Let's hope for a Secretary Bird!' Ilana said, in between gulps of wine.

'Why?' Joe asked.

'So that someone can take notes,' Freddie offered.

'It's a tradition that they bring you luck,' she answered.

'I'd rather have a more beautiful bird,' Clara protested, 'like a peacock.'

'Safety is beauty, Clara,' Li said. 'Especially when you're a parent.'

'Yes, safety is also dull,' Joe remarked.

Barbara, who had remained noticeably quiet, and who had consumed rather too much wine, waiting for a click of peace to be switched on in her head, tapped her, rapidly-emptying, wine glass with a knife, calling them to order. Her voice was throaty and somewhat slurred...

'I hope it's not out of order for me to say something at this point.'

'Mum, you're drunk,' Joe interrupted, fearing for her dignity and a little bit for his own.

Ben signalled for him to be quiet.

'Whilst the four or so months since we arrived in Namibia have been...' she fumbled for the words which Ben supplied.

'Stimulating?'

'Stimulating, thank you Ben. They have also been professionally challenging, to put it mildly.'

'What does that mean?' Clara asked.

'It means, my dear Clara, that my first hotel site yielded a Victorian explorer, a lot of controversy, but... no hotel.'

'Including an encounter with a vicious Namibian guide!' laughed Ilana.

'Exactly,' Barbara said, 'I couldn't have put it better myself. My second hotel site is a farm flooded with radiation and a rare leopard that doubtless will have to be protected, thus preventing building work. Apart from that, everything's perfect!'

Being able to view the last few months through the lens of

Barbara's disaster-prone, professional life triggered hysterical laughter around the room. She continued…

'But whilst my professional life has basically gone up in smoke, my personal life has rarely looked better. My husband is experiencing a fever-pitch level of excitement in hunting down a burial chamber… nothing entirely new in that, but lovely to behold. More importantly, I have rarely seen my youngest son so happy and with such good friends. And, finally…'

'Mum, enough!'

'No, Joseph!' Barbara always used the longer version of her son's name when she wanted to control him. 'Finally, I would just like to say how glad I am that I have found, in an obscure corner of Africa whose name I couldn't even spell a year ago, I have found friends – true friends – from around the world.'

'Hear, hear!' said Ralph, 'I'll drink to that.'

'You'll drink to anything at the moment!' said Anne, plucking a wine bottle out of his hand.

'Whilst we are on the subject of friendship,' Li started.

'Oh no, a chain-reaction!' Hannah muttered, fearing her father would cry, as he sometimes did after drinking whisky and turning red.

'I, er, want to thank you all for the amazing support you gave me during the genocide crisis,' Li declared. 'Especially after my deputy's …. suicide.'

'Li, not in front of…' Sarah said, gripping his arm.

'We're not children anymore, Mum,' Hannah said.

'I am,' Clara piped up.

'Anyway,' Li continued, 'although like Barbara, my career has seen better days, I am very grateful to all of you that I was not destroyed by shame. And seeing Hannah buried in friends rather than books, is a joy, much as I admire books.'

Hannah blushed.

'Dad!'

Sarah looked at Selima and Hannah holding hands and felt both joy and a deep sense of loss.

'Can I say something totally unconnected to this mutual admiration society please?' Joe enquired.

'Of course, you can Joe, 'Ben said.

'Can we get dessert now?'

15
The Discovery

Hannah awoke in the tent feeling unusually warm. Then she realised why. In the middle of the night, when she'd heard a pack of wild dogs howling and yelping under the full moon, she had hopped into Selima's bed and wrapped around her for comfort. Selima had reached out sleepily and held Hannah's hand to indicate that she was happy to be invaded, indeed understood her need for comfort.

It felt wonderful to be close to her, mingling warmth, intertwined; two tiny creatures under the vast African sky. She wondered how someone who had been thousands of miles and a cultural world away a few months ago, could now be her soulmate.

It made her think how many 'Selima's' and 'Freddie's' and 'Joe's' there must be in the world: people she could be close to in the right circumstances. We only scratch the surface of human intimacy in a lifetime. It was a thought that warmed the world and promised to send her back to sleep again.

However, she could already see through the tent walls the faintest glimmering of dawn and rolled on to her back. Then the soundscapes of dawn overwhelmed her. There were layers to it. In the 'foreground', there was twittering from all sides: the trebles of the dawn chorus: silly, nonsensical and constant. Threaded through them was an intermittent corkscrewing up and down: the chromatic scale of a practising bird. Piercing that occasionally was the percussive beat of wings: low-flying herons or egrets as they swooped low over the campsite.

The lapwing made its occasional single, tinkling note like a nervous child playing the triangle in a school band. There were also sounds like a boomerang being thrown and returning, whirring, back into its thrower's hands. The baritone grunts of a hippo in the river added an element of farce. Woven into this tapestry of sound, was warbling, cooing, the chirrup of insects and the soft padding and bracken-twitching of foraging kudu. All this on a single planet.

'What time is it?' Selima asked sleepily.

'Time for intrepid explorers to be stirring.'

'Stirring is what spoons do in coffee, not what I do in the morning.'

Hannah laughed.

'The sounds outside are extraordinary. To think they happen every day.'

'One day they might not,' Selima observed.

Hannah paused to take in the thought.

'In the city we wake up to mechanical sounds… even in Windhoek: cars, alarms, doors slamming, radios blasting. Out here it sounds like a different planet,' Hannah observed.

'No, it sounds like a planet, full stop,' Selima answered.

'It's like Eden.'

'Until you step outside.'

'Why have I spent so much of my life reading books?' Hannah asked herself, rolling on to her side to face Selima.

'Because books make sense of life. If I could read as fast and fluently as you, I'd devour them as well.'

'You're right. I take for granted that I can read quickly. Has my mum been good? With the dyslexia…'

'No. Better than good. She's been amazing. So patient…' Selima said.

'Glad she is with someone!'

A flock of birds unzipped the sky above them.

'Do you like Joe?' Hannah asked.

'What do you mean? Of course, I like Joe.'

'No, I mean do you like him…in that way?'

'He fascinates me. We're very different. Remember how aggressive he used to be? We're lock and key if you know what I mean.'

'I know exactly what you mean. That's what I feel about Freddie,' Hannah said, unable to resist smiling.

Joe had been awake since five o'clock. His mind was racing. He often wished he had another kind of mind. A mind more like Freddie's that took time, played with ideas, rolled them over and tested their texture. Joe's mind was always chasing answers like a wolf hustling sheep. It exhausted him.

Freddie awoke to see Joe already sketching in his notepad, his face aglow with the reflection of his head-torch. He had come to admire, even love, Joe's intensity, draining though it could sometimes be.

'How long have you been awake?' Freddie probed.

Joe checked his watch.

'Eighty-three minutes. Look, I'm sorry to bombard you as soon as you wake up, but I need to test this idea on you.'

'Shoot,' Freddie said, despite doubting whether he was compos mentis enough to focus on one of Joe's challenges.

'So, the computer analysis shows that there are twenty-eight different types of fairy circle. You suggested it might be an alphabet. But whose alphabet and why?'

'No idea,' Freddie said, trying to bury himself deeper into his sleeping-bag and stay out of the chill morning air. He felt like a larva that doesn't want to hatch. 'Ancestors? Tribes? Aliens?' he suggested,

'Aliens?' Joe said incredulously.

'Well, not all those UFO sightings can be fakes, can they? Haven't you ever had that feeling we're being watched? Or gazed into the sky and seen something that can't be a plane or a satellite, but then dismissed it? Statistically there must be other life in the Universe mustn't there?'

'Quite possibly. And look at Oumuamua?' Joe replied.

'What's that when it's at home?' Freddie exclaimed.

'Apparently, it means "distant messenger from the past" in Hawaiian,' Joe explained. 'It's the name they've given to this cigar-shaped object astronomers have spotted close to the sun. They think it might be an alien probe.'

'Why?' Freddie quizzed

'Because it's been seen to accelerate. Which suggests it has its own power, it's not just being pulled by gravitation. They think, from the way it reflects light, it might have a very thin sail.'

'So, a real space- ship,' Freddie observed, thinking of the words literally. 'We've sent two Voyagers out there with music and greetings in fifty-nine languages, and images, to communicate. Why wouldn't others do the same and seek us out?'

'So, here's my line of thinking,' said Joe. 'What is the best way to communicate to another race? Images of course.

Hannah was right, it's pictures and symbols that are universal.'

'We don't know that. How do we know if other races even have eyes? Or any of our senses?' Freddie pleaded.

'Ok, just bear with me. Do you know Seurat?' Joe asked

'The painter?'

'Exactly. You know the style he became famous for?'

'Dots. Hundreds of them.'

'Yes, he used hundreds of dots of paint to make up a picture. Like pixilation in a modern TV or computer. In fact, he effectively invented the TV before Baird. So, supposing you were to take satellite photos of the fairy circles and you pull back, reduce the scale until each circle becomes a dot…. would those dots form a picture?'

'You mean the Fairy Circles are a giant picture message?' Freddie asked.

'I sense you're not convinced,' said Joe beginning to sound frustrated: either because his friend was not logical, or because he was too logical. He couldn't work out which.

'Like a lot of the things you say, Joe, I'm bowled over by how clever it is. But, first of all, wouldn't it take the most monumental computing power to convert the hundreds of thousands of fairy circles into dots? Secondly, what kind of message is so important that you'd burn it on to the face of a planet?'

'Now that,' Joe said, 'is the most exciting question I have ever heard.'

Darius, Sarah, Barbara and Ilana, had prepared breakfast for everyone: fruit, bread, cereal and eggs.

Basarwa had already showered, eaten his own porridge,

and was busy checking torches and sharpening his bowie knife.

The other bushman 'Ace' - named in affection after his prowess as a guide - was preparing his Maasai-style belt of tools.

Hannah, Selima, Freddie and Joe appeared from their tents.

'You lot look bleary-eyed,' Darius said.

'My mind woke me up early as usual,' Joe said.

'Joe's mind then woke me up early as usual,' Freddie added.

'I've been awake for hours because of the dawn chorus,' said Hannah. 'Why are the birds so noisy at sunrise?'

Ace stopped cleaning his binoculars to answer.

'You need to think of the bush as a twenty-four-hour survival course. Different animals are stressed at different times,' he said. 'Many predators– the cats, hunting dogs, hyenas, for example – are most active at night when it's cool and they are less visible. Birds are therefore most in danger at night. Come the dawn, they celebrate being safe by singing.'

'As we all should,' Ilana pointed out.

'We should,' said Ace. 'However, as the birds relax, so others get stressed. The insects hide at dawn because the birds can now see them. The fish swim deeper in the river to avoid being caught by the birds. At dawn, the leopard and the wild dogs are active, and so the kudu and eland and baby elephants are stressed. And, so it goes on.'

'If you look at elephants when they are under stress, you will see a dark mark below their ears. But most anxiety runs under the skin…as with humans,' Basarwa added.

'I'll never look at the bush in the same way again,' Freddie said.

'We are at the top of the food chain. Think how stressed you would feel if you were in the middle!' Ace pointed out.

After breakfast, they were ready to set off from the camp.

Ace and Basarwa gave them all a safety briefing. They both spoke softly but firmly.

'Tracking on foot can be dangerous,' Basarwa said.

Clara clung closer to Anne.

'Are you sure Clara's all-right to come?' Basarwa asked.

'She's braver than all of us,' Anne replied, hoping this would bolster her youngest child, which it did.

'We walk in single file because if we encounter a dangerous animal, it will see one or two of us at most, not a whole pack of us,' Basarwa continued. 'Seeing all of us at once would throw the animal into a panic, making it more likely to attack. So, we trick them into thinking we're singular.'

Ace took up the theme.

'I will go in front and Basarwa at the back. Because they are alert to our voices, we must keep talking to a minimum. Cats can rotate their ears one hundred and eighty degrees, remember that. Instead, we will use signs.'

The five immediately thought of Namib, their own secret language, which included signing.

'If I put my hand up like this...'

He signalled like the Pope giving a blessing with one hand.

'It means we must stop and observe whether there is any danger. If I make a fist...'

His arm shot up like a black rights activist, fist pumping.

'It means we have a dangerous animal close. In which case you must freeze. Is that clear?'

The nods were solemn.

'What if our instinct is to run?' Joe asked, voicing the turmoil churning in all of them.

'Everyone's instinct is to run,' Basarwa answered. 'However, it is exactly what you must not do. If you run from a lion or leopard, even an elephant that's threatening to charge, they are likely to chase and kill you. Whatever you are feeling inside, you stand your ground, stare them in the eyes and slowly retreat…'

'And hope they've just had a good meal,' Freddie added.

Laughter punctuated their fear.

'Are you carrying guns?' Li asked.

'No!' Ace's answer was quiet but defiant. 'The best protection we have against animals is respect for them. Knowledge and a calm head also help. We have a sound-blaster and knives if we really need them.'

The adventure in their heads was rapidly being re-shaped into a harsher reality: the reality of being the hunted, not just the hunter. The fear of being prey seeped into their reptilian brains and nervous systems and took hold.

Joe pondered whether 'being prey' and 'to pray' were similar for a reason.

'Remember,' Ace said, 'that even a lion can be confronted. Everything runs from the lion. So, if you don't run, it will force the lion to re-think. "What is this creature that doesn't run from me? Perhaps I need to run from it!". It's like all courage: it's the resolve not to fear that saves us.'

Barbara found herself somewhat in awe of her guide. Ace was tall, well over 6 foot, and more like a Maasai than his fellow countrymen. He stood totally upright without it appearing military or forced. His face was bony and handsome, edged with a carefully trimmed beard. Whilst the bush was clearly his domain, his manner had a sophistication wholly lacking in Basarwa. For all their alpha male posturing, no other man she knew had this certainty, this core 'maleness' that didn't need to protest too much.

After a few more nervy questions, they set off single file, each with binoculars, a rucksack, water bottles and a determination not to fear.

Li carried a giant rucksack for the 'radiation suits.' Darius had rope ladders, rope, pegs and crampons in canvas bags over his shoulders. Thank God, he'd inherited his father's strong back. He and Ace carried the winch between them. Anne carried the medical kits in a bag slung diagonally across her chest.

After twenty minutes or so, they stopped by some animal tracks. Ace and Basarwa knelt to examine, Ben hovering behind them.

'A leopard has passed here recently, heading North,' Ace concluded.

'How can you tell it's recent?' Joe asked, fascinated by their skill.

'The outline of the tracks is still sharp,' Ace responded, happy to be asked. 'The wind hasn't loosened or disturbed them. If they were covered by insect tracks, we'd know they'd been made last night because, as I explained, insects are active at night.'

Joe loved the detail of their logic.

'We need to be quiet now,' Basarwa counselled.

Clara put her finger to her lips and started to giggle, largely from nerves. Freddie took her hand and frowned to control her.

There was a rustling ahead. Ace signalled to halt. Through her binoculars, Selima caught a glimpse of the leopard. She passed on the agreed, tapping signal from shoulder to shoulder, to the front of the line where Ace acknowledged her. He then checked in his binoculars and signalled to move slowly ahead.

For several hundred, short-breathed, metres, they tracked the leopard through thickets, seeing his fur ripple then disappear, repeatedly. Every twig-snap wrenched their heads one way or the other. Fairly close by, they could see a herd of elephants, but they were grazing peacefully. At one point, a young bull raised his trunk high and curvy in the air, taking on the appearance of a giant, ungainly teapot.

'He can smell us,' Basarwa whispered.

The bracken and thickets thinned, and they found themselves in a large clearing. Trees in the distance shimmered, touched by the morning breeze. The only sound was the swish of the elephants cleaning the sand off roots in the water before eating them. It was strangely like the sound of washing-up and might have been comforting and domestic in other circumstances. As they entered the clearing, they froze.

'Now that is something I've never seen before,' Ace muttered.

The Golden Leopard was walking slowly and majestically, flanked on both sides by a cheetah. Such was their elegance, they could have been processing down the aisle of an ancient cathedral, rather than a scrubby bush-clearing dotted with dead branches. The bush often had the appearance of a recycling centre for Nature, in which discarded items were slowly re-purposed and nothing went to waste.

One of the cheetahs turned on hearing them. The early morning light flashed across its irises.

The three cats continued, on their steady path, rising up a gentle hill to its brow. The Golden Leopard then turned and gazed intently at them, as if searching each individual face for its readiness, before proceeding on its way. It seemed to almost be handing over a baton of responsibility. This was a feeling they all had, but they didn't articulate it until months later, for fear of sounding foolish.

The three cats disappeared slowly as they descended the far-side of the hill, their muscular shoulders flexing, lowering and glowing in the sun.

They followed cautiously at first, Ace and Basarwa leading, and Darius offering to take the rear to help the trackers. Ahead of them rang the 'alarm-calls' of birds, spreading like beacons. They were triggered by the three advancing cats. The sound rose to a cacophony as they approached the brow of the hill.

They were so absorbed they broke the single file code, walking forward together, like a platoon entering a battle. The young ones interlocked arms. They were so engrossed that only Basarwa checked what was behind them. He learned to do it obsessively, like a driver checking his wing-mirrors.

Ace signalled to stop. He took his binoculars and scanned the trees. Basarwa and Darius did the same. He found the leopard and two cheetahs on the low-lying branches of an acacia tree. Their postures were relaxed if attentive. Ace sensed he could trust them, for now anyway.

'Move forward slowly,' he counselled. They walked in step, examining the ground in front of them carefully. Li checked the Geiger counters. The readings had suddenly shot up, edging the red.

'Radiation is very high here. We could be close to something,' he messaged.

They felt like a police force scouring for murder clues on some barren, murder-cursed heath.

Ralph's left foot suddenly disappeared beneath him, throwing him off balance. Li and Darius grabbed him as he fell and hauled him back up.

'Stop!' Basarwa called. 'Move back a couple of feet.'

They shuffled back like soldiers adjusting their positions in a parade.

The two Bushmen used their long walking-staffs to test the ground ahead. One punctured the undergrowth and threatened to disappear, like a punt pole plummeting in deep water.

'There is a concealed entrance here,' Ace said. He, Darius, Ben and Basarwa spread out, constantly prodding, testing the ground. They traced the perimeters of a covering with sticks and staffs whilst the others held back and watched. Soon they'd traced and marked its edges. It measured roughly four metres by three.

'We need to find a way to cut and lift the covering,' Darius announced. 'Can everyone gather some fallen branches – strong ones. We need them as levers.'

'No-one stray too far, please,' Basarwa instructed. 'And don't go anywhere near the edges we've marked. We don't know how deep it is beneath that covering.'

Because the elephants had stripped them, many trees had died in the vicinity and broken branches were plentiful. They slotted the biggest branches systematically under three sides of the covering's perimeter, their bases disappearing into the ground, as they penetrated the space beneath the covering. They were careful to keep the angle of the branches shallow to stop them falling in. Then they spaced themselves evenly along the three sides, each taking a branch as a lever. Freddie and Clara did theirs together.

'We'll use the fourth side as a hinge,' Ace instructed. 'On the count of three, lever the branches upwards but be careful to lean backwards. Otherwise, you might tumble in.'

'One, two, three!'

Plants were uprooted, roots stretched and snatched, grasses tore. They manage to lift the covering by almost a foot. It was clearly man-made not just a progressive build-up of fallen trees. Branches had been woven into a lattice and then bound with ropes, many of them now rotting. It had the thorough design of something military.

'Hold it there if you can!' Basarwa instructed. 'Here hold mine,' he said to Darius. Then he scampered round the perimeter, using all the skills he had honed in the Augustineum gardens, to cut stubborn roots and plants with his Bowie knife and a small machete. It was like releasing the guy ropes on a hot air balloon. The matted covering lifted higher as he cut his way round the edges.

The men ran to the longer, front side to maximise leverage and to lift the covering like a giant trap door, pushing it back on its 'hinge'.

'Let's get it upright to ninety degrees and then push it over on to its back if we can,' Li suggested.

They managed, despite its stubborn weight, to get it vertical so that a dark well appeared underneath it, seemingly sucking in its first sunshine and air for years like a rasping throat. The fourth side - acting as the 'hinge' - started to tear under the strain.

'Wait, wait!' screamed Darius. 'It's going to fall into the shaft and block it completely if we're not careful. Just let it lower a little for now.'

He ran to his canvas bags and pulled out ropes, pegs and rings.

Then he and Ralph pegged rings on to the top edges of the 'lid' and tied ropes to them.

'It looks like a giant spider's nest opening,' Joe observed.

'Let's hope there's no funnel-web that big!' Freddie added.

'I knew my father's knot-training would serve me well one day,' Ralph said. He felt exhilarated by the challenge. At this moment he silently vowed he would never return to a desk.

Four of them pulled on the ropes. It looked like a tug of war with the landscape.

The weight of the covering was immense, and the hinge started to tear, threatening to give way completely. Straining every sinew and digging their feet ever deeper and steeper into the ground, they managed to pull the covering backwards and away from the well down which it threatened to plunge. It fell on its back with a huge cloud of dust and soil, leaving them spluttering.

They all instinctively shrunk back from the well that had been revealed. It gaped like a soil throat.

'Don't go too close to the edge please,' Anne called out.

Ace, Darius and Basarwa tiptoed as close as they dare, testing the ground in front of them for firmness. Selima bellowed into the pit to hear if there was an echo. Instead the well swallowed her cry. Her voice was stolen underground.

Darius and Ace threw in stones and listened.

'No splash,' Li said. 'It's a dry pit. Above the watershed.'

A beeping sound rang out insistently from his belt. He removed a vibrating Geiger counter and looked again at the readings.

'We're going to need the radiation suits. Whatever's down there is emitting strongly. We can't take any chances.'

Li unpacked the radiation suits and they all donned them. Thirteen figures stood in snow-white suits. It was suddenly as if a nuclear laboratory had opened in the middle of the bush.

'Keep the headgear on, but unzip the top of the suit, to the waist. Otherwise, you're going to boil as the sun gets higher,' Li advised.

They shone the most powerful torches down into the shaft. Heavier stones were thrown in to judge depth and the well flooring.

'You hear that?' Ben asked. 'It's rock at the bottom not soil. I suspect it's a cave.'

After 15 minutes, Darius had firmly staked a rope ladder to the ground, rolling on a few boulders to secure it further. He threw its unfurling length down the side of the shaft. He was adamant that he should descend first. He zipped his radiation suit up to his neck, donned the white hood and sealed it around his neck and shoulder. He pulled on a safety harness and switched on his head torch.

Ilana felt panicky but knew she had to hide it for Selima's sake.

Ace and Basarwa attached climbing ropes with clips to his harness and he slowly descended the ladder, facing the wall of the shaft.

'Darius, wait!' Freddie called. 'There's a Secretary Bird. We're all going to be safe.'

Sure enough, there it was, its upper half like a bird of prey but its lower half comical: black pantaloons on the upper half of its legs and white sticks underneath. The upper legs and body leaned forward but the lower legs leaned backwards, creating a curious right-angle and a comical walk. Suddenly it took flight and then swooped low, picking up a sidewinder adder in its talons and carrying it like a dangling question-mark in mid-air.

Darius smiled at his lucky talisman and disappeared beneath the surface.

'Darius? Darius?'

Ten minutes had elapsed since Darius was presumed to have reached the bottom. There was no reply to their shouts down the shaft. The rope ladder was dangling loose, as was the rope attached to his harness, so they knew he'd either fallen or stepped off it.

'I'm going down,' Ilana said, unable to take the uncertainty any longer. Hannah was hugging Selima who was stiff with fear for her father.

'No, let me go,' Li said. 'I've spent half my working life underground.'

Li strapped on a harness, was attached to the rope and descended carefully. As he got lower, he could see the faint glimmer of a light beneath him: Darius's head torch he presumed. There was a curious noise. It was indeterminate, like an elusive butterfly of faint sounds.

He stepped off the ladder, worried by the absence of movement or a voice. He found Darius curled in a foetal position, sobbing uncontrollably. It had been barely audible through his head-mask until Li got close to him. He cupped his hands over

Darius's to comfort him and shuddered at their touch. They were clammy and cold.

'Darius, what's happened?'

He turned his head-torch slightly to the right and then he knew.

Lying next to Darius was an outstretched and badly contorted skeleton. In its sunken pelvis lay a rusted torch, a knife and the rotting remnants of a belt.

'Darius?'

'It's my father,' he sobbed. 'I recognise his belt and knife. He must have fallen down the shaft. He always was clumsy. A clumsy, rough, bloody farmer.' He wept uncontrollably. Telling Li had crystallised his pain.

Li embraced Darius, trying to hug away the pain. The ability to heal with touch was severely hampered by the radiation suits, but both the love and the comfort it provided were palpable enough.

'Li?' came a shout from above.

'He's all-right. He's found his father's body.'

On the surface, Ilana and Selima cried twice, once with relief and once with sadness for Darius's wretched discovery.

It took an hour for four of them to set up a winch system on the surface, secured by several taut guy ropes. This meant the others could effectively abseil down the sides of the shaft whilst being lowered by the winch. It felt, and was, much safer.

Ace agreed to stay on the surface, watch for animals and winch people and equipment up and down as needed.

'Underground isn't for me,' he said. 'This is my domain,' he added signalling across the open land.

Ben and Basarwa were the last to descend. Before they did, Ben set up an emergency transmitter to signal their position back to his department at the University. He had briefed his Deputy on the risky and peculiar nature of their mission. It felt like an umbilical cord to safety. Ace and Basarwa were just as in awe of the thoroughness and sophistication of Ben's procedures and equipment as he was of their tracking skills.

The bottom of the shaft opened out on to a giant catacomb. Once they were all down, they banged pegs into the rock and hung lanterns on the walls to light their path as they moved forward.

'Thank God, it isn't raining,' Darius said. 'This place would flood in a few hours.'

'The covering over the entrance would slow it considerably of course, were it still in place,' Li observed.

'Probably why it was put there,' Darius suggested.

'You think so?' quizzed Ben. 'I doubt that. It would have taken several men and some basic engineering knowledge to construct. It was only put there for one reason, in my view: to stop this being discovered.'

'Captain Alexander?' Joe asked.

'Seems very likely,' Ben replied, 'given everything we know from his maps and journals.'

'Why would he want to hide it?' Hannah asked.

'I suspect we'll soon find out,' Ben replied.

'If we find anything at all,' Freddie said.' 'This place could have been ransacked.'

'I don't think so. I think there's only been one visitor in almost two hundred years,' Darius said wistfully, 'and that was my father.'

'Alexander may have intended to come back,' Selima said. 'Doesn't one of the journals imply that?'

'It does,' verified Ben. 'He may well have returned to take out whatever he discovered and then to cover the entrance. He would have had help…probably his regiment.'

'Can we go ahead?' Joe asked, impatient to explore deeper.

'Just be careful. Stay where we can see you please,' pleaded Barbara. Sarah and Anne echoed her pleas.

Joe and Selima took the lead. Hannah and Freddie walked just behind, with Clara sandwiched between them holding Freddie's hand.

They'd soon forgotten the instruction to stay in sight.

'What if there are more skeletons?' Clara asked.

'Skeletons won't harm you, Clara,' Selima said and then screamed as something cold touched her head.

Clara screamed in sympathy and the piercing sound echoed around the caves until it sounded like the wailing chorus from a Greek tragedy.

'It's just a stalactite, Selima,' Joe said, casting his head-torch upwards.

There was a sound of footsteps running closer.

Li and Darius appeared.

'What frightened you, Selima?' Darius asked.

'Her imagination!' Freddie replied.

'It was just a stalactite, Dad,' she reassured, 'but it felt like the touch of a dead man's hand.'

'I think we need to stay together! You've had a terrible shock seeing your grandfather's body. Perhaps you should go back up to the surface.'

'No way,' Selima protested.

They proceeded further, lighting and hanging lanterns at systematic intervals.

Basarwa, who had deliberately stayed back, walked towards them from the shaft entrance and shivered. In their white radiation suits they looked like ghosts patrolling the underworld.

There were a few small side caves, like the chapels for private prayer in a cathedral, each of which they explored, eager to find something. Each cave disappointed, its bare rock, almost mockingly, reflecting back the child-like probing of their multiple torches.

'Where's the buried treasure?' Clara asked in frustration.

'Who says there's treasure, pumpkin?' Freddie replied.

'There's always treasure in caves,' Clara replied indignantly.

Then, the claustrophobic rock corridor that had run the whole length from the entrance, opened out into a magnificent space. A meteor shower of stalactites descended from the high ceiling. Stalagmites rose from the floor at one end like a vast church organ designed by Gaudi. The floor undulated like a tongue.

'It's like a cathedral waiting for its worshippers,' Ralph said.

Ben placed two torches in the rocks, twenty feet apart, both shining up to the ceiling.

'Wow,' Clara said. 'This is better than the meteors.'

Selima and Joe both saw something glint in the distance beyond the vast space.

'Did you see something white over there or am I hallucinating?' Joe asked.

'Well, if you are, I'm sharing the same illusion,' she responded. 'Come on!'

They left the others, rapt in awe at the vast space, and walked rapidly ahead.

They could see something reflecting through a narrow opening. It looked like the end of a smooth, white lozenge. They squeezed through the opening by turning sideways. Their breathing slowed, their hearts, slipped out of rhythm.

As they entered the cave, their head torches illuminated it whole. There were twenty or more white caskets laid in niches carved into the cave walls. They were beautiful, flowing organic shapes but plain, unadorned and smooth. There were no handles or hinges as far as one could tell. They were all different lengths.

'Are they coffins?' Selima asked.

'Perhaps. Somehow, they look more like eggs. Like something that could give birth,' Joe said.

A minute of silently contemplating was broken by the anxious voices of Hannah and Freddie.

'Selima?'

'Joe? Where are you, Joe?'

'We're in a side cave,' Selima called out. 'Don't worry we're safe.'

'We've found something,' Joe added. 'Something extraordinary.'

The others tried to follow the breadcrumbs of their voices, but their sound location was poor.

'We can't find you,' Hannah called.

Joe had an idea.

'We'll switch our torches on and off. Look for the flashing lights.'

The blinking of lights soon took them in the right direction.

'You have to squeeze in sideways,' Selima explained.

'Wish I'd had less breakfast now,' Hannah exclaimed as the rock forced her belly inwards.

As they entered the cave, each one of them fell silent.

The chamber was big enough to fit all fourteen of them but Basarwa wouldn't enter.

'I will not disturb the ancestors,' he declared. 'We came with you as a favour to Ubuntu and to help. But I will not enter a tomb.'

'You have already entered a tomb: the tomb of my father,' Darius pointed out.

'I realise that of course,' Basarwa answered respectfully. 'I am truly sorry for your loss, but he is your ancestor and not mine.'

Ilana, dug Darius in the ribs, and whispered 'Respect his culture as he respects yours.'

'Of course, I am sorry, Basarwa. And thank you, for guiding us here. We could never have tracked the leopard without you. I wanted you to share in the find that's all.'

'That is kind, but I will stay here and light more of the main chamber,' Basarwa responded with his usual quiet dignity.

'I doubt very much that these are the tombs of his ancestors,' Li said, as he laid hands upon one of the caskets, feeling its texture and exploring its contours. 'I have never encountered a material like this. It appears to be extraordinarily advanced.'

He removed his hands from the casket and then touched it again with both index fingers, followed by his two palms which he laid on in the manner of a priest.

'It absorbs the heat from your hand, as if it were using it

as energy. Then it slowly cools.'

'What do we suppose is inside?' asked Ralph. 'Ben?'

Ben was already sketching the arrangement of the tomb, and scribbling notes in a pocket- book.

'No idea. This is like nothing I have encountered,' Ben replied. 'But the arrangement in niches, the symmetry, the chiselling of rock, would suggest a highly organised burial ritual. Also, the caskets are of different lengths. This suggests there may be children, not just adults buried here.'

Everyone absorbed his diagnosis, some with a shudder.

'What is baffling is that these materials can't be Victorian. Or even modern,' Li said. 'This kind of thermo-sensitivity has eluded us so far.'

'What is also odd is the lack of any kind of painting or decoration. For a tomb that is most unusual,' Ben observed.

'Who said there's no decoration?' Clara asked.

They all stared at her blankly.

She mimicked Ubuntu at Ui Ais.

'Where do people look when they seek inspiration?'

Almost as one, they raised their heads and eyes up and their torches with them. The floor and walls darkened, and the ceiling became a beacon.

The rock had been plastered over to form a large, smooth dome. Arranged around the dome were a series of four paintings like frescoes.

They appeared to be in a deliberate sequence. The first was a highly detailed astronomical chart. It was of a solar system. One of the orbiting planets was highlighted with rings like a halo.

Next to that, was what appeared to be an enlarged painting of the same planet. It had a greater proportion of blue than the oceans of the Earth. It lacked the reassuring contours of six continents. Instead, it looked as if the process of continental drift had been more extreme than when Gurdwara, Earth's original, single landmass, had broken apart. On this planet there appeared to be eight small continents, more dispersed than ours. They were yellow shading into reds and ochres. There was little or no green. The, 'polar icecaps', had thinned to virtually nothing.

'I've seen computer projections of how Earth will look if global warming melts the ice-caps,' Joe said. 'It looks very similar.'

'That is a dying planet,' Li said. 'There's no mistaking it.'

In the next painting, there were a multitude of biomes and domes in which tiny figures – single, emaciated downstrokes of paint - appeared to live. The skies behind the biomes were blazing with light on one side of the planet, whilst on the other side, bathed in darkness, giant telescopes scanned the skies.

The last of the paintings showed a fleet of spacecraft fleeing the surface of the planet like a swarm of locusts, tiny in the vastness of space.

It didn't need to be said but Ben said it anyway.

'My friends, we are looking at the evacuation of a planet. One not dissimilar, it seems, to our own.'

They lowered their lights as one, as an instinctive act of respect, and stood in total silence, drinking in the truth.

Thirteen people in a cave in south-western Africa, tried to contemplate the fate of millions. The emptiness of Namibia as it spread out above them, took on another dimension.

'A planet is fragile by its nature,' Li said eventually. 'We don't think about that enough. Here we are, perched at exactly the right distance from a Sun. Move any closer and we'd burn up, and any further away we would be extinguished like a candle. We are like a molecule in the vastness of space.'

'Stop it, Dad,' Hannah said. 'When I start to think like that, nothing seems worthwhile. What's the point?'

'The point is,' said Ilana 'that we have to fight the darkness. We have to make sense of being alive, of having a conscience.'

'So, this is how a civilisation ends,' Freddie said. 'Twenty-one caskets and four cave paintings.'

'All along, I had thought the answer was in patterns,' Joe ruminated. 'But it's all there in paintings.'

'Paintings are patterns,' Clara pointed out.

'Yes,' Joe answered, touched, and not a little taken aback, by the simplicity of her wisdom.

'So, Earth was their new home. But where are the others? The paintings showed millions of them,' Freddie asked.

'Perhaps, these are the only ones to survive.'

'Think of what happened to millions of native South Americans when the Europeans arrived,' Ralph pointed out. 'They were exposed to new kinds of disease and were wiped out in their millions. The chances are that when they were exposed to Earth's germs, they also died in their millions.'

'There must be more caskets,' Ben said. 'It looks as if there are hundreds of caves in here.'

'What happened to their spacecraft?' Freddie asked.

'My guess is that they are in the craters south of here. The ones that fell along the path of Alexander's lines,' Ben answered.

'Why would Alexander want to hide his discovery?' Ralph questioned. Why not tell the whole world?'

'Think about the time he discovered this,' Ben said. '1838,

at the height of Victorian Christianity. Darwin wouldn't publish "The Origin of the Species" for another twenty-four years. In Christianity, Man is the unique creation of God. Yet, this challenges all of that…' He signalled to the caskets.

Joe had been puzzling something else.

'They must have been mathematically advanced. Otherwise, how could they have entered the atmosphere at the right trajectory not to burn up?'

'Remember Clara's meteorites?' Hannah asked, 'the ones that survived the atmosphere, on display in Windhoek… Perhaps they studied those.'

'Or arrived with them,' Freddie added, conjuring images of spacecraft and meteorites riding, side by side, like burning coals, through Earth's skin of air.

'Or it was trial and error,' Li suggested prosaically 'and only a few of them survived? Perhaps, millions burned up on entry, leaving no trace.'

'The question is what kind of creatures will we find in those caskets? Hannah asked. 'Could they even still be alive? They might be frozen in some way.'

'Let's not awaken them then,' Barbara suggested. 'Remember Frankenstein.'

'I hope they look like ET!' Clara said.

It was their first and only moment of laughter for hours.

'There's another reason not to open them,' Anne pointed out. 'We don't know what diseases it might expose us to.'

'Won't the radiation suits protect us?' Freddie asked.

'They won't even necessarily protect us from the radiation effects,' Li said. 'The readings could skyrocket if we open those caskets. How do we know?'

'I am happy to take the risk alone,' Ben declared. 'I don't want the younger ones to be exposed.'

'No, Dad!' Joe exclaimed. 'How can you put yourself at that kind of risk?'

'I have two heavy duty radiation suits back at the entrance,' Li announced. 'Why don't Ben and I put them on and try to open the caskets while the rest of you stay in the main cavern?'

The plan was agreed. Li and Ben emerged from the shaft opening like astronauts. The others waited for them in the 'cathedral cavern' as they had nicknamed it.

'Please be careful,' Sara said to Li.

He signalled thumbs up and they proceeded into the burial cavern.

Li and Ben looked for springs, catches, hidden compartments, buttons or levers. There were none. The caskets appeared to be hermetically sealed with no point of access.

'The only response has been to heat,' Li said through the helmet. 'I know it sounds mad, but let's lay our hands on a small area and see what happens.'

They removed their protective gloves and laid their bare, trembling hands at one edge of the casket. They felt it warming under their touch, as if from an unseen fire within.

'What if we get burned?' Ben questioned.

Li signalled to him to keep his hands in place. If Li hadn't been such a rational man, Ben would have taken his hands off. The heat grew more intense. They both started to sweat. Their hands were like coals. They stared intently at each other, each one mirroring the other's pain but willing the other to stay put. Just as the heat became intolerable, and they felt they would melt into the caskets like wax, a few cracks appeared. The fissures spread like ice cracking across a pond. They got deeper, wider, louder, faster until the whole outer layer shattered like an eggshell under a spoon and fell in fragments on the floor.

Underneath was another casket, made of, some kind of, metal. But this casket had latches.

After one hour, which seemed as if it were five, Li and Ben re-entered the cathedral cavern, helmets removed. Their faces were pale with shock.

'Why have you removed your helmets, Li?'

'Out of respect,' he replied.

'Have you managed to…?' Ralph asked.

They both nodded solemnly.

'We opened one large casket and then a small one,' Ben answered.

'And?' Hannah asked.

'You better come and look,' Li said.

'But be prepared,' Ben added.

'Should the children see it… then?' Anne asked.

Li looked at Ben who nodded.

'Yes,' Li said.

Clara clung to her mother as she used to when she was younger, face buried in her bosom, not wanting to look. There was silence. Then she felt Anne's chest heave. She was sobbing, quietly at first and then uncontrollably.

Clara hugged her tightly and then turned to look herself.

The figure was tall – perhaps seven foot – thin and gangly, but perfectly preserved by the casket. Its hands were long and bony and Clara, unsure if she was seeing things, counted six fingers.

Of one thing she was sure.

Inside the casket, was, to all intents and purposes, a human being. Its dimensions and features were different, but the essence was the same. It was like looking into one of those comic mirrors at a fair that distorts and elongates you.

Hannah, meanwhile, had gone to the small casket. Inside was a child not much older than her. The child was clasping something under her folded arms. Hannah lifted the stiff arms, and with Sarah's help, removed it.

It was a painting. It showed her parting, it seemed from her sister, leaving her behind on the dying planet. Hannah saw it and wept until her eyes had no more tears.

The wind blew gently through the palms making a sound like rain. It felt comforting.

Ralph, Li, Ben, Darius, Ilana and Selima carried the casket.

The owners had given permission for him to be buried on the perimeter of the farm he loved.

Inside the coffin lay the battered skeleton of Darius's father and his treasured possessions: those that had been found besides his body at the bottom of the shaft, and a few which Darius had always kept with him, but which he felt now belonged in the grave.

Selima laid her favourite necklace inside the coffin and a poem to the grandfather she had never met.

As they lowered the coffin, Ilana sang a traditional chant, her voice soaring to the trees. The landscape seemed to bow before the grave out of love for the man who had tended it.

Darius sang a Boer song his father had sung to him since the cradle. After scattering earth on the simple coffin, he felt strangely at peace, more than he had done for years. At least this was certainty.

The families decided to keep their find from anyone for a few days: until they were able to test Joe, Li and Ben's theory.

If hundreds and thousands had come to Earth, leaving their near-extinct planet, they must be buried somewhere.

The map of the patients with the radiation burns, when re-examined, showed that they lived close to a belt of the Fairy Circles.

A mechanical digger, commandeered by Li, dug deep underneath one of the Fairy Circles.

At a depth of ten metres beneath the sand and scrub lay a casket. They dug five more circles, a wide distance apart. The findings were the same.

The Fairy Circles were the graves of ancestors after all, as the San had always said. Just not the ancestors they had anticipated.

Clasped in the hands of each body was a globe. It glowed when touched. It appeared to be an 'Essence'. It emanated a circle of radiation, killing life above it and signalling death beneath it. Perhaps the Essence contained a record of that individual life were they ever able to decipher it; perhaps it was a transmitter for those who might follow them from the dying planet.

16

Exposure

By the time Ralph arrived at the Namibian Parliament, the police were struggling to hold back the throng of reporters. Many of them had camped all night, as was evidenced by the ragged tail of makeshift tents and smouldering campfires opposite the Parliament building.

As soon as Ralph's official car stopped, it was mobbed. A senior police officer radioed his driver, advising him not to leave the vehicle. Ralph felt far more claustrophobic with faces and cameras squashed against his window than he'd ever done in the caves. Nature was never as frightening as human beings en masse.

Ralph had spent many years dealing with the press. He knew when to drip-feed; when to trust an exclusive; when to do a live interview and when not. Yet nothing could prepare him for this.

Since the Namibian, Chinese, American and British, governments had jointly issued, a deliberately short, crisply factual Press Release to the news syndicates the day before, the four families had become famous around the world. Their solitary moment of touching another civilisation, deep beneath the Earth, had been ripped from their grasp, and processed into the 'sound-bites' of rolling 24-hour news.

Access to the burial cave and the Fairy Circles had been severely restricted. The Chief Scientist and Chief Medical Officer of the United Nations, plus their teams, had been granted access but no-one else.

The entrance to the burial site, had been covered by a hastily-constructed geosphere, to protect it both from contaminating and being contaminated.

Photographs had been released of a few of the caskets that were still intact. They also released pictures of the two caskets that had been opened but without their occupants.

They had coined the term 'extra-terrestrial humans' to describe the refugees from another galaxy. Out of respect, no photographs had yet been released of them. These were only to be shown after the medical and scientific teams had been given a chance to examine the bodies and come to some initial assessment. There was, a specially arranged, press conference organised for tomorrow.

Fairy Circles a hundred miles apart were being carefully dug up by scientists and medics and examined. Others, sadly, were being vandalised. As soon as the news broke, a flood of vehicles had entered the vast band of circles, determined to dig up the graves. They had calculated they could sell the first photographs of the corpses for a fortune.

The South African and Namibian Army had been drafted in to stop the looting and the President had made a national address on television pleading with people to respect the sanctity of the graves. He also warned that an emergency decree in Parliament had made it illegal and subject to arrest. Surveillance planes constantly patrolled the strip and army bases were set up at regular intervals.

The official digs, and those pirate digs that couldn't be stopped, both confirmed that this was indeed the burial ground for an entire civilisation, the remnant life of another planet.

Mainframe computers had been deployed to try to calculate how many Fairy Circles there were from satellite photos. This would then tell them how many extra-terrestrial humans had been buried on Earth.

A few of those they exhumed had been horribly burned, charred beyond recognition, presumably in their terrifying descent through the heat of our atmosphere. Their entrance to another mother planet in the hopes of a life-preserving embrace had killed them in their nerve-jangling moment of hope. Those who uncovered them, wept.

After several minutes, Ralph could see the blue Namibian sky again through his car windows: a sky he had already learned to love for its purity. He and his Head of Staff were able to pass through a corridor of policemen into the Parliament building.

He was ushered into the Prime Minister's private office. It was in a state somewhere between beehive and chaos. Doors opened at the back into two support offices and a constant flow of aides came and went: bright, young graduates with lanyards, folders and laptops, the cream of Namibia's future government. The Prime Minister was the calm at the centre of the maelstrom.

The Chinese, and American Ambassadors, and their teams, were already there and he shook their hands. They had spoken innumerable times over the last two days.

They sat around the Prime Minister's table. Sam Nashandi was there, doubtless eyeing the main chance that this global exposure might provide. He nodded as Ralph entered the room.

Nashandi had made sure he was sitting next to the P.M., with his private secretary conspicuously to hand as a power-play.

'Welcome, lady Ambassador and gentlemen Ambassadors,' the P.M. said. 'I apologise that you had to battle through the world's press to get in here. We find ourselves at the centre of the world's attention, which is unsurprising given what has been unearthed. I will start, if I may, by stating the obvious but for a reason. All of this has happened on, or underneath, Namibian soil. Although the Fairy Circles do extend into Angola and South Africa with whom we are, of course, collaborating. I would ask, therefore, that Namibia's rights are fully respected. We are a small country compared to your own.'

They all nodded respectfully.

'The sometimes-violent attempts to dig up the Fairy Circles is now largely under control, thanks to the Army. Hysteria though has predictably broken out amongst the world's press. It is our firm intention however, to give this moment the significance, but, more importantly, the dignity that it deserves. This is after all the discovery of another civilisation.'

Ralph coughed and raised his open palm.

'Ambassador Wilde, please...'

'If I may say in support, Prime Minister, that this is also a people that has, amidst their tragedy of not being able to survive on our Earth, made every effort to pass on their wisdom, their story, to us; in order that we may not suffer the same fate. This makes it especially poignant.'

'I agree,' the Prime Minister responded, 'and having been part of the group that uncovered the burial chamber, the full force of this must be haunting you, I imagine.'

Ralph smiled appreciatively at this perceptiveness and found himself wishing there were British politicians as empathetic.

'Tomorrow,' the P.M. continued 'we have the press conference. Firstly, let's discuss the venue. I have listened to all points of view on this and decided it would be wholly inappropriate to hold it here or in any of our official buildings. The world's interest is in the burial chamber and the Circles. So, despite all the logistical and security challenges, we will hold the press conference next to the biome protecting the chamber.'

The American Ambassador raised her hand.

'Madam Ambassador Klein…'

'Thank you, Prime Minister.'

Ambassador Klein was in her sixties and this was possibly her last posting. She wore her diplomacy with an elegance and surety that seemed effortless but had been learned over a lifetime.

'I think I can speak on behalf of the three of us and our respective Governments…'

She looked at Ralph and Gan Liu for agreement and found it in polite nods.

'Now that our Presidents and Prime Minister have received the UN reports, they recognise that, whilst there is much to be uncovered, there is no doubt that this is a race, remarkably like us, seemingly from another solar system. Originally, as you know, there was thought of our leaders flying in for the Press Conference. However, following your intervention and the heartfelt remarks of Headmaster Ubuntu, it has been agreed that this is not a moment for politicians, apart from yourself Prime Minister of course. The families, including your own Ambassador Wilde, should tell their story. Families from our four cultures speaking together, will create more unity than politicians ever can.'

'And,' Ralph added, 'the families would like our children to speak. They were the ones who were determined to unravel the mystery of the circles. We owe these discoveries to their persistence. They are also the generation that has to save this planet from dying in the same way.'

'Speaking of which, I need to counsel one thing,' Ambassador Klein intervened.

She shifted uneasily before putting on her official demeanour and voice.

'The President has made it very clear that he does not want this event to be turned into what he describes as "climate change propaganda." Indeed, he has said,' she coughed in embarrassment, 'that were the coverage to follow that path, he would be forced to stage his own subsequent Press event.'

Ralph found himself flushed with anger, despite all his training in restraint.

'This is monstrous!' he cried. 'If further proof were needed that we need to take immediate, global action to reduce global warming, clear our oceans of plastic, lower carbon emissions, protect our scarce resources, this is it.'

'Privately, I agree,' Ambassador Klein replied 'as do many of my fellow countrymen, perhaps most. However, this President's wishes are clear and always have been…'

Ambassador Gan Liu spoke up.

'As the world's most populated country, China has already recognised the need to change. We have poured record amounts of money and skill into renewable energy. This tragic discovery will only accelerate that process.'

'I am delighted to hear it,' Ralph said.

'And so am I,' Ambassador Klein added. 'Believe me the message is ringing loud and clear around Capitol Hill and I will do my best to add to it. America must curb its pollution.'

'We are agreed then that we leave the families and the scientists to tell the story,' the Prime Minister advised. 'What will follow, will follow. My role tomorrow will merely be to introduce.'

'If I may, Prime Minister…' Ralph said, fingering a dossier in front of him. 'We have a suggestion as to how our nations should pay tribute to the civilisation we have uncovered. Our nations have all agreed to take part if it meets with your approval.'

He distributed the dossier to everyone around the table.

The Prime Minister took out his reading glasses and read the contents of the dossier. Silence fell over the room, apart from the babble of twenty-four-hour news from one of the adjoining offices.

The Prime Minister closed the dossier, removed his glasses and pushed his chair back from the table.

'I can't think of a time in my political life, when I have seen something so apt. You will have our full co-operation and the use of our airfields.'

The Namibian, British, Chinese, American and United Nations flags all fluttered in the light breeze.

The press conference was held in a, rapidly-made clearing; in front of the geosphere built over the cave entrance, whose outline had already become iconic and instantly recognisable around the world.

A huge canvas roof stretched over the gathering crowd. Two tables had been stationed at the front, with multiple television screens arranged behind them in a triptych. To one side of the tables, covered in, beautifully-woven, Namibian fabrics were the two caskets the families had opened in the caves.

Once everyone was settled, Freddie, Hannah, Joe, Selima and Clara, filed into the whirr of cameras and a storm of flash-bulbs. They sat at the table flanking the Prime Minister. At one end of the table sat the two United Nations representatives. At the other sat Jacob Ubuntu. The parents sat in a row of chairs behind them like the back row in a game of chess, Ace and Basarwa amongst them.

The Prime Minister stood up.

'Welcome. Perhaps it is appropriate that it is in the least inhabited, and one of the least known countries in Africa, that we should find the vast burial ground of another civilisation. It seems that the population of our country was greater than we ever knew.'

Many in the audience wore a sad smile.

'So, it is also perhaps appropriate that the civilisation we have unearthed, chose to tell their story by painting on the ceiling of a cave; just as the ancient San and other tribes repre-sented here today have done.'

He turned to acknowledge Basarwa and Ace sitting behind him.

'Indeed, as long, as, ten thousand years ago, the Bushmen painted on cave walls near here... to teach their children how to hunt, but more importantly, to show us their vision of the spiritual world, not just the material.'

He paused to drink some water.

'We are going to hear from the young people who made this remarkable discovery, with their parents and guides who are seated behind us. But first, I would like to invite the Chief Scientist and Chief Medical Officer of the United Nations to address us. Please…'

The man and woman rose together and went over to the podium.

The Chief Scientist spoke first, with her reassuring voice of the factual.

'A week ago, in a cave turned burial chamber that is both behind and beneath us, four families found twenty or so burial caskets. They had entered what we now believe to be the Leaders' Chamber, a kind of presidential or royal chamber as it were. We have started to explore the other caves, beyond, and they are extensive. We think there may be up to fifty burial chambers beneath where we sit. Each chamber so far uncovered has contained simple, white caskets made of a remarkable, heat-responsive material that we are still trying to analyse. We also estimate there are hundreds of thousands of bodies buried under the 1,500-mile band of the so-called Fairy Circles. It is the largest and most tragic graveyard on Earth.'

Her first images flickered on to the screens behind, showing various caskets in their neatly arranged wall niches. Then close-ups of the caskets themselves.

'This protective material acts rather as an egg-shell does. Inside it has always been another metal casket. Because of these two protective layers and the dryness of the desert, the bodies are remarkably preserved. We are trying to determine how long ago they landed on Earth. One theory is that their arrival was the truth behind the so-called meteor storm of

1833. Carbon dating is already underway but feels crude to be honest, especially as we are dealing with a race that had advanced scientifically way beyond ours, with materials we cannot yet analyse.

There are astronomical drawings on the cave walls of the planet they left and its solar system. We are starting to compare those with the many galaxies our telescopes and voyagers have photographed. Given the vastness of our Universe it is probably unlikely that we will be able to determine which solar system was their…home. But we must try…'

She found herself reaching for a vocabulary that matched the scientific with the respectful.

'What we can say with certainty is that their planet was dying. I would now like to hand over to my colleague, Professor Abraham Guz, the U.N.'s Chief Medical Officer.'

'Thank you.' Professor Guz took the podium and coughed with nerves.

'We have deliberately not released any photographs of the extra-terrestrial humans until now,' he said. What I can now reveal is…'

His first slide was shown to gasps of recognition.

'These magnificent creatures are, to all intents and purposes, human beings, similar, to our-selves. So far, they seem taller, on average seven foot, probably due to more advanced nutrition than our own. Their lung capacity is bigger than ours possibly in response to breathing a lower level of oxygen than in our own atmosphere.'

Two more slides came up, showing details of the face and hands.

'They also have six fingers to our five which would have

made them more dextrous. That apart, they are remarkably similar to Homo Sapiens. We will be examining every aspect of their anatomy, in the coming months and years, including and especially their brain structures and DNA. We believe they died because of viruses and bacteria on our planet, against which they had no natural defences. They seem likely to have been able to breathe our atmosphere, rich in oxygen though it might have been for them. We have suggested to the United Nations, based on our findings to date, that we classify them as a new species: "Homo Super Sapiens."'

They both returned to their places at the table. It started like the pattering of a soft rain, then grew and grew, until it was like hail thundering on a tin roof. The whole audience had broken into applause, not for the scientists, but for a new race of humanity that now had a name.

It was time for the five to speak. The enormity of what they had unearthed made this moment seem both more important, but less daunting, than it would otherwise have been. Nothing could seem as significant again.

'This started as a school science project,' Freddie started. 'But it seems to have mushroomed into something else.'

Everyone in the audience laughed.

Hannah continued.

'We were fascinated by the Fairy Circles and why fifteen hundred miles of them appeared here and nowhere else on Earth.'

'We also wanted to know why they grew and died as it were, with the same average lifespan as humans,' Selima added. 'This we still can't explain.'

Joe continued the verbal baton pass.

'We tried to apply math to the circles at first. We ran computer modelling on satellite photos of the circles. The only pattern that emerged was that there are twenty-eight different types of circle.'

The press were furiously scribbling, in shorthand.

'So, we thought they might be an alphabet of some kind,' Hannah, said 'a way of telling their story.'

'And they have told us their story,' Clara added 'but not through words.'

At this point, Clara, Hannah and Selima got up from the table, stepped down from the makeshift stage and walked over to the two draped caskets.

They solemnly pulled the flowing fabrics from the caskets arranged them around their necks and shoulders as wraps.

They moved to the small coffin.

'This is the coffin of a young girl,' Hannah explained. 'In her coffin, held in her arms, was this painting.'

The picture flashed up on the trio of screens. Its simple naivete was heart-breaking.

'It shows the sister she had to leave behind on the dying planet,' Clara said.

'One of us has lost a sister,' Selima added, deliberately not looking at Hannah for fear of triggering her tears. 'But, in this casket, we have found another.'

Together they bowed to the coffin and each placed a flower on the casket lid, before returning to the stage.

Then, Freddie and Joe got up and walked to an easel at the side of the stage and placed on it a blown-up image from the chamber, which also came up on the screen.

Freddie started.

'This is a photograph of the planet they drew on the ceiling of the Leaders' Chamber. We can assume it's a depiction of the planet they left.'

Joe continued, using a telescopic pointer to highlight parts of the image.

'As you can see, it bears a strong resemblance to Earth. The continents have drifted further apart than ours and have started to become submerged. We can assume from the very thin ice-caps, and the dusty reds of the land masses, that this is a planet that has overheated.'

'This could be our planet in fifty years,' Freddie added, 'if we don't stop global warming.'

Several thousand miles away, a fist slammed into the desk of the Oval Office.

The questions from the press ranged from the scientific and medical to personal details about the five and their families: their occupations, why they came to Namibia and whether they would stay.

The Prime Minister sought to bring matters to their close.

'If there are no more questions, I would like to ask someone rather special to introduce our closing ceremony. Jacob Ubuntu, the Headmaster of the Augustineum school, where the young people met and now study. He is their mentor and guide in every sense.'

Ubuntu stood and slowly made his way to the podium.

'Good morning everyone. I couldn't be prouder today to be a Namibian. This may not be logical, but I see it as an act of benediction, an act almost of trust, that a dying civilisation landed in our country to try and make it their home.'

He had, as ever, commanded absolute attention.

'It is especially appropriate, as Africa is the land of our common ancestry as human beings. This is where we first hunted, gathered, farmed, painted, learned to speak...and still do. For between forty thousand and sixty thousand years this is what we did on this magic soil of Africa. But in the last hundred years we have managed to near exhaust the planet that nurtured us.'

He paused to gaze into as many eyes as he could individually reach.

'If there was an Eden, it was in Africa. If there were an Adam and Eve, they were black and were African, where people have grown darker from more exposure to the life-giving sun and for no other reason.'

The emphatic end to his sentence was designed to penetrate every racist's mind like a bullet.

'These five brave souls should remind us of the billion or more young people on this planet that deserve a future. We must accelerate our effort, apply every muscle and neural pathway in our collective bodies and brains, to save our planet.'

Ubuntu turned to a military General standing at the entrance to the conference to check all was ready. He nodded. Ubuntu continued.

'The nations of our planet would like to pay homage to the beautiful, tall, but doomed race who lie buried in our soil. Let us ensure that they have not died in vain, that their message, their story did not go unheard.'

A sound like distant thunder came from behind them. It grew louder and louder until overhead they saw military and commercial planes of every type, nationality, and description, flying low, and, in formation.

As they approached the Fairy Circles, the planes swooped lower and released their cargo: millions of flowers of every type, colour and description were scattered over the Fairy Circles, until the desert was a carpet of flowers.

The Zimbabwean side of the Victoria Falls had been spectacular as they walked along the theatrical cascades of water. The Zambian side was more intense however, closer to the knotted torrents.

It had been a month since the Press conference and the four families had come to escape at the end of term.

They would like to have remained anonymous but that was now impossible. As they walked past Livingstone's statue, there were high fives all around from the crowds.

It was late afternoon and the Falls were swollen with people, most of them women. Many were in costume, swaying and singing, snapping photos. High-pitched laughter rippled in every corner of the walkways, bouncing off the rocks. Excitement was rising to fever pitch as the afternoon headed inexorably towards sunset.

'Excuse me, but where are you from?' a man asked Ben. 'You look familiar.'

'I'm from Brooklyn, but I'm here with friends from around the world. Is there something special going on today?'

'Yes, this is a meeting of women from churches all over Zambia. It happens once a year. Stick around. We are singing the Eucharist at sunset. It's become a tradition. Now, I recognise who you guys are. Oh my God. You're the people who found the aliens.'

'Fellow humans,' Ben corrected.

The word that the Fairy Circle families were at the Falls jumped between groups like firecrackers and soon they were surrounded.

This had become typical of any outing they made, but the whole atmosphere of religious fervour lifted it to another level.

They finally managed to escape for a few moments.

'Just think,' Joe said. 'This planet is hurtling through space at sixty-six thousand miles an hour, whilst rotating, and we can't feel any of it. But if you look at the Falls you can see all that power, that incessant motion.'

They ran up the spray-soaked paths laughing, barely casting a glance at the railway bridge, built, with imperialist pride and Scottish engineering, to survey the falls. When Nature flexes its muscle, man is reduced to a mere spectator.

They danced in the spray, twirling in the late afternoon sun until almost in a trance. The Falls thundered their joy. The Zambezi so quiet and peaceful above the Falls morphed into patterns of furious water and spray as it leaped downwards, with a sound that could drown a hundred lions.

As the Sun started to descend, it lit up the spray that filled the chasm.

'Forget uranium,' Li shouted. 'Water is the world's most precious resource. I've handed in my resignation at the mining company.'

'What will you do?' Ben asked.

'Renewable energy grids, here in Africa. They need engineers like me.'

'Sounds like the future,' said Ralph.

At sunset, a gospel choir sang with a passion that rose with the spray from the Falls. The families, stood, watching, arms interlinked. A rainbow appeared in the Falls. Not a half-rainbow struggling to be seen in a rain-filled sky, but a total circle held in the mist, as if it would last forever.

Epilogue

There had been a flurry of fake news in the last two weeks: 'Namibian burial sites a hoax' and 'Four Liars of the Apocalypse'. Now they knew why.

The climate change deniers, the peddlers of so-called 'progress' and 'capitalism at all costs' were on the march again.

Rayon-Zentel, the multi-national oil-and-gas conglomerate, issued a Press Release.

'In the last few years we have discovered a vast oilfield under the Arctic ice fields. We are proud to announce that have now developed the requisite technology to drill in this threatening terrain. We will be constructing our first rigs in the next six months.'

That evening, it rained in Namibia for the first time in forty days. At first it was a hesitant shower tickling the ground. Then it grew to a through-the-clothes-and-skin-down-to-the-bones drenching. Finally, it gushed from the incontinent skies like a Biblical torrent.

The Tsumeb river burst its banks and flooded the dunes, gushing like a serpent through Langstrand. Dead Vlei filled with lithe, swirling water. Water lilies started to bloom. Birdsong sprinkled its magic.

It rained until the mummified trees were drowned, the birds fled and all that remained was the water, the sand and silence.

THE END